The Lipstick Diaries

The Lipstick Diaries

Lori Soard

Five Star • Waterville, Maine

First Edition
First Printing: November 2004

Published in 2004 in conjunction with Tekno Books
and Ed Gorman.

Set in 11 pt. Plantin by Christina S. Huff.

Printed in the United States on permanent paper.

Library of Congress Cataloging-in-Publication Data

Soard, Lori.
    The lipstick diaries / Lori Soard.—1st ed.
        p. cm.
      ISBN 1-59414-182-7 (hc : alk. paper)
      1. Female friendship—Fiction.   2. Single women—Fiction.
    I. Title.
    PS3619.O37L57 2004
      813'.6—dc22   2004043315

To my dear friend Sally Kale, who owns the other half of my brain. Your many hours as a sounding board and talking me through moments of panic made this book possible. You know how special you are to me. It isn't often in life that you find a friend who understands your heart and soul; who likes you even though they know how wicked and witchy you can sometimes be; who knows what you're going to say before you even say it; who knows that even while you feel blessed to have sold another book, you are a nervous wreck and worried about *this* book being the best it can be. Thank you for being my critiquer, my partner in crime, and my best friend. Your type of comradeship is the basis for the friendships in *Lipstick Diaries*—the kind of bond that lasts more than a lifetime.

Acknowledgments

A special thanks to my agent, Linda Hyatt, for believing in me and always looking out for my interests.

To Russell Davis, who trusts me to write the story my way and has faith that together we'll create a wonderful finished product.

I need to thank my husband, who took the kids away for a fun getaway and let me work on editing my book, and my children, who put up with my weird writing habits and have learned that ideas can strike at any moment.

A special thank you to my parents, who've always supported me no matter what path I chose.

And thanks to God for helping me through the hard times and giving me more blessings than I can count, the main miracle being the two angels he sent to me in the form of daughters.

Prologue

"Kiss it." Kate Tyler's blue eyes sparkled with laughter.

Rebecca swallowed her misgivings and puckered her cotton candy colored lips. Kate and Sarah forced her to go along with at least a dozen crazy ideas a day. This one was mild compared to most.

Her lips brushed against the cool, smooth surface that smelled faintly of sawdust. She kissed and opened her eyes. The page in front of her sported a pink imprint of her lips. Rebecca couldn't remember whose idea the lipstick diaries had been. They'd ridden their bikes to the local drugstore and chosen a shade of lipstick they liked—their "signature" color. The one they would wear forevermore and would sign the diary entries with each week.

"My turn!" Kate pulled the diary to her face and pressed her lips to the page. "Purple Passion Fruit. My favorite color. My signature color."

Kate turned the journal so that the open pages faced the other two girls and proudly displayed the bright purple lip marks next to Rebecca's pale pink ones. It defined the difference in their personalities perfectly. The bold purple reflected Kate's outgoing personality and fearlessness, while the pale pink mirrored Rebecca's cautiousness and shyness. Becca knew that shyness helped her create a shell that protected her from being hurt by anyone. She hadn't been shy before her father walked out on her and her mother. Sometimes she wished she could be as confident as Kate but with that self-assurance came too much risk. Kate's scribbling stopped.

"Your turn, Sarah." Kate handed Sarah the diary with the tiny lilacs on front and the matching satin ribbon that marked the last page written on.

"Do we have to do this?" Sarah rolled her gaze toward the ceiling, managing to look bored. Sarah always looked bored, as though she were waiting for something bigger and better to arrive. Her blonde hair lay in bouncy waves and her green eyes held a hint of mystery and wisdom beyond her years.

"I told you. This is the start of our adventures. Next year we'll be in eighth grade." The excitement in Kate's voice coiled around the room and settled around them like a lasso they couldn't escape.

"So? What's so great about eighth grade?" Sarah said.

"So?" Kate frowned and crossed her legs Indian style. "So? Boys and parties and sleepovers and everything else."

"Listen you two, why don't we go see if there are any cookies left." Rebecca tried to stop the argument she could see starting. Kate and Sarah could be the best of friends or the worst of enemies. When they fought, they both made Rebecca miserable, using her as a go-between. When the word "so" came into the conversation, a battle was imminent.

"Oh, give me the stupid thing. This is such a waste of time." Sarah grabbed the journal and laid it across her legs while she smeared the fire engine red lipstick on with quick strokes.

The pages rustled as she picked it back up and pressed her lips to the page.

"There. Are you happy? I 'signed' it."

"Every Friday, we'll meet and add a page to the lipstick diaries. Even when we're old. Like thirty." Kate's eyes grew wide at the thought of being that old!

"What if something else is going on?" Sarah asked.

"Cancel it. Friday nights are lipstick diary nights. Forever. Swear it." Kate placed her hand, palm down, in the middle of the circle they all sat in on Kate's princess pink carpet.

"I swear it." Rebecca laid her hand over Kate's. It wasn't as if she'd ever have anything to do other than hang out with her two best friends anyway. Her throat felt tight as she realized that she felt as though she was part of a group for the first time in her life.

"Oh, okay." Sarah laid her hand over theirs.

"Friends forever," they all said.

Rebecca wondered how long forever would last. Everyone else in her life had walked out on her, including her own father.

One

Sixteen Years Later

Kate Tyler threw the stack of mail on the small table in the entry of the apartment and lifted the heavy, sweat-soaked hair off the back of her neck. The sticky weather reminded her of August in Indiana, even though New Orleans was about as far away from the Midwest as one could get—not only in distance but in atmosphere.

"Becca? You home?" Her heels clicked over the polished oak floors. No one answered except for the faint hum of the air conditioner working overtime to stave off the heat.

She'd kept one interesting-looking envelope out of the stack of mail and now she carried it over to the sofa and sank into the comforting suede, cream-colored softness. The Vieux Carre never truly slept and even now, in the middle of a workday, the faint sound of street musicians and the bustle of activity below floated past the balcony and into her apartment. Kate didn't care. The noise never bothered her, even during Mardi Gras and the many other festivals that lined the streets throughout the year. She loved 'Nawlins. They'd moved here because of the two big colleges where all three could study what they wanted, fallen in love with the city, and stayed. Although she missed living close to her family at times, in this city she just fit like she never had in a small town.

The postmark on the shimmery white envelope was from

10

Greenfield, Indiana. There was no return address, which was unusual. The envelope had the weight and feel of a formal invitation, but they'd just missed their ten-year high school reunion because of work obligations and not much of a desire to attend, so it couldn't be that. She considered waiting for Becca and Sarah to get home before she opened the correspondence, but curiosity won out. Kate slid her fingernail under the flap and lifted it.

"Who are you from?" Memories of old fashioned, cobbled alleys and the clock tower rising over the town as though guarding its residents flooded her mind. She wondered if the urban sprawl that had just started a few years ago was now taking over. The fast food restaurants sitting like festering wounds on the outskirts, the crowded state road that ran through the heart of the small town, and the children that ran amok. She grinned. She'd been one of those children and she had to admit they were some of the best memories she had.

"Kate?" The front door slammed.

"In here, Becca." Kate opened the white vellum invitation; little metal confetti hearts fell out all over her lap and skittered across the floor. "I hate these confetti things. People who put them in invitations should be shot."

"I see you're in a good mood." Rebecca looked wilted in her sensible button up shirt, knee-length skirt, and matching penny loafers. Who wore penny loafers in this day and age?

"Always." The paper crackled as she held the invitation in her hands. The words wavered in and out of focus before her eyes.

"Kate? You've gone pale. What is it?" Rebecca waved her hand in front of Kate's face.

Kate forced herself to shrug but she couldn't swallow past the lump in her throat. Unable to speak, she handed the invitation to Rebecca. Surely it was a cruel joke of some sort—it couldn't be true.

"I'm home!" Sarah meandered through the front door. Her billowy blue and green dress seemed to float around her as though carrying its own breeze. Maybe it did. She didn't even look as though the intense Louisiana humidity affected her.

"Mark's getting married," Rebecca told her. She handed the invitation to Sarah and put her arm around Kate's shoulders.

A tear slipped down Kate's cheek and she swiped it away. Dammit. She wouldn't cry over him again. She'd shed more than enough tears over Mark Jackson back in high school. The tears were for his bride-to-be . . .

"I thought you'd gotten over that jerk years ago, Kate. Who would marry *him?*" Sarah's eyes narrowed to slits.

"My sister!" Kate swabbed away another tear, but it was replaced with one that followed closely behind. "I don't care about Mark, it's my sister I'm worried about."

"Jennifer? I can't believe she'd marry him, knowing what he did to you back in high school. I know you said they were dating, but Mark's dated everyone in Greenfield at one time. Oh, Kate." Sarah chewed her lower lip.

"I wouldn't say he's dated *everyone,*" Rebecca said.

"I didn't think their relationship was this serious. I warned her about his reputation." Kate shrugged. "Jen is a big girl. She can make her own decisions."

Mark Jackson had been a player in and after high school. Once a dog, always a dog. The thought of her baby sister married to him made her chest ache. The last time she'd tried to stay out of her sister's life, Jen had nearly been killed. The guilt of that mistake still weighed heavily and she wanted desperately to save her sister from another mistake. She didn't think Mark would physically hurt Jen, but emotionally he could devastate her gentle sister.

"Kate, are you going to the wedding?" Rebecca frowned.

"I don't know." Kate rubbed her arms, suddenly chilled. "I guess I'm still in shock. She never said a word to me about them being this serious and we talk every week. She's only been dating him for two *months!*"

Sarah threw the invite onto the floor and stomped on it. "Let's put a curse on him."

Kate laughed. "You always know how to make me feel better."

"I know a gypsy. She works outside my store. She would probably put a curse on Mark. Maybe make us a voodoo doll."

"Jen can't be thinking straight." Kate shook her head. Either her sister was confused or Mark had used Jen's trusting nature to his advantage and tricked her into thinking he was a changed man. If Jen truly believed that, then why the rush to the altar? Of course, Jen was sometimes reckless. Kate knew that about her sister and loved how different they were—between the two of them, they created a balance in the family. However, when each was on her own, sometimes those differences made for unwise decisions. Kate was the older sister and had learned her lessons the hard way. She just wished Jen could learn from her mistakes, but she knew her sister had to discover life on her own terms. It didn't mean she worried any less. Still, even with Jen's free spirit, things didn't add up.

Something niggled at the back of her mind but she pushed it away. Was she just feeling upset because her baby sister was getting married and she was a single, almost thirty-something? She'd thought she was fairly satisfied with her life here in New Orleans but on closer examination, it was clear that her life was something less than she'd hoped it would be by the time she'd reached twenty-nine years of age. Her career was going nowhere, although she enjoyed being a haunted history tour guide. Her sex life was going nowhere, actually it was nonexistent. And she was going nowhere near that wedding.

"Your turn, Rebecca." Kate passed the diary to Rebecca and then placed the cap back on the Purple Passion Fruit lipstick.

These days the tube lasted her for years since the only time she wore the hideous color was for their Friday night meetings.

"I'm not sure a paragraph will be enough this week." Rebecca gave a strangled laugh.

"Oh, c'mon, Becca. What could you have to report? Did a patient throw his bedpan across the room again?" Kate snickered.

"That was very traumatic at the time." Becca blinked several times as though she held back tears.

Kate swallowed, feeling immediately guilty for teasing her friend. She loved Rebecca but sometimes the girl's passivity drove her insane. She wanted to grab Rebecca and shake her until she put up a fight. But it wasn't in Rebecca's nature. Although she was a striking woman with her deep auburn hair and ivory skin, Rebecca hid behind a tight little bun and ugly clothes. It was almost as though she were afraid of being loved. Guilt burned through her for making fun of Rebecca's problems. Inside her friend lived a sensitive soul, whose feelings were sometimes hurt easily. Kate's sense of humor didn't always strike a chord with Becca and she hadn't meant to hurt her.

"I'm sorry, Becca. I'm just upset over the invitation and I took it out on you. You take as much room as you need.

14

That's what the lipstick diaries are for. To report important things in our lives."

Although Kate secretly wondered what was so important about bedpans, the diaries must remain pure and that meant that each recorded what was important to her—even bedpans.

"My date last night didn't go so well," Sarah said. "The jerk failed our basic dating test and didn't open my car door. He actually stood at the curb and waited five minutes before I finally leaned forward and told the cab driver to pull away."

"I always forget to use those tests Granny taught us. I can't even remember most of them," Kate admitted. "Of course, men always fail them. That may be why none of us are married."

"The few that I remember aren't difficult tests." Sarah frowned. "We just meet jerks. Speaking of jerks, did you decide about your sister's wedding?"

"I haven't decided." If Jennifer had bothered to use the dating tests their great-grandmother had taught them, she certainly wouldn't be marrying Mark. Her baby sister—married to a liar and a cheat. The thought left a bitter taste in her mouth. Jen deserved better, especially after Billy and everything she'd gone through last year.

"I think we should all go. It's been years since I've been back to Indiana. I'd like to visit my aunt. She's getting too old to travel here every year."

An image of Jennifer floating down the aisle toward Mark blurred Kate's vision. She didn't want Jen to get her heart broken, but she was absolutely furious that her sister was gullible enough to marry the man. She hadn't done a very good job as the older sister if she hadn't taught Jen to have better taste than this in men. First there had been the incident with Billy and now this. She hadn't shared her opinion last time and she'd regretted it every day since. Jen's life had been turned upside down and backwards and all because Kate hadn't wanted to interfere. Hadn't Jennifer learned anything from that horrible experience?

"Cotton Candy Pink." Becca smeared it on her lips. She was the only one of the three who still wore the original lipstick shade she'd started with so many years before.

"What did you write, Becca?" Kate leaned forward and tried to peer at the page.

Rebecca snatched it away. "Not until we're all done writing. You know the rules."

"I should. I made them up. If I'd been smarter, I would have insisted I know all the news first." Kate grinned.

"My turn." Sarah snatched the journal from Becca.

The sound of the pen scratching against the paper filled the room. After sixteen years the sound should be familiar, but it seemed fresh and new just as it had the first time they'd gathered and performed this ritual. It hadn't always been easy through the years to keep their Friday night lipstick diary dates. Sometimes they'd had to schedule them late in the evening to avoid missing school ballgames or dances. But they always managed to get together on Friday and perform the ritual. Other events were planned around the diary dates whenever possible. That they'd rarely missed a Friday was a testament to the strength of their friendship and their commitment to be there for one another.

"Finished!" Sarah laid the pen down on the floor and passed the journal to Kate.

"You forgot to sign it." Kate handed it back, determined to prove she wasn't anxious to read what Rebecca and Sarah had written. Her fingers itched with the urge to snatch it back as Sarah took the journal and placed a bright red kiss on the page. Sarah then held the book out at arm's length and tilted her head from one side to the other, stalling to drive Kate insane.

"Oh, gimme!" Kate grabbed it when Sarah didn't hand it back right away.

Sarah's entry was exactly seven words.

Remember, it's the rest of Jen's life.

The page was signed with fire engine red lipstick. A sick feeling crept into Kate's stomach.

"I can read the future." Sarah waved her arms in front of her forehead. "I see a long trip in our future. I see a wedding. And I see a man. A man who is humiliated beyond belief."

"Stop it." Kate glared at her. "I don't know if I can do it, Sarah. I don't think I can sit quietly while she marries that man. When the minister says, 'If there is anyone with just cause,' I won't be able to keep my mouth shut."

"Kate, I want to go. Becca wants to go. This isn't some stranger. This is your sister. Let's just go back and face our demons." Sarah grabbed Kate's hands and squeezed them. "Becca needs to know she won't always be deserted, I need to remind myself that I don't have to be like everyone else to be happy, and you need to forgive yourself for not saving Jennifer when she was dating Billy. It will be therapy for all three of us."

"And I'll help you find a killer dress to wear," Becca offered.

"We'd better get it here. Finding a killer dress in Greenfield, Indiana isn't very likely," Sarah said.

"Fine." Kate gritted her teeth together so tightly her jaw ached. "I'll go. I'll put on my fake smile. I'll pretend I don't care."

"Oh, honey, you misunderstand me." A slow, sly smile

lifted the corners of Sarah's mouth. "We are going to stop this wedding, not attend it."

Kate stared at Sarah for a moment. "I have to make my sister see reason, don't I? That's what you meant by 'the rest of her life.' "

As the big sister, it was her responsibility to save Jen. She'd let her baby sister down once before—she couldn't let her down a second time. Maybe her sister didn't know all the rumors about Mark. Or perhaps he'd tricked her into thinking he was a changed man. If she could just talk to Jen face-to-face, then she could convince her to at least postpone the wedding. She had exactly ten days to get to Indiana and stop her sister from making the biggest mistake of her life.

Two

In exactly ten days, he would be married to Jennifer Tyler. Mark Jackson parked his black Ford pickup and whistled his way into the *Daily Reporter*. His new job as the senior editor brought many benefits and perks—enough to support a new family.

"Good morning, Mark." The front desk receptionist batted heavily mascaraed eyelashes.

"Hello, Tara." He didn't stop to talk. He'd dated her two years ago and sometimes the heat of that hot fling almost seared him as he walked past her desk.

"Mark, Cynthia needs another day on that story about the school superintendent and how he never cancels school when the weather is bad." Tara followed him into his office and closed the door behind her.

He suspected she'd lock the door if there was a lock. He tugged at his shirt collar, wishing she would go back to the front of the building. He had a secretary, one who did an excellent job for him. Tara telling him that a reporter needed more time on a story seemed off-kilter and certainly wasn't part of her job description. It smacked of an excuse to get him alone and he didn't appreciate the temptation.

Mark sighed and moved behind his desk. He was tired of going through women like they were disposable cups. He'd dated nearly every single woman in town. Okay, maybe just the ones who were ready, willing, and eager. Since he'd started dating Jen, he wanted something more. He wanted a family. Tara wasn't making it easy to resist falling back into his old pattern of flitting to another woman as soon as things started to get serious. He'd made a commitment to himself to forget his old ways. Otherwise, he was going to wind up like his father—old and alone.

Her red dress was tight and outlined every curve in her body. He tugged at his shirt collar again, loosening his tie in the process. There'd been a time when he'd thought he wasn't capable of truly loving another human being. Loving and leaving was in his genes—a curse he'd inherited from his father. But, with Jen's love, he now believed that he could overcome his predisposition and give his heart to another person for the rest of his life. Sure, their relationship had advanced much more quickly than anyone had expected—including him—but he felt ready to commit to forever.

"Did you get the invitation to my wedding?" he asked Tara, hoping she'd leave.

"I did." She moved around the desk and leaned toward him. The heavy scent of some exotic flower wrapped around him, almost choking him. Jen always smelled fresh and clean, like she'd just taken a shower, and her scent wasn't overwhelming. "I am completely heartbroken, darling. But I'm not opposed to having one last fling before you settle down."

Mark shook his head and swallowed, resisting the temptation of her inviting, soft lips. The tip of her tongue darted out, leaving her sweet mouth moist and glossy. He groaned. Jen counted on him to be loyal. They were getting married in less than two weeks. He wouldn't ruin things now—there was too much at stake.

The phone on his desk shrilled loudly and he jumped as though he'd been caught in an indecent position. He'd done nothing wrong! He picked up the phone and barked a greeting into it.

"Mark? If this is a bad time, we can talk later." Jennifer's soft voice reached through the phone wires and instantly killed his attraction to Tara. The effect was immediate, as though a jug of ice water had been poured over him.

"I always have time for you." Out of the corner of his eye, he saw Tara shrug and head for the door. She turned just as she was about to exit, blew him a kiss, and mouthed, "Anytime." Then she swayed down the aisle toward the front desk. He released the breath he'd been holding.

"—do you think?" Jennifer finished.

Mark had no idea what she'd said. He blinked twice. *Get it together, buddy. She's your one chance at a normal life.* He wouldn't blow things now.

"Mark?"

"I'm sorry, Jen. Things are crazy here. Could you repeat the question?" He had to get a grip on himself or risk losing the best thing that had ever happened to him. Already, everyone in town expected him to cheat, break it off, or jilt her at the altar. Jen herself took many months of convincing before she'd even agree to go out with him. How he'd gotten lucky enough that she'd agreed to marry him, he wasn't sure, but he planned to race to the altar.

"This is a bad time. I can tell you later." She sounded hurt, her soft voice warbling at the end of the sentence.

"No. No. Of course it isn't a bad time. I'm sorry I wasn't listening. What is it?" Their relationship had gone from dating to engagement in less time than it took a season to change. The breakneck speed of their courtship left them both feeling uncertain and off-balance. The tremor in Jen's voice told him she was having doubts again.

"My sister phoned and said she's coming to the wedding. I

thought she'd be furious. She's been so protective since the Billy incident. I think she's realized you're a good match for me. What do you think?"

What did he think? His temples started a slow throb. He thought if Kate made it to town before the wedding and had five minutes alone with Jen, she'd tell her every rotten thing he'd ever done in high school. She'd also tell Jen every rotten thing she'd heard about him. He knew he had a bad reputation—some of it deserved and some not. She'd do the same thing he'd do if Jen were his sister—she'd do her best to stop the wedding. Part of him couldn't blame her. After what had happened with Billy, Kate had a right to be protective of her sister. That didn't mean he wasn't terrified of the havoc she might create.

"Mark?" Jen laughed. "You really *are* busy."

"Yes. I think it's wonderful your sister is coming. You'll let me know the minute she arrives in town won't you?" He needed to talk to Kate and convince her that he'd changed. Maybe it would be best to phone her before she ever left New Orleans. Once she arrived in town she'd be caught up in the whirlwind called their wedding. "It's great that she was able to get time off work from . . . where does she work again?"

"Ghost Hunters Tours." Jen lowered her voice. "I love you, Mark."

"I love you too, sweetheart." He placed the phone back in the receiver and wondered how he was going to stop Kate Tyler from ruining his wedding. He needed to phone her right away, but wanted to plan out his words very carefully. Would she be willing to listen to reason?

The white test stick showed a clear blue positive sign. Rebecca laid it on the counter next to the other two. Her red hair had escaped hours ago from its updo and now lay against her shoulders in disarray. She stared into her own gaze, realizing that her blue eyes were as wide and frightened as a child getting a shot. Pregnant. She sank onto the cool, tile floor and pulled her knees to her chest.

Her sobs were drowned out by the noisy overhead exhaust fan she'd turned on before entering the bathroom. The noise was simply to distract her, since her roommates weren't home. Kate's work started at nightfall and Sarah was out on a date.

The chilly, bitter taste of loneliness washed past her lips and almost choked her. What was she going to do? She'd played it safe her entire life. For God's sake, she'd been the one to choose cotton candy pink lipstick. You couldn't get much safer than that. All the nightmares of her own childhood came flooding back. *I can't raise a child by myself.* Her mother had managed it, but growing up without a father left more scars than Becca wanted to admit. She shook her head to clear her thoughts.

"Pull it together, Rebecca." She stood and unlocked the bathroom door. She'd leave the sticks where they were. It would save having to explain to her friends.

She needed to phone Jared and let him know. Would he be angry? He'd only worked at the hospital for six short months. She'd been so upset when he'd told her that he'd be gone for a month or two that the rest of his words were lost in a haze of hurt. He'd deserted her just like every other man in her life. Perhaps she should have paid closer attention to his words, but a part of her only heard that he was leaving—the rest sounded like an excuse. A man who left never returned. She'd learned that lesson at the age of five from her own father. *This is different, Becca. Jared isn't your father.* She had his cell number and his promise to phone when he returned to New Orleans. That day lay etched in her memory.

Punching the numbers into the dial pad with a trembling finger, she tried to compose herself.

"Hello?" The whiskey huskiness of his voice stretched through the phone wires and sent skitters down her spine as though he'd stroked her.

"Jared, it's Rebecca."

The long pause was followed by crackles. ". . . hear from you."

"You're breaking up, Jared." She frowned. Perhaps the bad connection was an omen.

"Sorry. I'm in South America. Can I see you when I get home?"

South America? Was he serious or making excuses to not see her? Why would he be out of the country? It didn't make sense to her. Besides, she wouldn't be home . . .

"I may not be here. There is a wedding in my hometown I may have to attend next week."

". . . can't . . ." A loud crackle popped on the other end of the phone. "Sorry . . . stupid . . ."

Becca's heart sank. Was it even possible to have a conversation with this type of connection? "Jared?"

". . . see you . . ."

A loud crackle filled the air and then the line cleared. She'd better tell him before they lost their connection again. She took a deep breath.

"Look, I hate to tell you this way and you are not obligated—I mean I know we talked about seeing each other when you came back to town—but the thing is—" she took a deep breath. *Just tell him, you wimp!* "I took a pregnancy test this afternoon and the stick turned blue."

The small, crystal clock on the mantle ticked off the seconds of silence. She swallowed. She was a nurse. He was a doctor. Of course they'd used protection. It just hadn't worked. She waited but the only sound was a slight crackle over the wires. With every moment that passed, her heartbeat quickened, dread filling her mouth with ash.

"I guess we're through then," Jared said. The phone crackled one final time and then went dead.

Rebecca held it out from her ear, stunned. Of course she hadn't expected anything of him, but she'd thought he'd have more of a reaction than to just say they were through. The rejection cut deep. Her hand crept over her still-flat stomach, resting there protectively. Had she just consigned her child to a life without a father? She knew how difficult that could be. While she hadn't expected an offer of marriage, some small part of her must have thought he'd make a good father to her child whether they were together or not. The realization that he'd not only rejected her but their child almost brought her to her knees.

The lock on the front door clicked and slid out of its socket. Sarah threw her handbag onto the floor and kicked it.

"Stupid jerk. If you can't pass the basic Lipstick Diary test, then you aren't worth my time." She slammed the door behind her and then looked up to meet Rebecca's gaze. "Becca? What's wrong?"

"What makes you think s-something's wrong?" She hiccupped.

"Oh, I don't know. The tears. The red nose. The puffy eyes." Sarah left her purse lying in the middle of the floor and walked Rebecca to the couch where they sat down.

How would she tell Sarah she was pregnant? She was supposed to be the responsible one of the three. The one who led the straight and narrow life, but there were a few things even her best friends didn't know. For one, they didn't know about Jared. Their love had been so new and she hadn't been ready to share the news during their weekly diary writings. Now she wished she had. It would make explanations simpler. Her hours at the hospital varied so widely that the other two never knew if she was on a date or at work, and she hadn't volunteered the information.

"Honey, what is it?" Sarah hugged her. "Whatever it is, we'll help you. It can't be that bad. Are you in love? Did he break your heart? I'll kill him."

"No." Rebecca shook her head, unable to speak for a moment.

"Is someone sick? Dead? Hurt? Are you hurt?"

"No. No. No. I'm pregnant." She couldn't meet Sarah's eyes. She looked at the crystal chandelier hanging from the fifteen-foot ceiling.

"You?"

"You don't have to sound so shocked. I do have female organs, you know." Dammit. She knew this would be hard. Her friends had her pigeonholed. It wouldn't be easy to break out of the mold they had all gotten used to. Her pregnancy shouldn't be this much of a surprise. Maybe for a change she wanted to be the daring one of the three, instead of reserved. If they knew what she'd done two years ago when she went home for a visit, they would both fall over in a dead faint. That was one secret she could never tell them. Kate wouldn't understand and maybe not even Sarah.

"I didn't mean that. I meant you are always so careful about everything. Why not this?"

"I can't talk about it." She stood and walked to the balcony doors, swinging them open. She needed air. The street below bustled with activity at a time in the evening when many cities rolled up their sidewalks and went to sleep for the night. The spicy, sultry sounds of jazz echoed up from the nightclub around the corner.

"Of course you can talk. We've known each other forever, Becca. What's going on?"

"I *was* careful, Sarah. The protection failed. I'm a statistic." She turned to face her friend. "And what's worse, I'm not really all that sorry. I loved him desperately and I'd do it again."

"I'm sure as soon as you tell him about the baby—"

"No." Rebecca shook her head. "I phoned him. He said we were through and hung up on me."

"Becca, forgive me for asking this, but where on earth did you meet this guy? You never go out."

She felt the heat creep into her cheeks. "He's a doctor. He was filling in for a colleague for a few months. Now he's gone."

"Becca!" Sarah stared at her. "I'm so shocked, I guess I don't know what to say."

"I don't know what to do, Sarah." She crossed her arms over her midriff. There—that was the look—the intense shock over Rebecca being the one who was pregnant. She'd see the same look when she told Kate. Well, she was tired of it—it was time she stopped hiding behind her shell and learned to express herself. "I'm not twenty anymore. What if this is my last chance to have a baby?"

"Do you really want to raise a baby by yourself?" Sarah frowned. "I mean, if that is what you want, I'll support you. I'll support you whatever you decide."

"I know that." She'd always known that. Sarah and Kate would be there for her no matter what she chose.

Deep in the innermost recesses of her heart a tiny voice cried out that she wanted a child. But she wanted the white picket fence and loving husband too. She didn't want to raise a child alone. Her mother had raised her alone and no mother or child should have to go through that. But her options were few unless she could find someone else to marry her in the next few months. Someone who didn't mind that she was carrying another man's child. Fat chance.

There were few times in her life when she'd been unable to judge the true character of someone. Sarah crumpled the notice from the bank and threw it behind the counter. If she didn't figure a way out of the mess Daniel had gotten her into, she was going to lose everything. Already, she owed two months on her mortgage. If business didn't pick up soon, she'd never come up with the funds to cover her bills. What was she going to do?

"How could I have been so wrong about him?" she muttered. Her love for him had made her blind to his faults—a mistake a twenty-nine-year-old woman shouldn't make. What she'd thought were a few eccentricities grew over the months of their relationship until the darker side of his nature seemed to take over and obliterate everything good in him.

The whirring overhead fans in the shop did little more than stir the hot air and send it back down. The air conditioning worked overtime but couldn't really cool the interior. It only made the soul-sucking heat bearable. The marble floor seemed to create a haze in front of her eyes, the heat almost making the air waver. Scents of the freshly dried herbs that lined her back wall created a heady aroma that nearly overwhelmed the interior of the store on this late summer afternoon.

"I have to figure out a way to get that café next door out of here." She glanced out the front window as a man with black hair, black eye makeup, and black clothes walked by.

A shiver skittered up her spine as he turned. Cold, blank eyes looked through her. She wanted Daniel and his strange customers out of the shop next door.

"This second wouldn't be soon enough," she muttered.

"Talking to yourself again?" Kate stood in the open doorway, her chin-length bob swinging in dark waves against her face as she tilted her head.

"Maybe I was talking to the spirits." She wished it were true. Maybe spirits could make Daniel vacate the building.

"Whatever." Kate shrugged. "You know I don't really believe that mumbo jumbo."

"Yes you do. You just won't admit it." Sarah pulled a tray full of stones toward her and picked out several.

"What are you doing?" Kate narrowed her eyes.

"Making you a present." Sarah placed the stones into a tiny velvet bag, pulled the gold drawstring and handed it to Kate. A sixth sense told her that Kate would soon need the protection these stones offered. "Put this in your pocket."

"Oh, Sarah. Those stones will make my back hurt. They're way too heavy." Kate grinned and her blue eyes sparkled with mischief. She loved to tease Sarah about her mysticism.

There were times when Kate needed to take her warnings a bit more seriously, and this was one of those times. "This isn't funny, Kate. Put them in your pocket. Now." The tiny hairs on the back of her neck rustled as though brushed by an evil hand.

"Geez. Okay. I was just kidding. You usually aren't so touchy about this New Age—"

The doorbell chimed over the antique wood door. It creaked on its hinges, pulling what little cool air there was from the inside and replacing it with damp heat. She tried to breathe but the vile stench of death wrapped around her neck, cutting off her air. Sarah's fingers closed around a stone that lay on the tray she'd just finished sorting through for Kate's pouch. It offered scant protection from evil, but any protection was better than nothing.

"Daniel, what rock did you crawl out from under?" Kate stepped in front of Sarah. It was a move Sarah recognized from their childhood. Kate, ever the protector of her and Rebecca.

"I need a spell book." Daniel tried to step around Kate but she scooted in front of him.

Daniel had romanced Sarah, talked her into leasing him the precious space next door and then opened a Goth café. While she believed that they had the right to be as strange as they wanted, the truth was that the café was not a business she would ever have granted a lease. Her own customers, mainly tourists, were frightened to come near her store because of the dark, fear-provoking appearance of the café's customers spilling onto the street day and night. Of course not all in the Goth culture were evil, but Daniel and a few of the others were. Their evilness stretched out across several hundred feet, creating a thick, dark taste in the air and a fetid smell that made her want to retch.

"Tell your friend to back off before I rip her throat out, Sarah." His words hissed past his black lips like flames from hell.

Sarah could feel the putrid scorch of death on him. How had he disguised this from her? Had she not wanted to see the true Daniel? Had she been that desperate for love? No. She didn't need a man to feel fulfilled. She never had. He'd changed since she'd first met him and fallen in love. His involvement in dark magic killed all that was once good and kind in him, leaving an empty, evil shell of a man.

"Your business isn't welcome here, Daniel." Sarah moved to stand in front of Kate. She was no longer a second-grader needing protection from the taunts of school children who didn't understand her connection to the supernatural. Kate probably needed protection worse than Sarah from this man.

Kate seemed completely oblivious to Daniel's black heart and the possibility of violence that dripped into the room.

"I need a spell. Someone pissed me off." He made another move toward the books on the back wall.

Sarah put one hand up, her other hand clutching the talisman the gypsy woman had made for her. It was her own personal shield against evil. She just hoped it was strong enough.

"We don't deal with that type of thing here, Daniel. This isn't a voodoo shop. It isn't for black magic. It's a New Age shop. You should know the difference. We deal in good, white magic. Not evil. That means you don't fit in here. So leave."

He glared at her. His eyes had once been a soft, gentle brown. When they'd first met at a Tennessee Williams Festival, she'd felt safe and warm in his presence. Now his eyes were two bits of coal, flat and without life. Had he hidden this part of his soul from her? Or had he changed so completely? Sarah wasn't sure. She bit her lip, sending a prayer to God that Daniel would leave. Years ago, she'd learned to imagine herself inside a white bubble of protective light where only Christ's love was allowed to enter. It was the first time she'd been faced with such intense evil, and her concentration didn't allow her to throw up the protective armor quickly enough. She would never admit it or give the man the satisfaction of seeing it, but she was terrified of him. Deep within her soul, she knew he was capable of anything.

"Your refusal to embrace the darkness will be your undoing," he said. Then he turned and left the store, the door slamming behind him.

Sarah released the breath she hadn't realized she was holding. She might sometimes joke with her friends about curses or voodoo but she'd never seriously fool around with any type of dark magic. This last encounter with Daniel was as close as she ever wanted to stand to evil again.

"You okay?" Kate still watched the front of the store as though ready to do battle.

"I do think you were a warrior in a past life, Kate. You always jump into the fray."

"Only for my friends."

"Well, you should be more cautious. Take a breath before you say what you're thinking sometimes."

"You know me." Kate shrugged.

Sarah did know her. She had a heart as big as the sky and a fierce desire to defend those she loved. The protectiveness often got her into trouble. Sarah started to throw in an additional caution, but decided to change the subject instead. Kate's nature was to save those she loved from any possibility of harm, and you couldn't change someone's true nature.

"You never did say what you were doing here," Sarah said. Kate sometimes stopped in for lunch but never this late in the day. It was nearly time for her to start her evening ghost tours.

"I had an idea that I think will help both of us. It will get me out of my rut. It will bring you more business. Although I can't promise it will get rid of the café."

Sarah waved her hand. "I only have to survive for a year. Then his lease is up and no matter how charming he pretends to be, he won't fool me a second time."

Kate had enough to worry about, she wouldn't tell her just how serious her financial situation was, or that she'd lose the building if things didn't improve soon. She'd rather change the subject and work out the problem on her own for now. If necessary, she knew she could count on her two best friends to do everything in their power to help her.

"And you aren't in a rut, you're running from your manager because you're scared of love. Things are starting to get too serious for you, aren't they?"

"Forget love. It doesn't exist. I'm starting my own business because I want to, not because I'm scared of Ian." Kate snorted through her nose as though that would prove her point. "I've got some money saved. If I can work for six more months, I'll have enough to cover start-up costs and a little to live on."

"This is wonderful." Sarah grabbed a money stone and slipped it into the pouch that Kate still held in her hand.

"Stop that." Kate slung the pouch onto the counter. "There is no such thing as luck or elements or any other brouhaha. We make our own luck."

Sarah grabbed the pouch and slipped it into Kate's purse while her friend stared into space as her idea took shape. Kate might not believe in magic, but she did. She'd seen the power of positive thought and too many unexplainables to overlook the possibility of a simple bag full of stones.

"I want to start a new kind of tour service. I plan to do early morning tours when the dew still glistens on the moss-hung oaks. And the ghost tours when the deep shadows of the river creep across the city. Then, we'll traipse into the cemeteries at dusk and have a short candlelight tour."

"I love it." Sarah smiled. Kate had yet to realize her full potential. She was like a bird just learning to spread its wings and fly. Every once in a while she tumbled to the ground, other times she soared into the air. "You have to include a history of the famous voodoo queen, Marie Laveau!"

"I also want to focus on stories like the Axeman, who terrorized the Italian community during the turn of the century. Maybe a few of the less famous ghosts and legends. The other tour companies all cover similar material—I want to do something different."

Kate still stared into the distance and Sarah knew she'd gone off into a world of her own, filled with stories of times past and ghosts that still walked the cobbled streets of the city.

"The tours have a twist. I'm calling them Fondest Wish Tours. They will start right here." Kate seemed to come back to the present and spun around in a slow circle, her arm extended to encompass every corner of the store. "You'll meet with each client for a moment and create a pouch for them based on their life. Then we go on the tour. We end up back here where each will sign a book and explain how the stones made a difference that day."

"Kate, you don't have to do that." She'd dug herself into this grave, she'd pull herself out. Kate didn't realize how dire the situation or she'd know that a few sales from stones wouldn't help her enough to make a difference. She loved her for trying, though.

"I know I don't have to. I want to. And here is the best part . . ." Kate rubbed her hands together and grinned. "I want to use the space over your store and I want to put a tea room up there called *Tea Leaves*. I want to hire the gypsy woman to come in and read the leaves. I know the clientele is different, but maybe all the activity will run off Daniel and his cronies or at least convince him to leave you alone."

Sarah stared at Kate a moment, utterly speechless. "You have the most diabolical mind of anyone I've ever met."

"Yes, and that is exactly what you love about me."

Sarah wished she could get as excited as Kate about the entire idea but a vague feeling of unease settled onto her shoulders. She knew herself well enough to know that she should pay heed to the subtle warning of impending doom. She knew Kate well enough not to say a negative word. Kate wouldn't hear her anyway.

★ ★ ★ ★ ★

Jared Wells unloaded several large bags of donated clothing off the back of the truck and stacked them inside the door of the mission. Sweat trickled down the side of his face and he swiped it away. It was a good thing he'd had his brown hair cropped short before this trip; he couldn't imagine dealing with a thick head of hair in this heat. His pulse still raced from Becca's telephone call. His cell phone had cut out. She probably thought he'd hung up on her, although it hardly mattered after what she'd said to him.

Anger drove his movements as he hefted bag after bag of donated items.

"Hey, partner, slow down before you collapse." Pastor Wayne Brown laughed, his rounded belly jostling with the movement. He slapped Jared on the back. "Anything you want to talk about?"

"The woman I've been dating called on my cell phone and dumped me." Jared could still feel the sting of her words. The phone had crackled and at first, he'd been thrilled to hear her voice until he'd heard her say, "Look . . . hate to tell you this way . . . the thing is . . . we're through."

He threw another bag on the pile.

"I know quite a few single women who would love to date a doctor, a good Christian man they might settle down with."

"None like this one, Pastor." Becca wasn't like any other woman. "She's the most gorgeous woman I've ever met, but not vain. She's quiet but has a wit about her. She makes me laugh." And in the bedroom—he couldn't share that part of their relationship with his pastor.

Not many women could put up with his strange work hours as a doctor. The ones that could usually just wanted someone who would give them a cushy living, and he was more interested in helping people than taking huge amounts of money for his work. He'd thought in Becca that he'd finally found his soul mate.

"She sounds like a keeper."

Jared nodded. He'd been thinking this was the woman he'd spend forever with—that made her rejection sting even more. Visions of a little house near the hospital and family vacations to the beach already filled his head. He'd already created their children in his daydreams.

"How many mission trips have we gone on together, Jared?"

"Five." Jared grunted as he lifted a particularly heavy bag. The sun scalded down on his head.

"In all the years I've known you, I've never known you to give up so easily. You usually go after what you want and you usually get it."

Jared paused mid-throw and stared at the pastor. A slow grin tilted up his lips as determination filled his chest.

"You are absolutely right, Wayne." Where had Becca said she was headed? Home. He tried to remember where home was. Some small town in Indiana and she was always talking about the flower parades for a poet.

"Go get her, boy." Wayne winked at him.

Three

Ian Fields leaned back in his well-worn, leather-covered swivel chair. Kate should arrive at work anytime and he could hardly wait to see her. She'd been so busy lately that they hadn't spent much time together. It was a good thing she worked for him or he might not see her at all.

He frowned. Maybe he needed to send her flowers or something. Two years ago, his wife had walked out of his life and into his best friend's arms. As she'd left, she'd made it clear that it was because he worked too much and didn't romance her enough. He'd lost his best friend and his childhood sweetheart in one heartbeat. He'd never seen it coming. He'd believed that if he worked hard to make sure she could have a nice house, nice cars, and any other thing she wanted that everything else would work itself out.

"What an idiot I was." He rubbed his hand over the back of his neck. His hair was longer than normal and he could feel the ends curling against his nape. Time for a haircut. He wouldn't make the same mistakes with Kate that he'd made with Angela. Not that Kate was anything like Angela. The two women were as different as Vanilla and Rocky Road— one was bland and common and the other full of surprises. He'd loved Angela, but it was a familiar, comfortable feeling. With Kate, their relationship was intense and touched him on a deeper level. Her ability to laugh at herself was one of the things he loved most about her. Her devotion to her job and friends made it clear that she had staying power.

The phone jangled, interrupting his thoughts. He picked up the receiver, expecting to book another tour group. "Ghost Hunters Tours."

"I'm looking for Kate Tyler. Is she there this evening?" A man's deep voice thrust across the phone wires. It was probably a client from a former tour, but something about the man's tone sent Ian's blood boiling. During the last few months of their marriage, Angela often whispered secret conversations on the phone. How many times had he answered the phone only to hear a swift click as the person on the other end hung up?

"Ms. Tyler is not in yet. I'm the manager of Ghost Hunters. Can I help you with anything?"

"Afraid not. It's personal."

Ian's chair was already tilted back on two legs and when the man's words registered on his brain, he almost sprawled backwards. He slowly set the chair down on all fours and pulled the receiver closer to his ear. Personal? Was Kate seeing another man? True that she'd seemed busy lately, but it wasn't fair for him to assume it was because she was seeing someone else. *She isn't Angela.* Perhaps the man was a relative of Kate's. Ian refused to picture Kate with another man—not until he heard solid proof of the other man's intentions.

"Would you like to leave a message for her?" Ian asked, hoping for a hint of who the man was.

"I'll just talk to her when I see her," he said. "Thanks."

The phone clicked in his ear and then went dead. Ian set the receiver slowly back in the cradle. If it had been a relative, Ian was fairly certain the man would have identified himself.

He'd never made it clear to Kate that he wasn't seeing other people. Perhaps Kate assumed he was and was seeing other people as well.

Ian jumped from his chair and paced the room. He wasn't sure if he should approach the subject with Kate or wait and see if she did. What if she fell in love with this other guy? What if she was *already* in love with him? The thought made Ian's head and heart both ache at the same time. No, if she was in love with the other man, she wouldn't still be dating Ian. At the same time, he knew that if she was in love with him, she wouldn't be dating another man. He'd have to wait and follow her lead, but at least he was forewarned. He could pour on the romance and see what happened. At least he wouldn't make the same mistake he'd made with Angela.

There was no time to waste if Kate wanted to get to Indiana and have enough time to convince her sister not to marry Mark. She'd need at least nine days off work and more luck than Sarah's stones were capable of producing.

A breeze had kicked up from the northwest, making the weather perfect for the walking tours she conducted five evenings a week. She loved her work as a tour guide, but her relationship with Ian was becoming too intense too quickly and a short break while she attended her sister's wedding was just what she needed to clear her head and figure out her true feelings.

Ghost Hunters Tours resided in a three-hundred-year-old building made of red brick, with intricate wrought iron balconies, and a huge hundred-pound door that creaked as she entered. Her shoes squeaked across the recently polished slate floor. She winced. The nursing shoes weren't the most attractive footwear she could have worn but she'd learned from

Becca that they made hours on your feet easier than just about any other type of footwear. She was willing to sacrifice a little fashion for comfort.

"Full tour tonight, Kate." Megan, a young woman who Kate'd just finished training as a new tour guide, greeted her with a wide smile.

"The more the merrier." A full tour meant twenty-five to thirty people. That many people meant a lot of questions. A lot of questions meant she could get her mind off Ian and off her sister for the rest of the evening. She felt some of the tension fall from her shoulders.

"Kate, can I see you in my office for a minute?" Ian stood in the doorway leading to his back office; his dark brows were lowered in a scowl. Dark stubble covered his square jaw, even though Kate knew he shaved twice a day. He had a rugged handsomeness about him that made her heart race. The tension hopped back onto her shoulders and perched there as though roosting permanently.

"Of course, Ian." She followed him into his office.

He stood just inside the door and, when she entered, he closed the door swiftly and hauled her into his arms. This wasn't fair. His body was hard and warm and all she really wanted to do was rest her head on his chest and cry out all the frustration of the past week. His lips brushed over hers in a feather light kiss as soft as the brush of butterfly wings.

"Come over tonight after your tour." His deep brown eyes reminded her of the box of Swedish chocolate Jen had sent her for her last birthday. "I'll light some candles and put on some soft music."

"I can't. I have to pack." She pulled away.

"Pack?" Ian reached out and brushed the back of his fingers across her cheek.

Her abdomen clenched in excitement. "Yes, I was going

to talk to you about it earlier, but things have been so hectic. I need nine days off work."

She knew she owed him more of an explanation. Even if they hadn't been dating for the past few months, she should tell him about the wedding as his employee. But she'd spent so many years answering only to herself. And she'd had one too many relationships not pan out—she wasn't sure she knew how to open up any more than this. Fear fluttered up her throat and she coughed. She was terrified to open up to him, terrified he would hurt her, and terrified that she would deceive herself into believing there was more of a relationship between them than really existed.

His eyes narrowed to two dark slits, a look she recognized as raw jealousy. She'd never been able to put up with a jealous man because of her independent nature. Yet, Ian struggled with that issue because of his ex-wife. From his expression, she knew he was wondering if she was leaving town with another man. She'd never offered him a commitment or promise; she was never available for Friday night dates but hadn't told him about the Lipstick Diary meetings. He probably thought she was dating a lot of men. But the truth was that she hadn't been able to think about another man since the first time they'd kissed.

"Where are you going?" he asked.

"Home." That much was true. *Just tell him about the wedding, Kate. Share a piece of your life with him. Ask him to go with you.* But she couldn't. She wasn't ready. She swallowed down more panic.

"Indiana?" He moved to the other side of the room and shuffled some papers on his desk. "Are you going alone?"

"No." She opened her mouth to tell him Sarah and Becca were going with her, but he slammed the papers down. While he was jealous at times, he wasn't normally this intense. The move shocked her into silence.

"I see." He swung back around. "The answer is no."

"Excuse me?"

"No. You can't have the time off. I need you here. It's too short notice." He waved his hand. "You have a tour starting in ten minutes."

"You are telling me no and dismissing me? As though I'm a pest?" White hot anger sang in a high soprano voice through her veins. A red fog lowered over her vision.

"I can't spare you right now. I have a commitment to the company to keep a certain number of tours running during our tourist season. Sorry." He didn't sound or look the least bit sorry.

She didn't have a choice. If she wanted to save Jen, she had to go to that wedding. She couldn't wait and go just for the ceremony. If she waited until the day of the wedding and flew in, then all would be lost—no, she had to go now while there was still time to convince Jennifer to call the whole thing off. Her sister's future was at stake. She'd made a promise to herself that she'd never let her sister down again.

"Ian, please. Megan can take over my tours until I get back. She's fully trained. She's wonderful with the tourists." She swallowed. "This—this is really important to me."

Her vocal cords barely formed the words. It was hard for her to admit that to him. She wanted desperately to keep their work and professional lives separate until she could save up the rest of the money to strike out on her own. Then, she would be able to explore how she felt about him when they weren't working in such close proximity. Maybe then, she'd be able to start to trust him and open up. She wanted that very much. She couldn't remember ever wanting it more with any man, but he needed to be patient with her.

"I'm sure it is important to run off and have whatever fling

42

you want to have." He crossed his arms and leaned back against his desk. "The answer is no."

"You think I'm leaving to have a fling?" At least his words were honest, if a bit raw and edgy.

"I really don't know what you're doing, Kate. You don't tell me anything. All you do is run from any real relationship." He sliced his hand through the air. "But that has nothing to do with this. I can't spare you."

She wasn't going to tell him anything now either. He could trust her or not, she didn't really care. They weren't married and she didn't have to answer to anyone—didn't *want* to answer to anyone. That was one of the reasons she was still single. She shifted from foot to foot. He was right that she didn't share anything with him, but she was trying to overcome her inhibitions and learn to open up to him. Right now, though, she didn't have time to argue with him. Her tour started in a few minutes and she *would* attend that wedding.

"I'm going, Ian. Make sure I'm covered." She moved toward the door but he took three quick strides and stepped in front of her.

"If you go, you won't have a job when you get back."

"You're firing me?" The heat of unshed tears burned her eyes. She refused to let them fall. Not only did his words put their relationship on the line, but in six more months she'd have enough money to realize her dream. If she lost her job now, she'd have to live off her savings. Everything was on the line.

"I'll be forced to replace you. I'm not firing you. It's your choice." He opened the door and held it for her. She walked out, and he closed the door firmly behind her. Stay and her sister was lost. Go and her future was lost. Either way, she'd have to make her decision soon.

★ ★ ★ ★ ★

The numbers in her savings book register swam in front of her eyes, taunting her. Kate closed the cover, leaned back in the chair, and rubbed her temples. Either she stayed and let her sister marry a man who would make her absolutely miserable. Or she left and gave up her dream of owning her own business.

Fury over Ian's ultimatum sing-songed through her. "Jerk." She stood and crossed the room to where the eighth-grade picture of her younger sister hung lopsided on the wall. Braces covered a wide, thirteen-year-old grin.

Jennifer was only two years younger, but at times it seemed as though decades separated them. She'd vowed never to allow her sister to be hurt again, if she could prevent it. The terror of a year ago came back in full force and she closed her eyes against the sting. If she knew a man was bad news, she couldn't just sit quietly at home and do nothing to save her sister. She'd done that once before and it had almost resulted in disaster.

"I love you, Jen." She brought her fingers to her lips and then transferred a kiss to her sister's forehead. "I'm coming home."

Four

The flat, green plains of central Indiana spread out across the horizon like green sheets of construction paper. Sarah pressed her forehead against the cool interior glass of the Ford Mustang they'd rented. Returning to Indiana was therapy as much for her as it was for Kate. She'd escaped small town life for college and never regretted the move. People in New Orleans didn't look askance at her weird ways. She fit perfectly into the city. There were times, though, when her throat ached with longing for home and family. Not that she'd ever really had that. It didn't mean she didn't want it. And deep inside the little girl who'd been the outcast still cried out for acceptance and a place to belong.

If she wanted to be honest with herself, part of the reason she'd fallen so hard for Daniel was because he'd told her he loved everything about her and wouldn't change a thing. She'd never had a man feed her that line before and because she'd wanted it to be true, she'd overlooked signs she might otherwise have picked up on.

Now, in the middle of a full-blown, Midwest heat wave, the stalks of corn that blurred together along the sides of the road seemed a bit dry for this early in the season. Sarah took a deep breath, imagining the smell of the freshly reaped crops in the fall and the scent of freshly turned dirt in the spring. She hadn't really missed her hometown, but there was a sense of proverbial life that reached out and reminded her that not all the times she'd spent in this state had been bad—thanks mostly to the other two women in the car with her.

"How am I going to convince my sister not to marry Mark? She's so stubborn." Kate's fingers gripped the steering wheel so tightly that her knucklebones stood out in sharp, white re-lief.

"Just like her big sister," Rebecca reminded her.

Kate jerked her hand up and pushed an escaping strand of hair back into place. "This isn't going to be easy is it?"

"Is anything ever?" Sarah leaned forward, grabbed a bot-tled water, and handed it to Kate. She knew her friend well enough to know that Kate did not like to lose. She'd figure out a way to convince Jennifer to call off the wedding.

She leaned forward to grab another bottle for Rebecca, but her hand slipped as a frisson of foreboding stole along her nerve endings. Closing her eyes, she wished she could under-stand what these moments of vague unease meant. At times, it was as simple as a flat tire. Most of the time, the warning re-garded something far more ominous. She shivered and handed Becca the water she finally managed to grip and pass back.

Kate's emotions were in high gear. The waves of tension bounced off her and echoed through the car. Perhaps that was all that had her on edge—she hoped.

Kate pulled the car off an exit ramp just a few miles to the east of the Shelbyville/State Road 9 exit. She stopped in a gas station parking lot and put the car into park. Her head dropped onto arms crossed on the steering wheel. Her breaths came fast and shallow, her back rising with each movement.

"I can't do this. Jen will hate me."

Sarah patted her on the back. "You can do this. We're here with you."

"Why did I agree to come for an entire week before the wedding?" Kate groaned. "Because I'm insane. Completely insane."

Rebecca scooted forward and spoke from the back seat. "Jen will understand that you only have her best interests at heart, Kate. After what happened last year with Billy, how could she think anything else?"

"Are you sure Mark is such a bad guy?" Rebecca asked.

Kate lifted her face and glanced at Rebecca in the rearview mirror. She took a deep breath and nodded her head. "He cheated on me in high school, which was a long time ago and I wouldn't think that much of it, but from what I hear he hasn't exactly mended his ways. He's known as the town playboy."

Sarah glanced over her shoulder at Becca, who shook her head. "You make him sound like Satan," Becca said. "He isn't that bad or Jen would never have dated him."

Since when did Becca stand up for Mark Jackson? When he'd cheated on Kate in high school, it was Becca who had helped Sarah console their best friend. Her behavior was extremely out of character. Perhaps the hormones coursing through her body were making her more giving and trusting than normal.

"I should just turn the car around and go home," Kate said.

"If you don't show up at the wedding, then Jen'll never forgive you," Sarah said.

"You're right. I know you're right. I'm just dealing with a lot at the moment. I'm worried about my sister. Worried about Ian. Worried about my job. And now I have to deal with Mark Jackson, someone I thought dead and buried from my life."

There had been times when she'd felt slightly jealous of Kate. Everything Sarah longed for had always come easily for her friend. Dates, friends, family, fitting in. Mark was the one blip on an otherwise perfect horizon. At least he hadn't tried to destroy Kate's livelihood the way Daniel had tried to destroy hers.

"Stop whining," Rebecca mumbled from the backseat, echoing Sarah's own thoughts.

"Excuse me?" Kate twisted in her seat to glare at Rebecca.

"You heard me. I'm tired of hearing you whine. You've always been the popular one. The pretty one. The one who got the dates. The one who won the trophies. The one who graduated as valedictorian. You are an overachiever in the worst possible way. You have outshone me over and over and you want to complain about the one man who dumped you. Get over it—for your sister's sake. We have bigger problems. Focus on the here and now."

Rebecca's chest heaved with the power of her words and her eyes glittered with anger. *Whoa, girl. Those hormones are raging.* The topic of Mark Jackson certainly seemed to set off fires in Rebecca's veins anymore. Kate shifted sideways in her seat and looked at Sarah.

"Do you feel the same way?" she demanded. Tears glistened in her eyes.

Sarah bit her lip. One of their unspoken rules as friends was to always be honest with one another.

"Never mind. Your silence speaks louder than words. Thanks so much for all your support." Kate rammed the transmission into drive and squealed out of the gas station. Her jaw lifted into the air and she clenched her teeth tightly together.

Sarah sat back and released a long breath. Right now she was more worried about facing a town full of people who'd always looked down on her than she was about Kate being angry. Kate would get over her anger. She could never stay mad for long or maintain a silence for long. For now, she planned to use the break from Kate's chatter to think about what she wanted out of her own life. She'd be thirty soon and she wasn't about to go into her thirties without having a firm grasp of who she was and where she was headed. One thing she was certain of—in the past, she'd been entirely too trusting of others. She'd given the benefit of the doubt too many times. All that was about to change.

Walking away from her job in New Orleans was the worst mistake Kate had ever made. A twenty-nine-year-old woman should have more sense. She took a deep breath, dreading the wedding that loomed just over a week away, feeling in her gut that trying to stop it was tantamount to trying to stop a freight train with her bare hands. She didn't want to see Jennifer and have her suspicions confirmed. What if her sister was head over heels in love? Kate remembered the glassy-eyed looking Jen just after she'd started dating Billy. That madly-in-love expression was one of the things that had stopped her from expressing her misgivings to her sister. She should have spoken up then, but hadn't.

As much as she dreaded confronting Jen with her thoughts about Mark Jackson, there was nothing else to keep her from going home—Sarah had been dropped off at her aunt's house and Rebecca was with her mother. That didn't leave her many choices in a small town where her own mother had probably been notified the moment she'd rolled into Hancock County.

The familiar landmark sign marking the location of the former home and birthplace of the beloved poet James Whitcomb Riley stood out in green relief against the dull modern concrete sidewalk. Just across the street, a local pizza place still sported a neon "OPEN" sign. How many half-pepperoni, half-mushroom-and-green-pepper pizzas had she, Becca, and Sarah shared over the years in that very restaurant? Too many to count. She wondered if that old Hank Williams song was still number 149 on the jukebox. She turned down a cobbled alley, her wheels bumping gently over the rough road. How many times had she ridden her bike down this alley on her way to Sarah's house?

The white, two-story, turn-of-the-century home captured the corner lot and stood like a regal ruler over the smaller houses on the quiet, suburban street. Vivid pink and white petunias cascaded from large planters which ran up both sides of the steps leading to a large wraparound porch. It was unbelievable but it could have been today or twenty-four years ago. She could almost picture her father teaching a five-year-old version of her to ride a bicycle along the sidewalk that crossed in front.

Kate blinked a couple of times and then pulled her car into the long driveway that ran beside the house. A low fence surrounded the back yard. She wondered if her father were working in the garage as he often did during warm summer days. He had a bright yellow hot rod he'd been building for as long as she could remember. She considered going around back and seeing if he was there, but knew her mother would be hurt if she hid out in the back yard instead of going inside. She didn't want to face her sister—didn't want to destroy the happiness she knew Jennifer thought she'd found.

Grabbing her heavy suitcase from the trunk, she pulled out the handle and dragged it behind her on the wheels. If the outer appearance of the town and her childhood home hadn't changed, then the inside dynamics would most definitely be the same. She would play the role of big sister and Jennifer would ignore everything she had to say. *You aren't a child anymore. Play your game, not hers.*

Feeling out of place and wishing she could run back to New Orleans, she lifted her fist and knocked on the glass pane in the center of the heavy wood door. The sound of footsteps shuffling across the floor signaled her mother's arrival. She saw through the pane of glass that her mom was wearing navy blue slacks and a white, button-up blouse. Her hair was cropped short but died dark brown and her blue eyes lit with happiness when she saw her daughter through the door.

"Katie." Her mother opened the door and took Kate into her arms, patting her on the back as though Kate was still a small child. "Why are you knocking, child? This is still your home, you know. I won't want you to knock when you bring my grandchildren to visit—hopefully soon."

"Hi, Mom." Love, resentment, and confusion all rumbled around inside her. She hugged her mother back, pushing the feelings aside. She loved her mother and knew the woman only wanted her to be happy, but the constant questions about who she was dating and when she would settle down were starting to wear thin. They were questions she'd often asked herself in the last couple of years. But she wouldn't marry the first man who came along to please her mother. That's exactly what Jennifer was doing and look what a mess she was in.

"Noah, come here. Katie is home." She held Kate out at arm's length and looked her up and down. "Have you been eating? You are so thin."

Kate smiled. She was at the upper limit of her ideal weight range, but could never convince her mother of that fact. She worked out, ate healthy, but indulged in the occasional hot fudge sundae, no nuts, whipped cream on the side. She was happy with the way she looked. The extra weight gave her some soft, feminine curves but she still liked the way she fit into her favorite pair of tight blue jeans.

"Kate." Her father stepped onto the porch and took her in a big bear hug, lifting her slightly off the ground just as he had when she was a little girl. "It's so good to see you."

"Daddy—" Her throat closed off with emotion. Her father's love was like a warm blanket of acceptance and approval that she could wrap around her when she felt particularly low. She'd seen Rebecca grow up without a father—knew how deeply the scars stretched from that abandonment. Tears of thankfulness welled up in her eyes. She hugged him back tightly.

As he set her back on her feet, she noticed his hair had gone completely gray in the year and a half since she'd seen him and his shoulders were a bit more stooped. For the first time, she realized that he was becoming an old man. Panic flitted through her, setting her pulse soaring. It was as though the certainty of his death was something she could no longer ignore and her future seemed bleak without her parents' love.

"Tears?" He brushed the moisture off her cheek with his thumb. "None of that. We've got a wedding to plan and you know what that means . . ."

"Parties," all three of them said at once.

Kate laughed. Her parents craved good parties. Some things never changed.

"Where is Jennifer?"

Her parents exchanged a glance that told her they'd been discussing Kate and her unmarried state and probably a whole lot more.

"Jennifer and Mark are in the city getting a license and then she's staying overnight in Indy with some girlfriends and doing some shopping for her honeymoon."

They gave licenses to men with cloven hooves? She figured that would automatically exclude you from marrying a human woman, but that was bureaucracy for you.

"I'll get your bag." Her dad grabbed her suitcase before she could protest and carried it up the long flight of stairs just inside the entryway.

"Stop standing on the porch and get in here," her mother said. "No matter how old you get, this will always be your home, you know. By the way, there is a small party on Friday."

Her mother took her arm and led her toward the kitchen, which she'd always made into the heart of their home.

"Can't do Fridays. You know that, Mom." She had a standing date with Sarah and Rebecca every Friday, and they didn't break their lipstick diary dates.

"Oh, those silly lipstick diaries. I never will understand you girls. You will all become childless spinsters and you'll have those diaries to thank for it. I suppose you can write about how much you regret never marrying in those ridiculous journals." Her mother grabbed a glass out of the cabinet and slammed it down onto the counter with enough force that Kate was surprised it didn't crack. She yanked a jug of milk out of the fridge and filled the cup.

"Please send my regrets to the hostess." Kate took the glass of milk from her mom and grabbed a couple of cookies from the plate sitting in the middle of the oval, oak table.

Her mother stared at her as though wanting to argue further about the diaries but gave her head a slight shake instead. She sighed deeply, probably wondering why she'd been unfortunate to have a daughter who didn't have common sense. "I just worry about you, honey. I want you to be happy."

"I am happy, Mom." But she wasn't. She couldn't remember when she'd felt more miserable.

"That's all I want." Her mother patted her hand, but looked as though she wanted to say more. She probably wanted to mention that she had at least half a dozen men lined up who were eligible and willing, but Kate wasn't going to bite.

Her mother had Jennifer to bend over backwards in her people pleasing manner. Jennifer would marry, give her the grandchildren she wanted, and be miserable her entire life all for the sake of their mother. But not if she could help it. She'd talk to Jen, tell her what a clod Mark was, maybe she would cancel the wedding. And her mother would kill her. She suppressed a dry laugh.

"Anyway . . ." Her mother grabbed a third cookie and slipped it onto Kate's plate. "The party is at noon and it's here at the house. Sort of a bachelorette party."

"Well, why didn't you say so?" Instead of almost starting an argument over the diaries when she knew that Kate wouldn't cancel that date for anything or anyone.

Her mother shrugged. "I have a lot on my mind. You wouldn't believe the preparations for this wedding. And then I've been concerned about the restraining order expiring—"

Her mother stopped mid-sentence, which wasn't like her. Instant worry coursed through Kate. "Billy hasn't been around, has he? You know what the judge said—"

"We haven't seen him."

They hadn't *seen* Billy, but they all knew that didn't necessarily mean he wasn't stalking Jennifer. She still couldn't understand why the courts chose to let Billy remain free, but apparently there hadn't been enough proof to convict. Surely after a year, he'd moved on to some other obsession? Kate set the remaining cookie back down on the plate, her appetite completely gone.

"I'm really tired, Mom. I think I'll head upstairs and lie down."

"It's only seven o'clock. It isn't even dark outside. I wanted to hear how Ian is doing."

And there was yet another topic she had no desire to thrash out. Her head ached from the tension of the last few days and she knew if she didn't get a good night's sleep, she was going to wind up with a migraine. Then, what good would she be to Jennifer or anyone else?

"It was a long drive." She needed her rest to deal with tomorrow.

"Okay, I thought you could bunk up with Jennifer."

"Bunk up? Why can't I just sleep in my old room or on the sofa?" She'd been out on her own for eleven years but desperately wanted to escape to the haven of her childhood bedroom. The last time she'd been home, her bedroom remained the same as always. It was a throwback to her childhood. She felt safe and protected in the refuge of her room, surrounded by trophies from happy times and favorite toys her mother had kept all these years.

While her old room sounded like a sanctuary, the truth was that if her sister hadn't been getting married she probably wouldn't have come home at all this year. They came to the south to see her at Christmas and she'd always told herself it was a nice winter vacation for them. But Jennifer was starting her own life now. Soon, she'd have her own family and children and probably wouldn't want to travel. What would Christmas be like if Jen married Mark? Uncomfortable—particularly since she was marrying a man that Kate despised.

"Of course you can sleep in your old room, if you prefer. All your stuff is still in there. I just thought sharing a room would be a good chance for you girls to chat and catch up." Unshed tears shone in her mother's eyes.

"You are absolutely right, Mom. I'll just crash in Jen's room." And it would give her more time with Jennifer to try to convince her that this wedding should be called off.

★ ★ ★ ★ ★

Years of feeling as though she didn't quite belong and wondering why her father hadn't wanted her rushed back to greet Rebecca as she stepped through the front door of the tiny apartment that sat above the old Pickett Hardware store.

The same shabby furniture she'd grown up with filled the tiny living room. Her mother tried to brighten up the faded material with a colorful, crocheted throw but it only made the material underneath look dingier. She could see into the kitchen from the doorway and the same chipped Formica table with the thin stainless steel legs sat in the center of that room. She wished for the hundredth time that her mother would allow her to do more in the way of sending money or buying her things. The television she'd purchased on her last visit sat on a rickety, wooden stand that seemed to almost groan under the weight of the black box. It didn't matter how much her mother argued this time, she was buying her a new couch while she was in town. She wouldn't take no for an answer.

"Hi, Mama." She embraced her mother, who had been a couple of inches shorter since Rebecca hit thirteen, but now felt tiny and frail with the osteoporosis that had caused her back to hunch slightly. The pretty, velvet bathrobe she'd bought her mother for Christmas last year clashed with the rest of the apartment. She wished her mother would let her do a little more. But she was filled with pride—always had been.

"It's so good to see you, sweetheart." As her mother squeezed her, the scent of roses and sugar cookies filled the air. "You have such a glow about you."

Rebecca felt the heat rise in her cheeks. She was still coming to terms with the fact that she was going to be a single mom. She wasn't ready to tell her mother the news just yet. In fact, she wasn't sure how the news would be received—her mother of all people knew how hard it was to raise a child by yourself.

Jared's words echoed through Rebecca's head. *I guess we're through then.*

Fresh anger bubbled in her stomach, causing a low rumble. Whatever kind of reaction she'd expected when she told him she was carrying his child—it hadn't been that. She'd thought he loved her and at the very least would try to support her through the pregnancy by helping her find the best doctors. Not that she really needed him for that. She straightened her spine. No, she was capable of caring for this child on her own—she'd just wanted her baby to have more than that—she'd wanted the happily-ever-after dream.

"How are Kate and Sarah?"

Her mother led her to her old bedroom, which was exactly as she'd left it when she'd taken off for college eleven years ago. The frilly white lace on the canopy bed had yellowed a bit with age, but she immediately remembered the feeling of being completely safe and loved in this tiny home she and her mother had created. It was only when she left the apartment that the reality of not having a father intruded. As much as she loved Kate's dad, he'd been a reminder of exactly what she missed in her own childhood. He'd been a father-figure when she'd most needed one throughout the years. Would her child have anyone like Noah Tyler in his or her life?

"Kate isn't happy about Jennifer marrying Mark, but Sarah seemed happy to see her aunt."

"Such nice girls." Her mother had always liked her friends, and was happy to have them all over for some rather cramped slumber parties. Many times, they'd had their Friday lipstick diary nights in her cozy bedroom.

"They're good friends." And they'd be there for her through this pregnancy. Her hand dropped to her stomach.

What had she done to her child? It would be raised the same as she had, without a father. Father/daughter dances would be a nightmare for the baby if it were a girl and if it were a boy, then there would be no father/son camping trips or Boy Scout outings. She hadn't really expected Jared to do cartwheels over the news that he was unexpectedly a father, but she'd thought he was a responsible, loving man. If she was going to be honest with herself, she'd thought he'd offer to marry her. She'd wished he would. But he hadn't. She sighed.

"Something the matter, Becca?" her mother asked.

"It's nothing, Mama. Everything is fine." But everything wasn't fine and she wasn't sure how to fix it.

Sarah hated everything about this town and the people who lived in it. Years of torment clouded her thoughts as she unpacked her clothes and hung them in the closet of the guest room she'd occupied for most of her life. Before she'd become friends with Kate and Sarah, she'd spent most nights in this room alone, crying. After she'd become friends with them, she'd spent far fewer nights in tears—but the pain of rejection had still smarted, even with the support of their friendship to take the harshest edge of the sting away.

"It's so wonderful to see you, Sarah." Aunt Mary placed fresh sheets on her bed and opened a window to air the room out a bit.

Even at seventy, Aunt Mary's curly blonde locks had a life all their own. Rather than turning gray, her hair had darkened to a deeper blonde. She was the only woman over fifty Sarah had ever known who didn't have to either dye her hair or go completely gray. She hoped her own hair turned the same color when she got older.

Sarah lifted her hair off her neck, thinking it was hot and

sticky even for summer. In Indiana, you never knew what the weather might bring. She'd seen snow in early May and heat in the middle of winter. New Orleans was much more predictable, if a bit more humid. She longed for the rumble of their air conditioner in their wonderful apartment. Without the sounds of jazz, everything seemed slower, as though someone had given the world a sedative.

She loved her aunt's house, which had been built around 1902. Wooden, glass-paned transoms sat overtop each doorway and allowed the heat to travel from room to room during the winter. She didn't think the transoms were much help in the dead of summer, but even then they were attractive and made the doors look taller and wider than they actually were.

"I'm glad to see you too, Aunt Mary." She was happy to see her aunt but she wished it could be anywhere but here. The only good memories she had of Greenfield were of Kate and Rebecca.

Her aunt stopped making the bed and turned to look at her, hands on her wide hips. "Oh, Sarah. You haven't worked through all that angst yet?" Aunt Mary clucked her tongue. "Honey, you know you have to get over this and rid yourself of some of this karma before you can move on."

Sarah blinked in surprise. She'd forgotten how easily her aunt could read her. In fact, when she'd been little, her aunt had encouraged her eccentricities—her ability to sometimes see things a heartbeat before they happened, such as knowing someone was going to call before the phone rang. But those very peculiarities that Aunt Mary embraced were the things that caused the other children at school to make fun of her.

"I am normally fine, Aunt Mary. I just don't like coming here. I know some of the kids who were so cruel to me are married and living here now and I have no desire to see them."

"Then you haven't truly forgiven them for their immaturity. For their mistakes. And until you do, you can't move on with your life."

Sarah shifted uncomfortably from foot to foot. She hated it when her aunt was so right, but she wasn't ready to give up her anger just yet. That anger had helped her survive the two horrible years before Kate had befriended her and her world had become a little easier. The anger had helped her through four dateless years of high school, because none of the boys wanted to be known as the one who dated "the freak." And the anger had even helped her survive Daniel and his betrayal.

Her aunt nodded, almost as though she'd read Sarah's thoughts and went back to making up the bed. "It's okay. You'll forgive when you're ready. Tell me about Daniel and his Goth café. Have you found a solution?"

"I'm not certain, but Kate and I have some ideas. I think it may work out and his lease is up soon, so I only have to survive until then." She wouldn't worry her aunt with her troubles. There wasn't anything Aunt Mary could do to change the situation anyway. She'd never have told her aunt about the café in the first place, if she'd thought things would get this dire.

"Be careful of him." Her aunt shivered. "He sounds positively evil."

"He is." And a severe lapse in her judgment that would never happen again. In fact, after her rotten date last Friday, she didn't really care if she ever saw another man again.

"You just haven't found the right one yet," Aunt Mary said.

"Perhaps." Or maybe, the right one wasn't out there. The

thought of living the rest of her days without a companion was like a swift kick to her heart. As much as she loved sharing an apartment with Rebecca and Kate, she knew that one day they would marry and have families. Rebecca had already started on the family part of the equation. She, Sarah, would be left on her own. Could she stand that? Or did she want something more? She wasn't sure, but knew that she needed to figure it out—and soon.

Rebecca's heart pounded in her chest. She couldn't lose this baby. Just a few hours before, she'd been worried about raising a child alone. She'd woken at one in the morning with severe cramps. Now, panic fluttered in her chest, replacing the worry. Already, she loved the tiny life growing inside her. The child she hadn't known she wanted. Her training told her what cramps at this point in her pregnancy might mean.

She swung her legs out of bed and picked up the bedside telephone and dialed a number she remembered even after eleven years away from her home town. When she heard her friend's voice, she breathed a sigh of relief. Thank goodness she hadn't woken Kate's parents with her late call. "Kate?"

"Becca, what's wrong?"

A bittersweet smile rose to her lips. The three of them had made a vow to always be there for one another. Even when it interrupted a date; even when it was inconvenient; even out of a dead sleep at one in the morning.

"I think I'm losing the baby. Come with me to the hospital?"

"I'll swing by and pick up Sarah and we'll be there in ten minutes."

Becca took deep breaths, praying for the pain to go away. She wrapped her hands around her middle and stood carefully, the spasms still strong. She dressed and then tiptoed into her mother's room.

"Mom?" she whispered. What would she say? She'd never lied to her mother and she wasn't about to start.

"Becca? Honey, what's wrong?"

"I need to go to the hospital, Mama. But I don't want you to worry. I'm okay."

"Becca, I know you. You are my baby girl and the look on your face tells me that you aren't okay. What is going on?" Her mother got out of bed and placed her hands on her hips. "I hope you know there isn't anything you could tell me that would make me love you less."

Becca swallowed. She did know that and it should make telling her mother about the baby easier, but somehow it made it more difficult. She didn't want to disappoint her mother. The woman had lived her entire life in this small town, with small town values. Women didn't have babies out of wedlock and if they did they usually kept it quiet or moved to the big city where it was more acceptable. Of course, things that weren't acceptable eleven years ago were more common-place today.

"I'm pregnant, Mama." There wasn't an easy way to break the news, so she just blurted it into the room.

"I'm gonna be a grandma?" Her mother's grin seemed to stretch wide across her face, overwhelming her small features.

"Y-yes." That wasn't the reaction she'd expected. After Jared's rejection, her mother's happiness over the news was a relief.

Her mother cupped Becca's chin. "Then why the tears, child? A baby is always a blessing."

"Because the father doesn't want us." Becca bit her lip. Just like her own father hadn't wanted her or her mother.

"That's his loss, sweetheart. You're going to be a wonderful mother." Her mom hugged her close and Becca felt a little of the tightness that had been pressing against her chest ease.

"If I get the chance. I'm having cramps. I didn't want to tell you about the baby this way." Becca stared at the toes of her sneakers. Shame filled her. Throughout her teen years, her mother had cautioned her to be careful about getting pregnant. She hadn't wanted her daughter to be forced into marriage with a man who would desert her as Becca's father had deserted them both. Well, it might not have happened in high school, but the result was exactly the same. Except that her child might never have a chance to survive much less know life without a dad.

"It's okay, Becca. I'll get dressed. I'm coming with you."

"No, Mama. You have to work tomorrow—"

"Nonsense. You are my daughter and that is my grandchild. I'm coming."

"Thanks, Mama." A tear fell slowly down Becca's cheek and dripped off her chin. She might not have had a father, but always her mother had been there for her. Sleepless nights; worrying and caring; teaching her to be a good person; constant, steady, strong, and always there.

Would she be as good of a mother? She hoped to God she got a chance to find out.

Five

Kate couldn't help but feel responsible over Rebecca. Had the long drive caused the baby to miscarry? Becca and Sarah loved Jen too—they'd all grown up together—had the stress of the wedding caused problems? Rebecca was so sensitive but kept things inside. That wasn't good. She took a deep breath and blew it out slowly. It was too soon to know if the baby was going to be okay. *Slow down, Kate. Becca needs you right now.*

She remembered the shy, red-pigtailed seven-year-old who had hid behind a tree at recess. Becca had come a long way since grammar school, but Kate couldn't help but think she still hid behind the proverbial tree a bit too often. Becca was rarely a risk-taker. Of course, a baby could change all that.

"It's going to be okay." She squeezed Becca's cold hand.

Becca nodded but her gaze indicated that she was somewhere else than the examination room.

What was taking the doctors so long? Didn't they know that a precious life hung in the balance? She glanced at the clock for the umpteenth time since they'd been shown to the room. Becca's mom and Sarah had agreed to stay in the waiting room since the cubicle they'd put Becca in was so small. Kate knew they were just as worried as she was and waiting for a report. And waiting and waiting.

"C'mon," she whispered.

"Low priority," Becca said, a hollow look in her eyes.

"What?"

"I'm low priority. I'm not bleeding to death." She tried to smile but the tears glistening in her eyes halted the grin. She swung her legs over the edge of the examination table and grabbed a nearby stethoscope and blood pressure cuff. "I do know how to take my own blood pressure though."

"Oh, Becca. That's just—it's lousy. Your baby is important. I'm going to find someone and—"

Becca grasped her hand. "Don't leave me alone, Kate. I thought I could do this by myself, but I can't. Even though I didn't plan this baby, I have fallen in love with it. The thought of losing it . . ." Her throat worked as she swallowed several times.

Helplessness tightened Kate's insides, making her want to scream. She had to get Becca help, had to fix things, had to take action. She blinked, realizing it was a role she'd taken on over and over again during their friendship. She always wanted to fix things, but some things couldn't be fixed. Maybe this was one of them. Then again, how would they know if the doctors didn't come and look at Rebecca? She had to *do* something, she couldn't just sit here while Becca's baby died. Becca, seeming to sense her indecision, squeezed her hand.

"They'll be here soon, Kate. Tell me the story about the day the three of us became friends." Becca closed her eyes.

"Becca, you know the story, you were there." Kate glanced at the clock again.

"Tell me again. I need something to take my mind off things."

"You and I were friends in the first grade. Then, the first day of second grade, we met Sarah, who was in our class. The other children were mean to her."

"And you stepped in and punched Billy in the nose." Becca smiled. "We knew that day he was bad news even without what he did later to Sarah or what he did to your sister last year."

"I punched Billy in the nose, the three of us walked off, and we've been fast friends ever since and forever more."

"I hope my baby has your courage, Kate."

The words hit Kate in the gut. Although she seldom cried, she felt the hot wetness of tears spring to her eyes. She blinked several times, wishing the weakness away. Tears wouldn't help Becca.

"I hope my baby has a chance to have your courage," Becca added.

"That's it. We've waited long enough." Kate jumped to her feet and stuck her head out of the curtained cubicle. A nurse with thick, white-soled shoes zipped past her. "Excuse me?"

"One moment," the nurse said.

"We don't have any more moments," Kate responded. "My friend needs help. This baby is very important."

"So are everyone else's babies." The nurse's mouth was tight, as though she'd heard it all, seen it all, and hadn't liked any of it. Or maybe the tight stretch of her hair into a formal bun had caused a severe headache.

Kate glanced over her shoulder at Becca, who shrugged. No way was she going to resign herself to watching Becca lose this baby. A child that was going to have her courage, Sarah's faith, and Rebecca's gentleness was too important to the world. She took another step toward the nurse and looked her in the eye.

"This child *is* special. My friend is special. I want you to help her and I want her helped now."

"I'm sorry—" The nurse didn't look sorry.

"Kate, I actually feel a little better." Becca tried to rise from the examining table but collapsed again on her back and grabbed her stomach. "Oh!"

The nurse moved quickly to Becca's side and wrapped the blood pressure cuff around Becca's upper arm. She grasped Becca's wrist and took her blood pressure.

"Is it normal?" Kate frowned as the nurse removed the cuff and placed it back in its holder on the wall.

"It's slightly elevated. I'll let the doctor know she's still cramping. He should be here soon."

A few minutes later, a silver-haired man pushed back the curtain and smiled gently at them both. "I hear someone is very concerned about their friend."

"Dr. Edwards." Kate reached out and hugged her childhood doctor. She couldn't believe he was still practicing. He should have retired ten years ago. "Rebecca couldn't be in better hands."

"What seems to be the trouble, little lady?" He moved to Becca's side and leaned over the bed.

"Spotting, and cramps."

"How far along are you?" he asked.

"I'm not positive. I just took an at-home test. I think around the end of the first trimester, but my cycles have always been irregular."

"Well, we'd best order an ultrasound. They can do it up in OB. That will tell us how far along you are and let us see if there are any other problems. I'll have them send you up there and then I'll be back shortly to check on you."

"Thank you, Dr. Edwards." Kate gave him another hug, remembering childhood visits where he'd made her feel better just from his gentle presence. He'd always had stickers and lollipops and he always had a smile. This time was no different.

"Grape, right?" He pulled a sucker out of his pocket and handed it to Kate.

She laughed. "My favorite. Thanks, Dr. E."

She turned back to Becca. "Let's get you up to OB."

Thirty minutes later, the sound of a gentle but rapid heartbeat filled the new room where they'd wheeled Becca. This room was larger, so Becca's mother and Sarah had been allowed to accompany them. The walls were an antiseptic, pale green, but a border with bunnies and teddy bears broke through the middle of the wall and gave the room personality.

The sound of a new spirit beating with determination filled Kate with awe and started a fierce longing she hadn't realized she was capable of. The wonder of a life growing inside Becca's womb, a separate little person, made her wish she'd taken things to the next level with Ian. White picket fences and happily ever after might not be for everyone but if she could just learn to open her heart a little more, she could create her own version of the happy family. She swallowed.

"Oh, Becca. That is amazing."

The ultrasound technician smiled and pointed to a screen. "Look at this. This is the baby's head, an arm, a tiny hand. Looks like you're just over three months."

"Does the baby look okay?" Becca asked, a worried frown puckering her brow.

"The doctor will have to review the tape but it looks like the placenta is attached firmly, heartbeat is strong, that's all good."

Becca let out a breath and Kate wondered how long she'd been holding it. As happy as she was to be here with Becca, the truth was that the father should be here. Rebecca had said she loved him—Jared. Kate narrowed her eyes. He'd better hope she didn't get her hands on him, because she wasn't happy at all with the way he'd hurt her friend.

"Baby is fine," Dr. Edwards pronounced, after reviewing the tapes. "It's normal for some spotting in some women. The cramps do concern me, though. I don't want you to travel for a few days. How long are you girls here?"

"Just over a week. My sister is getting married." The words left a sour taste in her mouth and reminded her that she still had a job to take care of—convincing Jennifer not to marry Mark.

"That should be fine, but if you have any more trouble, make sure you call my office." He wrote out a prescription and handed it to Becca. "Prenatal vitamins. I'm sure you know how important they are."

Becca nodded. "I've been taking some over-the-counter ones but this will be better."

"Good. Good." He patted Kate on the head, making her feel like she was ten again. "You girls take care of yourselves."

Kate watched him disappear, a bittersweet image of him etched on her brain. Something in her gut told her she wouldn't see him again. He was in his seventies and they lived on opposite ends of the country. She straightened her shoulders. Becca was going to be okay; now she had to make sure her sister would be okay as well.

"Kate!" Jennifer squealed, skipped down the stairs of their parents' home, and threw herself into her sister's arms. "If I'd known you were arriving yesterday, I wouldn't have stayed in Indianapolis last night. You won't believe how much shopping I got done, though. I found the cutest pantsuit for the honeymoon at Nordstrom's."

"No worries. If I had a chance to go shopping with my girl-friends and stay in a posh hotel, I'd take it."

"I was worried you wouldn't come when you heard who I

was marrying." Jen shrugged. "I should have known my big sister wouldn't miss my wedding."

Kate felt a stab of guilt. The truth was that she'd struggled over whether or not to come home. The only thing that had motivated her was the fact that she absolutely did not want Jennifer to marry Mark and she knew she had the power to influence her sister. But she couldn't start the conversation there.

"Of course I'd come home for you. Anytime," she said. *You don't know how much this is for your own good, Jen. I just hope you don't hate me for it.* She'd worried about interfering in her headstrong sister's life once before, and had regretted it every day since.

"This bachelorette brunch is going to be a hoot." Jen looped her arm through Kate's and dragged her to the kitchen. "I'm sure you'll see a lot of your old friends. It will be like a mini-reunion for you."

"I need coffee." A reunion was the last thing she wanted to deal with at the moment. The two A.M. visit to the emergency room, which had lasted until seven this morning, meant she'd spent a sleepless night.

"You look terrible. You should try to get a few hours of sleep before everyone gets here. Some of your favorite snoots will be here," Jen said, with a wicked grin.

"I should, but I doubt I could sleep now. I'm too wound up." A born night owl, their mother said Kate hadn't actually slept through the night until she was four or five. Even then, she'd often crawled out of her bed in the wee hours of the night and sat up playing. She'd spent many nights wide awake. When daylight hit, she was never able to get back to sleep. She knew from experience that she might as well stay awake, be a little groggy, and get a good night's sleep this evening.

"Good, then we'll have a chance to talk and catch up." Jennifer grabbed two bowls, filled them with cereal and milk, and pushed one in front of Kate.

"I miss our morning chats now that I live so far away." Kate picked up her spoon and dug into a bowl of her favorite cereal. "I can't believe Mom still keeps this around."

"Habit." Jennifer waved her hand. "So, want to hear about my wedding?"

Kate forced herself to swallow a mouthful of cereal. It suddenly tasted like bird seed—the kind they threw at weddings. Did she want to hear about Jennifer's wedding? Only if it was news that the wedding was off.

Jennifer didn't seem to notice Kate's hesitation but chattered on. ". . . and no roses for this girl. Don't you think roses are boring? We're having orchids flown in. They are very expensive, but Mark said—"

Kate couldn't take any more and interrupted. "Jen, how well do you really know Mark?"

"What do you mean? We've known him all our lives. Look, I know you two had a falling out in high school. That's why I was a little worried about telling you."

"I do have to say that an invitation with his name on it came as a shock. I knew you were dating, but this happened so fast." Kate pushed the bowl of cereal away. That was the understatement of the millennium. Jen's relationship with Billy had been just as rushed, but she refrained from saying as much. "By the way, next time you send out invitations don't put those irritating confetti explosions inside."

Jennifer laughed. "I knew you were going to say something about that."

"It took me fifteen minutes to vacuum them up." She'd spend fifteen days cleaning confetti off her floors if it meant she could protect her sister.

"Look, Kate, Mark loves me—"

"As much as he's capable of loving." She sighed at the stricken look on Jen's face. This wasn't going to be easy. The last thing in this world that she wanted was to hurt her sister in any way. She knew her sister wanted a family, wanted to be happily married. She also knew Jen was scarred from the experience with Billy, which was even more reason for her to help her sister find a man who would make her happy and not wretched—Mark wasn't that man. "Look, Jen, all I'm saying is that I think it would be wise to postpone the wedding. Get to know Mark better. Make sure he's the one. Why do you always have to rush?"

"Postpone?" Jen shook her head. "I can't do that. The invitations have gone out. The church has been reserved. We've spent a fortune."

"It's just money," Kate argued. She had to make Jen see sense. Mark would break her baby sister's heart. Then, she'd have to break his face.

"I don't want to postpone the wedding." Jen rose to her feet. "Kate, I think maybe we'd better end this conversation right now. I am marrying Mark and I expect you to be happy for me. Don't you think I learned anything after Billy?"

Jen walked out of the room and Kate put her head in her arms and wondered how a conversation with such good intentions could go so wrong. There were exactly eight days left until Jennifer's wedding. That wasn't much time to convince her sister to change her mind. Especially when Jen was being so stubborn.

Six

"Remind me again why we have to be here," Sarah asked Kate. " 'Cause I really *don't* wanna be here."

"Because it's my sister's bachelorette brunch and I have to be here. You're here for moral support."

"Who ever heard of a bachelorette brunch?" Sarah frowned.

Kate knew Sarah was dealing with a lot of emotions, including resentment. The partygoers who had assembled included every girl from their high school graduating class who'd ever insulted, tormented, or scoffed at them. In a small town, it was inevitable that many of their classmates would be at a party. She was dealing with the same emotions herself and they hadn't taunted her the way they had Sarah.

"Kate Tyler!" A slightly older, still fake Eloise Dillon grabbed Kate's hands. "It is still Tyler isn't it?"

Oh yes, it was still Tyler, and Eloise was perfectly aware of that fact. However, just as in high school, the girl hadn't been able to pass up the opportunity to rub some salt into the wound. Kate wasn't fifteen anymore. She knew exactly how to handle Eloise's type. The worst thing she could do is pretend to not know who the woman was. That would be a complete slap in the face to someone like Eloise, who lived for her reputation and popularity.

"You'll have to forgive me, but I can't quite place you."

Rebecca and Sarah knew her inside and out and they caught onto her game with the quick wit that made her love them both.

"Kate, it's Janie." Rebecca smiled. "You haven't changed a bit."

"I am not Janie," Eloise sniffed, obviously insulted at being compared to the class secretary. Janie had been worth ten of Eloise, just not as flamboyant.

"You'll have to forgive Rebecca." Sarah stepped into the conversation. "She can't remember her own name half the time."

"Thank you, Sarah." They were the first three civil words Eloise had ever spoken to Sarah and Kate wondered at her friend's poise.

"Not a problem, Samantha."

"What?" Eloise screeched, her face tightening.

"Oh my. Did we get it wrong again?" Kate sighed. "We have so many friends from college and in New Orleans that it all gets jumbled."

Kate barely held in her laughter as Eloise's face turned a dull shade of red. Puffing her chest out in a good imitation of an angry gorilla, she said, "I'm Eloise Dillon—Dillon-Jones now."

The three girls stared at her blankly. Kate shook her head slightly. Sarah shrugged. Rebecca grinned.

"Eloise Dillon! Captain of the cheerleading squad junior *and* senior year? Prom Queen."

"Of course," Kate murmured. "Excuse me. I need to see if my mother needs help in the kitchen."

She escaped around the corner, with Rebecca and Sarah on her heels. The three of them barely made it to the kitchen before erupting in giggles.

"That was sweet," Sarah smiled.

"How many times did she insult us in high school?" Rebecca asked.

"On a daily basis. But it was rather mean. I feel a little guilty." Kate fanned herself, wishing this day could be over. She pushed the thought of her sister's wedding back to the forefront. It loomed just a week away. Bright and early a week from tomorrow morning and she would be married to Kate's high school sweetheart, a man who had cheated on Kate and had developed a rough reputation over the years. Kate couldn't care less that he was the first boy she'd ever loved. That love had been killed years ago, but more than that, her baby sister would be married to a cheat and a louse.

Out of the corner of her eye, she glimpsed a dark figure bolting through the back yard and over the low fence. She frowned and tried to catch a better view of who might be racing across their property. Typically, it was Sarah who felt when things were off kilter, but Kate felt menacing warnings punch into her gut with the force of a freight train. There was only one person who had reason to skulk around and race from sight, and the thought that he might be in town didn't bode well for any of them. The word "danger" flashed in front of her eyes. Perhaps she was just imagining someone was lurking in the shadows because she knew Billy James no longer had a restraining order on him to keep him away from her sister—not that it would have worked anyway had he truly been determined. Surely enough time had passed that he had lost his obsession for Jen?

"What are you girls doing here in the kitchen?" Kate's mother bustled in with an empty punch bowl and interrupted Kate's thoughts. "Get out there and socialize with your friends. You haven't seen some of those girls in eleven years, Katherine Elaine. The least you can do is be social."

"Yes, Mom." She turned from the window. She'd probably imagined the figure. It had been a long few days. The last thing she wanted to be was social. But her mother was right. Many of those people in her mother's formal living room had been her friends. Besides, her family had enough to worry about with planning the wedding. She'd avoided her sister fairly well since the party had started, but she wouldn't be able to continue that forever. She had to face Jen and the words that still hung between them.

Taking Sarah and Becca's hands as they stood on either side of her, she drew in a deep breath. "Here goes nothing. Stick with me, pals."

"We're like glue." Sarah's green eyes sparkled with mischief.

"Like super glue." Becca squeezed her hand.

"What would I do without you two?"

"Go stark raving mad, darling." Sarah smiled, showing two straight rows of very white teeth from a recent bleaching.

Kate laughed and knew that Sarah was one hundred percent correct. Her mother's Victorian decorated living room was filled with women their age mixed in with aunts, Mark's mother, and a few other family friends. The conversation level had reached a low hum that reminded her of a jet plane taking off.

She might as well talk to her sister and get it over with. She made her way to where Jennifer sat on the low, nineteenth century reproduction sofa. Jennifer's dark hair had grown to a length that allowed bouncy waves to brush against her shoulders. She looked like any other blushing bride. She looked happy. Kate swallowed. She wanted her sister to be happy—she did! Just not with Mark.

"Jennifer, I just wanted to wish you the best."

Her sister's eyes narrowed as though she were suspicious of Kate's motives but she nodded her head. "Thanks, Kate.

You know I wanted you to be a bridesmaid but I wasn't sure if you'd make it on such short notice."

"Always the bridesmaid but never the bride?" Eloise sat on the arm of the sofa, holding a saucer with a tea cup. She raised the cup to her lips.

The urge to tilt the cup and send the liquid inside spilling onto Eloise's pale ivory blouse was almost more temptation than Kate could resist. Out of the corner of her eye, she saw Sarah's hand twitch and wondered if her friend was thinking the same thing.

"When are you girls going to settle down?" Kate's great-aunt Virginia piped up. "You're almost too old to marry. Why in my day, if a girl wasn't married by the time she was twenty-four or twenty-five, she was considered a spinster."

"A spinster?" Sarah gasped and then coughed to cover it.

"I'm taking my time and finding the right man," Kate said. Someone better than Mark. She didn't say it but everyone in the room knew that Mark had been her high school sweetheart, that they'd planned to marry the summer after they'd graduated, that he'd cheated on her with Eloise Dillon in the back of his pick-up truck one steamy June night, and that Kate'd broken up with him. There were no secrets in this room or this town.

"Better hurry, honey." One of Jennifer's friends patted her own bulging stomach. "I'm already on number two. The old biological clock ticks louder and faster the older you get."

Kate's head pounded. Were they crazy? Twenty-nine was hardly over the hill. Well, maybe in small town Indiana it was, but in this day and age a woman could marry or not; could have children or not; could be perfectly fulfilled just on the merits of her own accomplishments—with or without a family. But the truth was, she'd wanted a husband and children for a very long time. She just wasn't willing to settle for anything other than what she truly wanted. An image of Ian's handsome face flashed in front of her. When he smiled, his warm brown eyes crinkled at the corners and two dimples appeared in his cheeks. It never failed to increase her heart rate. How many times had they gone out? How many times had he begged her to move in with him?

She shook her head to clear the image. It didn't matter. She'd told him no. No matter how attractive he was, she wasn't ready to trust another man. Especially one as good-looking as Ian. No, the next time she fell in love, it would be with an ugly man. With an ugly man, you didn't have to worry about other women wanting him all the time. Personality counted more than looks anyway.

"If Kate doesn't want to get married, it's her choice," Jennifer said. "Soon, she'll have her nieces and nephews to dote on. Mark and I plan to have children right away."

Kate gritted her teeth to keep from screaming. *Over my dead body.*

"Kate, you really should consider it." Linda Cowen touched her on the arm.

Kate had always liked Linda. She was gentle and kind, never making fun of Sarah or being cruel as some of the other cheerleaders had.

Linda pulled a photo out of her purse. "This is my little Benjamin. Isn't he adorable? There is no feeling in this world like holding your child in your arms, nursing him, and knowing that there is this tiny being with your eyes and your husband's smile. The unconditional love you give and receive." Linda's gaze turned dreamy. "There's nothing like it. You simply don't want to miss this in your life, girls."

Who had said they wanted to miss it? Kate crossed her arms over her chest to ward off the chatter that followed Linda's statement.

"Walking down the aisle toward the man you love is amazing."

"I love waking up in his arms."

"The first time he had to change a poopie diaper, I laughed so hard."

"Benjamin laughed for the first time this week."

Kate rubbed her temples, trying to erase all the words being thrown at the three of them. While some of the women, like Eloise, were smug, others simply wanted to share their joy and satisfaction with their lives. But their words were like tiny arrows shooting straight into Kate's heart. The final blow came from her sister.

"The anticipation of growing old with someone who loves you and will remember what you looked like when you were young is the most satisfying feeling of all."

All the other women sighed and smiled. Kate grimaced and wished this brunch was over. She didn't know how much more of this she could take.

"That was a complete nightmare." Sarah leaned back on her elbows, lounging on Kate's bed. She hadn't felt under such attack since she'd been a child. Even though she knew a woman didn't have to be married to feel fulfilled, seeing their happiness brought out longings for family and a home of her own.

"Tell me about it. I thought my brain was going to explode." Kate set the journal across her knees, as though not quite ready to write. "You would think that eleven years would change some of the people we went to school with. They are just as judgmental as ever. Don't they realize that women have choices these days? And that twenty-nine is hardly too old for anything? Geez!"

"I wanted to tell them to shut up, I was pregnant already."

Rebecca giggled. "And that I didn't need a husband to accomplish it."

"That would have really set their tongues wagging," Kate said. "It just infuriates me. We are three smart, successful women. Okay, maybe the successful part doesn't apply to me, but I'm self-sufficient. Why can't they appreciate that?"

"Can you believe that smug Eloise?" Sarah jumped to her feet and pretended to hold an invisible tea cup and saucer, her pinky extended. "Always the bridesmaid, never the bride."

Kate laughed, but it wasn't the strong, robust laugh that Sarah was used to hearing. As much as they hated to admit it, the other women had gotten under their skin. They had reached down to a level that the three of them rarely admitted they felt and twisted in tiny daggers of longing, pain, and wishing. The truth was that they all had been raised with small town values, and even though the edge of such limited thinking had been honed away from their years of living in a big city, each of them one day wanted a family.

"Linda's words made me want to cry," Rebecca admitted, her eyes downcast. "I want a family, a home, a husband to snuggle up to. I know she didn't mean to be cruel, but her words stung."

"Honey, did you try to call Jared again?" Kate set the diary aside and leaned forward.

"No." Becca crossed her arms. "I told him. He made it clear that he doesn't want us."

"From what you've told me, he sounds like a responsible man. What if he didn't hear you right? What if—"

"No! I spent my entire childhood waiting for my father to come home again, telling myself that it was a mistake. That he'd misunderstood something. Or that he was hurt and had amnesia and once he remembered he'd be home. I waited from the day he walked out when I was five years old until . . ." She paused. "I'm still waiting, to be honest. I still expect him to find me."

"I'm sorry." Kate stood up and walked over where Becca sat. She gave her friend a hug from behind. "It's going to be okay. We're both here for you."

"I know that."

"Thank God you had your mother and I had my Aunt Mary. If she hadn't been there to raise me after my parents died in the car crash, I don't know what I would have done." Sarah swallowed and tried to force a smile. "Look at how serious we got all of a sudden."

"Can you believe Lizbeth was trying to give us advice on marriage? She's been divorced five times." Kate changed the subject, obviously sensing Sarah barely held onto her tumultuous emotions.

"Right, like if you marry and divorce a week later, then you're no longer considered a spinster like we are." Sarah blew her hair out of her eyes. "We should get married and then divorce right away just to show them. Not that I really care what they think."

Kate laughed as she paced the room. "No. We should all three find a husband in the next week and get married before the wedding. That would really show them that being single isn't the Greek tragedy they think, but our choice."

Silence filled the room. The rustic slice of a tree stump clock ticked as the minutes passed. Kate stopped pacing and looked at her friends. "I was kidding."

"I know, but it's brilliant." Sarah smiled and sat up on the bed. The thing she loved most about her time with Kate and Becca was that she could say any goofy thing in the world and they understood when she was serious and when she wasn't. "We don't have to marry for love. We can marry, divorce, say we're divorcees, and continue on in our wonderful apartment without the aggravation men bring."

"That's insane." Becca sat up.

"Think about it, Becca." Sarah wasn't really serious, but they'd always discussed what-ifs in this way. "You could marry and say that you and the baby's father were divorced. Kate could marry and show her sister and Mark that she couldn't care less about him. What could make that point better than showing up at the wedding—already married?"

"What's in it for you?" Kate asked.

"The competition. The thrill of the hunt. We'll see who can get married first. We'll make it a bet. We all love that Ford Mustang we rented. The first one to find a husband, the other two will buy her a brand new, cherry red, Ford Mustang."

"I do love that car." Kate picked up the diary. "Let's write it out and sign it with our 'signatures.' "

She scrawled an oath on the page, and inserted a deadline of midnight the night before the wedding. Opening her tube of lipstick, she smeared the purple color on her lips and kissed the page. Sarah rubbed her lips together as Kate passed the diary to her and then puckered up and "signed" the page. Becca looked from one to the other as though they were crazy and then shrugged and placed her own lips on an empty spot.

"It's a deal," Sarah said. "The clock is ticking. Tick tock."

They all laughed, knowing it was a joke and no one was going to find a husband in seven days.

"Seriously, how am I going to stop my sister from marrying Mark?"

"Beats me," Sarah said. "I'm looking for a husband."

"Stop it," Kate laughed.

"I think you need to talk to her again but maybe start the

conversation differently. Tell her you're concerned and don't ever mention Mark's name."

Sarah knew Kate was desperate to stop her sister from making a huge mistake. She only hoped there was still time to convince Jen that Mark was a big jerk.

Out of the three of them, Rebecca figured she had the most reason to find a husband. Only, she had no intention of divorcing him the next week. If Jared wouldn't offer her the happy family life she wanted, then she'd find someone who would.

"I'm done being shy, average, and living for tomorrow. I will live in the moment." She was taking their joke more seriously than her friends realized. She didn't expect them to buy her a new car, but she did need to give her child the life he or she deserved. Of course it wouldn't happen in a week, but she did plan to find Mr. Right eventually.

Rebecca stopped just under the marquee for the old theater in the middle of downtown. She'd worked here her senior year of high school. The bold, black letters proclaimed that the theater was now an arts center. She tried the door and it opened easily. Wandering from display to display of artwork by area artists, she remembered the last time she'd been in this theater.

It had been just before their high school graduation. Mark and Kate had broken up and she and Sarah had been trying to cheer their friend up. Mark, a football player who'd been told he was less than graceful, had taken a ballet class to improve his balance.

"He was so drunk, he never questioned Sarah and me when we asked him to put on that tutu." Rebecca giggled, remembering the image of Mark doing a pirouette in a pink tutu.

Sarah had taped him and they'd intended to show only Kate before the movie started. But the movie started twenty minutes earlier than they'd thought and instead of a single, laughing Kate in the audience, when she and Sarah had returned from the control booth, half the town sat in the theater.

Rebecca grinned. Part of her felt bad—they'd never intended to humiliate Mark, just to make Kate laugh. But part of her also felt it was poetic justice. And it was mild compared to what Kate would do to Mark if he hurt her sister. But Mark wasn't the same boy he'd been eleven years ago. Now, he was a man and what she knew of him told her that he wouldn't hurt Jen intentionally or play with her emotions.

She left the theater and walked toward home. Perhaps she should try to phone Jared again, but no sooner did the thought occur than she pushed it away. She refused to subject her child to the same disappointments she'd had. This baby would not sit and wonder when or if Daddy might come back. She'd make it clear that he wasn't in the picture. At the same time, she fully intended to be on the prowl for the perfect father. She didn't care what the man looked like, she just wanted someone who would be a kind and loving parent with staying power.

The apartment was silent when she entered, using the key she'd kept from her childhood. She took a deep breath, remembering too many times when she'd come home to an empty apartment. It wasn't her mother's fault. She'd done everything she could to keep food on the table, and that included taking some evening shifts. But she'd been at every major event in Rebecca's life. She'd been a good mother, just gone a lot. Becca didn't want to be an absent mother. Perhaps, if she didn't marry, she could start a home-care nursing service and take her child with her. She'd figure it out somehow. The baby would need someone there at all times, at least until she or he started school.

"Jared, why couldn't you just have cared enough about me to at least offer to be part of our child's life?" Renewed fury beat through her. She'd read him completely wrong. She'd thought he loved her. In fact, she'd almost expected a marriage proposal within the year. She gave a short laugh. "Boy did you deceive yourself, Becca."

No more. She knew what and who Jared was now. She would make it without him. He wasn't part of her future.

Jared Wells slapped the ticket against his thigh while he waited in the line for security. A woman in the front of the line kept taking off jewelry, beeping, removing more, and waiting while airport security ran the hand wand over her again. He glanced at his watch. He couldn't miss his flight. As it was, his plane wouldn't set down in Indianapolis until nearly ten tonight. Then he'd have to rent a car and figure out how to find Becca. He had no idea where her mother lived, other than the name of the town and the little bit she'd told him of her childhood. But he was determined to find her.

He wasn't going to let her blow him off that easily. He was certain they'd been in love. No, she was going to have to look him in the eye and tell him she didn't want to see him anymore. He wasn't going to be dumped on a cell phone with bad reception.

The scanner beeped again. The woman shrugged and they scanned her a final time, finally allowing her through. Once she'd gone through, the line moved more quickly.

It had taken Jared thirty-four years to finish medical school, get his career going, and find Becca. "Why would she dump me?"

When he'd left, she'd kissed him as though she couldn't

get close enough. "I'll miss you," she'd whispered with those soft, sweet lips.

What had happened in the last month to change her mind? He thought he'd been clear that he had to be out of town for two months, but then he'd come back. But maybe he hadn't been clear enough. What if she'd met someone else? The thought made him feel sick to his stomach.

He should have told her he was crazy about her. Should have asked her to marry him. Now, he might have lost her. But he was going to give it one final shot. If she was with another man when he arrived, then he'd walk away and leave her alone forever.

Seven

Jennifer breezed into the kitchen, and grabbed a slice of toast off Kate's plate while she tried to pull the back of her shoe onto her heel.

"Where are you headed?" Kate asked. When they'd been in high school, Jennifer often snatched food off Kate's plate instead of taking time to fix her own. It had become such a ritual with them that Kate had automatically fixed an extra helping this morning.

"I have last minute wedding errands. A final fitting for my dress, visit to the church to make sure all the details are correct, and then I'm meeting Mark for lunch."

Kate's appetite vanished. She lowered her fork and pushed the plate away. The china scraped across her mother's Formica countertop. Last minute wedding errands—time was ticking away as fast as a summer day. She needed to talk to Jennifer and try to get her to postpone this wedding. Unfortunately, she wasn't sure how to start the discussion. The last thing she wanted to do was hurt her sister.

"Earth to Kate." Jennifer waved her hand in front of Kate's face. "Where did you go?"

"Just thinking." Kate shrugged. When she looked at Jennifer, she often still saw the toothless seven-year-old sister she'd felt she had to protect. When Jen started first grade, it had been big sister Kate who had made sure she got to her classroom safely each day and got on the right bus in the afternoon. In high school, Kate had made sure Jen didn't get involved with troubled kids. It was her job to protect her baby sister. The only problem was that Jen was no longer a baby and she had a heart and mind of her own. Kate sighed. How did you tell a grown woman you didn't think she made good choices?

"Come with me," Jen said. "It'll be fun. A girls' day out—well except for the lunch with Mark, but that's only an hour or so."

"Great idea. Give me ten minutes to go brush my teeth and grab my purse." Kate left the room, determined to use their time together to talk some sense into Jen.

Talking to Jen would be easier if she didn't look so perfect and happy in her flowing, white wedding gown. Tiny crystal beads glittered on the bodice. The train fell like a waterfall and pooled on the floor in a graceful arc behind her sister. A tiny, beaded headband pulled her hair back and allowed yards of gauzy veil to drape down her back. Kate looked into Jen's eyes, which sparkled with tears. She wondered if they were from happiness or fear, but the smile on Jen's face made it clear that she was thrilled over her upcoming nuptials.

"Jen, you look absolutely beautiful." Was this really her baby sister? Of course she knew Jen was grown up, but there was a new element to her maturity. Maybe that was good because she hoped Jen would listen to what she was about to say and see reason.

"Oh, Kate. This dress is better than I imagined. I can't wait to walk down the aisle next Saturday."

The words were like a swift kick in Kate's heart. *Forgive me, Jen. I'm doing it for your own good.*

"Kate, you look so serious," Jen laughed. "You aren't going to cry are you?"

"Maybe. I need to talk to you and I don't think you're going to like what I have to say." Nausea settled in the pit of her stomach.

Jen moved to a small bench and sat down. "C'mon. Sit down and talk to me. Stop looking so serious."

Kate sank into the chair across from Jen. Her sister grabbed her hands and waited for her to start speaking. Jen wasn't making this any easier. Knowing her sister as she did, Kate understood that Jen would feel swift fury when Kate told her she didn't want her to marry Mark. But she had no choice. To sit back and do nothing wasn't an option. She couldn't let her sister marry a cheat without trying to warn her.

"I wonder if you remember how much Mark hurt me in high school."

"I know." Jen glanced away, as though she couldn't quite stand to look into Kate's eyes.

"I also wonder if you realize how much I wanted to warn you about Billy, but I bit my tongue."

"I know," Jen repeated her earlier response. "Surely you don't think Mark is anything like Billy?"

"I don't think he's a psycho, but I don't think he's right for you either. He cheated on me, Jen. And from what I hear, he hasn't changed a bit." That sounded harsh. She needed to tread carefully. Jen thought she had deep feelings for Mark or she never would have agreed to marry him.

Jen's eyes glistened with tears, but this time no smile accompanied them. "Oh, Kate. You don't believe everything you hear, do you? You know how gossipy this town is. Don't you think I have enough sense to not get involved with a liar and a cheat?"

"I think Mark has tricked you." *You always were too trusting.*

Jen dropped Kate's hands and jumped to her feet. "You're wrong about Mark. I don't know what happened in high school, but that was forever ago, and I don't believe he cheated even then. I learned a lesson after Billy. Don't you trust my judgment?"

"Jen, take the rose colored glasses off." Kate rose and followed her sister. "You're going to get hurt. He is a snake."

"I won't listen to this." Jen shook her head. "I'm getting married in one week and that's all there is to it."

That discussion couldn't have gone worse. Kate sat in the passenger seat of Jen's compact car. Her sister's silence and clenched jaw spoke volumes about her deep hurt and anger. Kate opened her mouth to say something and then closed it again. Now wasn't the time to bring the topic up. She needed to let Jen's anger subside and then try again to get her sister to see reason.

She glanced out the mirror on the passenger side of the car and spotted a dark sedan as it zipped around a corner behind them. She frowned. She'd seen the same car parked just up the street from the bridal shop when they'd arrived and again when they'd left, but hadn't thought much of it. There were a lot of dark sedans around, but not too many appeared everywhere you went. Was she being overly suspicious? After what had happened with Billy last year, perhaps her imagination worked overtime. The sedan went straight when Jen made another turn and she relaxed. *Stop imagining things, Kate. Everything is fine. Billy is long gone and out of the picture.*

Jen rocketed into a parking spot in a parallel parking maneuver that caused Kate to close her eyes and wait for the inevitable crash. It didn't come. Without a word to Kate, Jen got out, slammed her door and went into Annie's Restaurant.

Kate followed more slowly, dreading the lunch with Mark more than she'd thought. She really did not want to sit through lunch with that man.

The interior of the restaurant buzzed with conversation and laughter, which mixed with the smell of hamburgers and fries. Kate smiled. The restaurant reminded her of a similar one that had been a regular hangout when she was in high school. She spotted Jen already seated at a table in the back. *Thanks for waiting for me, Sis.* Jen was angrier than she'd thought.

As she approached, she saw that Mark was already here. He leaned across the table, listening as Jen spoke. When she stopped at the table, Jen stopped talking.

"Kate, nice to see you." Mark rose to his feet. "Have a seat."

Don't pretend to have good manners with me. Kate nodded and sat next to her sister. Silence fell on the table and seemed particularly loud compared to the chatter of the other diners. Kate read the menu to cover the awkwardness but was acutely aware that the atmosphere in this corner of the room was chilly enough to make it snow indoors.

"What's going on?" Mark asked.

Kate laid down the menu. He stared intently at the two of them with his vivid blue eyes. Age had brought mellowness to his rugged features that he hadn't possessed in high school. Tiny laugh lines fanned out from the corners of his eyes, as though he laughed often and robustly. Kate shifted uncomfortably, realizing that she really didn't know this Mark. Even his voice was different. Once a cheat, always a cheat, she reminded herself. She'd seen it happen too many times—one of her friends thought they could reform a cheat and it never worked. It always ended in heartbreak for the woman.

"I know you two are fighting. The tension almost knocked me out of my seat."

"Kate thinks I shouldn't marry you," Jen said.

Great. This was going to be a fun lunch. Jen was absolutely right about her opinion, though, and she wouldn't apologize. She crossed her arms and met Mark stare for stare. When it came to her baby sister, she wasn't ever backing down again.

"Is this about that Eloise thing back in high school?"

"That was forever ago and barely a blip in my present life. Even with the rumors I've heard about you in recent years, I'll concede that you could have changed. You may even make a wonderful husband for some woman—I just don't think you're right for Jen." There, she couldn't have been more diplomatic. She clenched her hands together and placed them on the table.

Mark burst out laughing. He reached across and put his hands over hers. "I'm perfect for Jen. You haven't been around, so you don't see it."

Fury pumped through Kate's veins with enough force to launch an instant headache. She pulled her hands away. He might think he was charming, but she knew better.

"All I'm really asking is that the two of you consider postponing this wedding until Jen's family feels more comfortable."

Jen let out a low, feral growl. "I think you need to back off, Kate."

"You mean until *you* feel more comfortable. The rest of the family knows me well and they approve of the union," Mark said.

God, she hated his guts. Her emotions had absolutely

nothing to do with the fact that he'd cheated on her some long ago time when they were both kids. She didn't like his smug attitude and assumption that everyone in her family liked him. Kate didn't like him. Didn't her opinion matter?

"Everyone loves Mark," Jen added.

"Not me." Kate rose to her feet. "I think this wedding is the worst possible idea and I'm going to do everything I can to see it doesn't happen."

"You'll be wasting your time. I am marrying your sister in exactly one week and there is nothing you can do to stop it."

"We'll see," she said.

"I can't believe you are doing this to me, Kate. I really can't believe it." Jen's eyes glittered with anger. It wasn't going to be fun sharing a room with her sister tonight.

"I have your best interests at heart, sis. I made a vow never to let you be hurt again if I had any say in the situation. I'm walking home. I'll talk to you later," Kate said.

The sidewalks were familiar even after all these years. Kate's feet moved toward home with little thought about her destination. She muttered to herself. How was she going to convince Jen to wait? At this point, any delay at all in the upcoming wedding would be a victory—not for Kate but for Jen. It would create more time for Mark to show his true colors.

A skateboarding youth zipped past her and into an empty parking lot where a local grocery used to sit. Now, the building sat empty and the blacktop served as a perfect spot for teens to hang out. The wail of a firehouse truck faded around the corner behind her. The old church on the corner reminded her of the prayers she'd said when her sister's life hung in the balance at the hands of Billy James.

God, if you'll just spare my sister's life, I promise I'll be there to protect her the next time. I won't stay silent when I should speak up. Just keep her safe. The words echoed through her head as fresh and raw with passion as they'd been the day she'd uttered them. God had sent her sister home in one piece, and she had every intention of keeping her part of the bargain. It was impossible to know if she was right about Mark, if she was doing the right thing, but she thought she was. At this point, all she really wanted was to get Jen to wait a few months, maybe even a year, and get to know her fiancé better before committing the rest of her life to this person.

It was time to call in the big guns. Because only two years separated them, Jen was close to Sarah and Rebecca. As children, the four of them had often played together and as teens they'd hung out. She was going to need some moral support. Maybe Rebecca and Sarah could make Jen see sense. Perhaps a third and fourth viewpoint would help show Kate wasn't being completely unreasonable. And the sooner they had the intervention the better. Tonight, if possible.

"What is this? An attack?" Jen narrowed her eyes and glared at Kate, Rebecca, and Sarah.

"No, this is two friends and your sister begging you to reconsider this wedding," Sarah said.

Kate knew this "wedding intervention" was a risk. Jen would either listen or become so furious she'd ban Kate from her wedding. It didn't matter. She didn't have a choice. Her sister's very future was at stake. She couldn't bear it if she didn't at least try to warn Jen. For her sister to marry Mark and live miserably-ever-after was not an option.

"Don't include me in that," Rebecca said.

Kate glared at her. What was Becca's problem? Had Mark fooled her into thinking he was Mr. Perfect as well?

"I love Mark." Jen pounded her chest with a clenched fist.

"You don't know how many frogs I dated to find this prince. You don't know!"

"Honey, we know. We've been there. I know you think you love Mark—"

Jen interrupted Kate. "No, I love him. You don't know him the way I do. He's kind and gentle and loyal."

"He does seem that way," Rebecca said. Then she frowned, as if reconsidering. "But he could be tricking all of us. I'm going to let you in on a little secret only my closest friends know. I'm pregnant."

"That's wonderful!" Jen eyed Becca suspiciously. Her crossed arms indicated that she felt assaulted.

"Yes, well, I thought the baby's father loved me. I thought he was kind and gentle and loyal. Guess what? He wasn't. He dumped me the second he heard I was pregnant."

"No." Jen shook her head. "That isn't Mark."

"You haven't known Mark long enough to really know if he's right for you," Kate chimed in.

"But we've known him for years, Kate. You forget that this is a small town. Mark and I have had the same friends. We've seen each other every Friday night at Zoobie's, at local football games, and we were friends before we ever dated."

Kate sighed and rubbed her eyes. Jen had never been this stubborn, only a little headstrong. In fact, growing up, she'd almost always let Kate have her own way. She wished she could threaten to not play with Jen anymore and get her to agree like she'd done sometimes when they were children.

"I know Mark isn't perfect." Jen sat back down, but leaned forward as though trying to impress the importance of her words on the three of them. "Have any of you found a man who is perfect?"

"Of course not." Kate paced the length of the room. If

she'd known about the wedding sooner, she could have stopped it. But that was probably why Jen hadn't told her. She'd known how Kate would feel about her marrying Mark. She'd had to have known.

"I really don't think you can tell me if my decision is a mistake or not, when you can't even find a man you want to marry yourself." Jen raised her hand as Kate started to protest. "I'm not saying you should be married or that you've failed. All I'm saying is that you don't understand where I'm coming from, because you haven't been in love."

An image of Ian flashed in front of Kate. She pushed it away. She couldn't allow herself to stop and think about Ian or what she was going to do about their relationship when she returned. He wouldn't let her put him off forever. Ian was going to want some type of commitment and she wasn't sure she was prepared to give it, especially after his possessive temper tantrum when she'd asked for time off work.

"We've made mistakes. That's why we want you to be more careful." Sarah swallowed several times and Kate knew she was thinking about Daniel. "I don't want to see you get hurt like I've been hurt."

"I've been hurt, Sarah. I know that type of man, intimately. Mark won't hurt me."

"I said Jared wouldn't hurt me. He did." Rebecca's words seemed to have the most impact on Jen. Becca rarely overdramatized and Jen knew that. "I agree with you that Mark seems like a nice guy. But I also know where Kate is coming from. This wedding happened *fast*. I guess I just want to know that you are really sure of him."

"What about Mark don't you like?" A single tear escaped from the corner of Jen's right eye, but Kate couldn't let her sister's emotions deter her. This was for Jen's own good.

Where to start? "I believe he is a cheat. I think he's smug.

He thinks he is better than anyone else. And I believe deep in my heart that he will make you utterly miserable."

"You're wrong about him, Kate," Jen said. "Do you remember Granny's tests?"

"About finding a man who would make a good husband?" Kate laughed. Before they'd even hit their teen years, their great-grandmother had taught them eight simple tricks for spotting a loser. "We've used them off and on a few times over the years."

"Well, I used the ones I could remember on Mark and he passed most of them. He did think I was insane when the food thing occurred, but the rest he took in stride."

"Didn't we write those down in the diaries at one point?" Rebecca asked. "I can't remember them all."

"I've used one or two of the tests a couple of times," Sarah admitted.

"Yes, we did write them down. Our old lipstick diaries are tucked safely into the attic." Kate wished she could turn back the clock and see their great-grandmother. The smell of corn sticks baking in the oven and a memory of the gentle rumble of Granny's voice brought a smile to her face.

"Remember how Granny always tucked snuff into her apron?" Jen asked.

"Yuck. She was a wonderful lady though. She taught me to play crazy eights." Sarah smiled.

"She taught me to play poker," Kate said. They all laughed.

When the laughter subsided, Jen spoke into the silence. "I love all of you. More than anything, I want you to be happy about this wedding. Right now, I see that is impossible, so all I'm asking is that you accept my upcoming marriage, be there, smile, and pretend to be happy for me."

"Jen—"

Jen held up her hand to stop Kate's words. "Because I want you to accept Mark, I'm willing to make a little wager."

"A wager?" This could be interesting.

"I challenge any one of you to find the perfect man before my wedding. If you do, I won't get married Saturday."

Eight

Was Jen really serious? How hard could it be to find a perfect man? Okay, maybe perfect was stretching it and that might be Jennifer's point, because Kate was certain that her sister had no intention of canceling her wedding. She'd made it perfectly clear that she intended to marry Mark. But she knew too that she could use Jen's wager to her advantage and get her to at least postpone this wedding.

"Whose definition of perfect?" Kate asked, hoping her sister took the bait.

"What about Granny's? If you wrote down the tests, then we'll use them. If any one of you can find a man who can pass more of the tests than Mark, then I'll wait to get married."

"How many tests are there?" Sarah asked.

"Eight, I think." Kate moved toward the stairs and motioned for them to follow. "Our old diaries are in the attic. C'mon."

"We should burn those things." Sarah followed on Kate's heels. "There is no telling what kind of incriminating evidence is in them."

"Let's read through some of them. I love to do that," Rebecca said.

"We know," the other three sang in unison.

The small stairway on the second floor led up to the

dingy, dusty, rarely-used attic. Kate sneezed when the dust mites hit her square in the face. What was it about attics that made them all smell the same? It wasn't exactly an unpleasant smell, just different. Dust, old papers, and moth balls combined to create an aroma that reminded Kate of a winter day when she was nine that she and her sister had spent up here. They'd played dress up and house. She glanced at Jen. God, she loved her baby sister. With everything that was in her, she wanted to ensure that Jen was never hurt again, never experienced any grief and lived her life happy and healthy.

Fresh determination sent her to a small trunk just to the right. She flipped the lid up and gazed down at the eight diaries in various sizes and colors. The first diary they'd ever written in stared up at her with its lilac covered wrapping. "Do any of you remember what the diary looked like when we wrote the tests?"

"I think it was orange," Sarah said.

Becca shook her head. "No, it had marigolds on it."

Kate shuffled through the diaries and pulled one out that had deep yellowish orange marigolds scattered across the cover. "This one?"

"Maybe."

The four of them sat down on the dusty, wood floor. Kate sneezed again and opened the journal she now held in her lap. A childish scrawl crawled across the page, ending with the impression of deep purple lipstick.

November 6th, 1986
Dear Lipstick Diary,

Tuesday, I got to sit next to Craig on the bus. He is so cute! I didn't know what to say to him. My tongue got all twisted. So, I decided to write in my notebook. I couldn't get

my pen to work. I started to shake it and black ink spewed
out and went all over Craig's white shirt.

Guess that's the end of our romance.

The entry was signed with Kate's lipstick color.

"This is so much fun." Sarah giggled. "I'd forgotten all about the 'ink' incident."

"Here is test number one. Spill a drink on your date. If he gets angry, then he has a bad temper."

"Seriously?" Becca frowned. "That seems mean and underhanded."

"Oh, it works," Jen said. "I've done that test on every man I dated and until Mark—" She stopped in mid-sentence and then crossed her arms.

"There are eight tests. How many did you do, Jen?" Kate asked.

"Six. Mark passed all but one with flying colors and it was minor. Best score a man has ever gotten."

"Okay, then we will use all eight and if any one of us finds a man who can pass seven, you don't get married Saturday. Is it a deal?" Kate prayed hard that her sister would accept the challenge because she was determined to stop this wedding.

"It's a deal. Good luck." Jen leaned back on her elbows and laughed.

A feeling of unease skittered up Kate's spine, but she pushed it away. She didn't have time for self-doubt. She had to find some men to date.

Test # 1—spill your drink on your date. If he gets angry,
then he has a bad temper.

Kate could almost hear her great-grandmother's voice calling to her. Granny had always insisted that the tests worked. As a youngster, she'd thought they were funny and antiquated and hadn't taken them seriously. As an adult, she'd felt they were underhanded. As an almost-thirty-something, she saw more wisdom in her great-grandmother's words. After all, who wanted to marry a man who had a bad temper or was possessive? Wasn't dating all about testing the other person?

Now, she just had to find a date. That might not be as easy as it sounded. Everyone in this small town would probably know what they were up to in a matter of minutes rather than days. Of course, Indianapolis was just a short twenty-minute drive from Greenfield. She just preferred to prove her point closer to home. Perhaps she could find the perfect mate and talk Jen into marrying him instead of that loser Mark.

Sarah and Becca had agreed to help by dating men as well. They had exactly one week to find Mr. Right. It wasn't much time, but how hard could it be?

He couldn't eat. He couldn't sleep. He couldn't concentrate. Ian threw the itinerary he'd been working on down on his desk. He shouldn't have given Kate an ultimatum. The thought of her slipping off for a tryst with another man was more than he could bear and he'd lost his head. Not having her around at all was far worse than dealing with a little competition. Now, he had no idea what she was doing and she hadn't bothered to phone him of course.

"Argh!" He stood and moved to his office window. The street below was dark black from a gentle rain that dripped down the window pane in tiny rivers. Why hadn't he fought to save his marriage to Angela? He could have fixed what was broken if he'd tried, maybe. But he'd just accepted that she didn't love him and let her walk away. Perhaps he'd never really been in love with her—he'd cared for her, of course. But love? He wasn't sure he'd experienced love until he'd met Kate.

He'd known Kate wasn't ready to settle down. She'd made that clear to him from their first date. But somewhere along the way, he'd come to care for her more than she cared for him. He was successful in business and in every other aspect of his life, except with this one woman. So why did he want to torture himself by dating her and hoping for a future that might never happen? Because she was worth it.

Who had she taken home to meet her parents? It should have been him. *He* should be the one meeting her parents. He was the one in love with her. The thought brought him up short. He hadn't yet admitted to himself the full depth of his feelings for Kate. The idea of getting married again rather terrified him after his first experience, but the thought of spending the rest of his life with Kate was comforting.

"You are in serious trouble, my friend, because the lady doesn't feel the same way." The rain continued to drizzle down.

Now that he knew his true feelings, he couldn't just keep them to himself. He knew professing his love might scare Kate but it might also give him an edge over the competition. He sure as hell wasn't going to let the other man spend an entire week in Kate's hometown—meeting her family and friends. No, he would have to follow her and he had every intention of winning her heart once and for all.

"You did what?" Mark felt his chest tighten with fear. If Jen's sister was able to find a man who passed some dating test, she was going to call off their wedding.

"Don't worry, Mark. She can't find a man who will pass all the tests. It's impossible. I think the lesson that Granny was

103

really trying to teach us was that no one is perfect. You get the best you can and you work through the rest."

"What if she does, Jen?" Mark took her in his arms and held her close, breathing in the sweet, green apple scent of her shampoo. "I want to have you by my side every day and every night for the rest of our lives."

"She won't." Jen chewed her bottom lip. "But if she does, I only agreed to postpone, not to cancel the wedding."

"I don't even want to wait until Saturday to marry you." Kate hated him and she'd do everything in her power to try to stop him from marrying Jen. Jen claimed her sister hadn't been so protective before Billy had almost taken Jen's life. He'd thought they could put the past behind them, but it was clear that Kate had no intention of forgiving or forgetting. He couldn't lose Jen. He just couldn't.

"It's okay, darling. How much can they accomplish in one short week?"

A lot. That was the problem. He wouldn't put it past them to try to dig up dirt on him, to make things up if need be. Not that they'd have to dig too hard. His past wasn't perfect, but he'd been honest with Jen about his failings. Pulling her closer, he stroked his lips down her neck in the way he knew she liked.

"Run away with me, Jen. Let's forget the big wedding and just elope. Forget your sister and her friends. Forget everything. I just want you to be my wife."

It was the smartest thing he could have said. If he could convince Jen to elope, then he wouldn't have to worry that her sister would use the next seven days to sabotage his wedding.

As she approached the room she was sharing with Jen, Kate thought she heard soft sobs. She stopped and listened at the door for a moment. She raised her fist and rapped her knuckles lightly on the wood.

"Come in."

Kate opened the door. Jen had her back turned, obviously wiping tears away. An open suitcase lay on her bed but it was empty. Kate frowned. It was too early to pack for a honeymoon that Kate hoped wouldn't happen. She hated to see her sister in pain, though, and she knew that she was the cause of some of it because she'd made Jen doubt Mark's love.

"What's up?" Kate pointed at the suitcase.

Her sister took a deep breath and let it out in a broken rhythm that proved she'd been crying deeply. Jen shrugged and sat down on the bed, looking down at the floor.

"Talk to me, Jen. I love you. I'm not trying to hurt you. I want to help."

"You could help by minding your own business," Jen said softly. She lifted her face and looked at Kate, the emotions ripping through her evident in her eyes.

"I'm sorry." Kate moved to sit next to her sister and hugged her close. She should just call off their stupid wager. As much as she didn't want Jen to marry Mark, she didn't want to be the cause of all this misery. There weren't many people in this world she loved as much as she loved Jen. To know that she was the cause of Jen's pain made her heart ache.

"Mark wants me to elope." Jen laughed but choked halfway through the laugh and coughed.

"What? Why?"

"He thinks you're going to stop our wedding."

Fury rushed through Kate's veins. Oh, he was a sneaky one all right. He knew just how to push Jen's buttons. He was trying to force her to choose between her sister and him and it was completely unfair. If she stood in Jen's way, then she would be forever responsible for Jen losing the "love of her life." If she didn't stand in Jen's way, then she was responsible for Jen marrying someone who would use her and then toss her aside as though she were nothing more than a second-hand tissue.

"He gave you an ultimatum. Well, if you love him, then you have to go."

She opened Jen's closet and tossed a couple of shirts and a pair of jeans in the suitcase. She couldn't look at Jen again. She'd failed. It was over. Mark and Jen would marry and there wasn't a thing she could do about it. Although Jen's life wasn't in danger this time, the memory of feeling helpless when Billy had kidnapped her sister came rushing back. She'd wanted to do something but there'd been nothing she could do but sit by the phone and wait for news.

"Where are you going? Vegas? It's hot there this time of year. You'll need shorts." She would just have to pray harder than she'd ever prayed and hope that things worked out for Jen.

"He didn't give me an ultimatum." Jen brushed away fresh tears.

"Then why are you so upset? You don't have to protect him, Jen. If I were him, I'd probably do the same thing. You're pretty terrific."

"So is he, Kate. You're still freaking out because of Billy's insane stalking of me and you're prejudiced because of something you think Mark did years ago, and it hurts me that he is worried and hurt. I don't want him to doubt us—ever."

"Jen, of course I'm freaking out over Billy. I thought I'd lost you. I kept my mouth shut last time—and look what happened. I know that Mark won't physically hurt you. It isn't just what he did to me. When I heard you were dating him, I hoped it was casual. I have friends here. They talk to me. I know all about his reputation. I know how many women he's dated since high school."

"They're rumors, Kate. Mark was honest about the women he's dated. He never lied to me. You, of all people, should know how this town likes to gossip and judge. Look at what they did to Sarah all those years. If you can see past the town's opinion and love Sarah, why can't you do the same with Mark?"

"Because it's different." The words sounded hollow, even to her own ears, and she made a face.

"How?" All the tears had washed Jen's eyes more brilliantly blue than normal and they glittered with emotions that threatened to bubble over.

"It just is. Look—if he isn't giving you an ultimatum, then I don't understand. You promised me a week to find a perfect man. I mean, I *understand*. He's pushed your buttons. He knows that if you think he's upset that you'll want to fix it."

"He's not going to be able to win with you, is he?" Jen shook her head. "I won't elope, but not because you don't want me to. I've spent a lot of time and effort planning this wedding. People are looking forward to it. Mom is looking forward to it, and it *will* happen on Saturday. You aren't ever going to find a perfect man. That was Granny's point—there are no perfect people or marriages. They all take work. I figured that out while using the tests."

"I don't want you to marry someone perfect." She was going to throw up. What was she doing? Her sister would hate her after this was over, especially once she found several men who passed Granny's tests with flying colors. She didn't know now if she could insist that Jen stick to her end of the bargain and postpone the wedding. And what was to stop him from eloping with Jen the next day even if she succeeded?

"You just don't want me to marry Mark. I get it. I just wonder if you do." Jen hung her clothes back up, closed the suitcase, and slipped it under her bed. "I won't elope. You'll get your chance to prove me wrong."

Kate watched as Jen held her chin up high in the air and walked out of the room. She may have won this round, but she wondered exactly what she'd won. She hoped it wasn't something more than she'd wanted.

"Do you have any dates lined up, Kate? We have to get on this immediately. There isn't much time." Sarah jotted some notes in a journal.

Kate smiled at her friend's tendency to organize everything. Sarah was typically the one who got them all in motion on any project and kept things structured. Since many places were closed on Sunday, they'd chosen to get a fresh start today.

"No dates. Actually, I'm worried about this whole challenge."

"I do think you should forget the challenge, because Mark's a nice guy." Becca scooted forward in her chair. "But I am kind of looking forward to maybe finding Mr. Perfect. I hate the fact that this baby might be raised without a father. A new car might cheer me up."

"Very funny, Becca." Sarah scribbled across the page. "How many dates for you?"

"Two today." Becca grinned and Sarah high-fived her.

"I don't know about this, guys," Kate spoke up again. "Jen was really torqued at me. I'm worried I'll destroy our relationship. I win nothing if I get her to postpone the wedding but make her hate me."

"She'll understand later, Kate. She knows you love her and have her best interests at heart. Now, back to our planning. I have one date lined up and lined another up for Kate because I suspected she wouldn't have time."

"A blind date?" Kate wrinkled her nose, thinking of Ian. She really didn't want to date someone else. She should probably call him. She didn't like the way they'd left things. She knew she wasn't open enough with him. How hard would it have been to tell him that she was coming home for Jen's wedding and that Becca and Sarah were traveling with her? Or to just invite him? She could have introduced him to her parents . . .

"You'll be fine. The goal is to get them to pass test one and then we'll have to probably pick up the pace and conduct several tests per date. We only need one guy to pass seven of eight." Sarah laid down the journal and pen. "Questions?"

"How do I spill a drink without making it look deliberate?" Becca asked.

"Who cares? You are trying to see if he has a temper. If it looks deliberate, it will make him angrier. That's sort of the goal at this point."

"Sarah, you're enjoying this way too much." It was good to see her friend laugh again. She'd been way too serious since Daniel had betrayed her. Kate wished she could enjoy the situation as much but niggling doubts kept her from being sure if she was doing the right thing . . .

"It's going to be okay, Kate." Sarah patted Kate's shoulder. "We will save your sister and who knows, maybe one of us will find a husband and win that little ante of a new car."

"That was a joke and you two know it."

"Was it?" Becca winked.

Nine

Mark hung up the phone and leaned back in his chair, defeat pressing down on the top of his head. Jen didn't want to elope.

"I'm afraid it will ruin my relationship with Kate," she'd said.

What about her relationship with him? Didn't that matter anymore? Kate had only been back in town a short time and already Jen wasn't as open. He picked up the photograph of a smiling Jen with her arms wrapped around his waist. It had been taken four weeks ago. He'd just proposed and her happiness was evident from the glow on her face and in her eyes.

No, he wouldn't lose her now. He would marry Jen and there wasn't a thing that Kate or anyone else could do about it. You couldn't mess with fate.

If Kate and her friends wanted to date the eligible men in this town and test them, then he'd help them along a little. He felt a bit surprised that Rebecca would participate in the challenge since he'd dated her a couple of years ago and thought they'd parted on good terms. Perhaps Kate convinced her that he'd done her wrong—who knew? One way or another he had to find a way to stop them from wrecking his wedding. An idea started to form . . .

Devilish delight surged through him. He knew nearly every bachelor in town. He'd let them in on the wager and the tests and tell them his predicament. Men stuck together, so they'd help him by proving that all the other men were jerks and he actually was right for Jen.

He picked up the phone and punched in Todd's number. "Todd? Hey. Mark here. I have a problem that I need your help with."

"What do you need?" Eleven years after graduation, and Todd's voice had a youthful quality as though he was always on the edge of another joke or prank.

"Jen's sister and her friends are trying to stop my wedding. You know how crazy I am about Jen." He filled Todd in on the details. "Can you get the word out to the other guys? If they can just react badly to the tests, it will help me a lot."

"Sure thing."

Mark hung the phone back in its cradle and sat back with a smile of satisfaction. Kate Tyler was about to get a taste of her own medicine.

Rebecca took a deep breath and stepped out of the apartment. She'd agreed to meet Keith Alexander at Blue Moon Rising, a local bar, for drinks. Of course, she couldn't have real alcohol. She had to be careful because of the baby.

What was she doing? Did she really think she might find a father for her baby through this process? She knew it was crazy but desperation sang through her veins. She could not repeat her mother's mistakes. She couldn't watch this child sit alone through events where a father should have been present. The pain on her child's face would surely kill her.

It was too far to walk to the Blue Moon Rising, so she'd arranged to borrow her mother's car. The traffic on State Street was heavy this time of night. When she'd moved away from Greenfield, the traffic hadn't been nearly as heavy. State Street, which was State Road 9, had always been traveled by truck drivers looking for a shortcut or straight route to Shelbyville, but it hadn't been clogged from stoplight to stoplight.

"This is crazy," she said. "New Orleans isn't this bad." Okay, maybe that was an exaggeration, but she wasn't sure she liked all the changes the town was going through. This one was certainly for the worse, although she'd have to admit that the Starbucks on the corner was for the better. Then again, she couldn't have caffeine right now, so who cared?

She parked in the Marsh Shopping Plaza and entered Blue Moon Rising. Even on a Monday night, the place was crowded. The interior was filled with neon blue moons and cigarette smoke. She coughed a little, wishing there were a nonsmoking section. Would this hurt her baby? She'd better cut this date short. She wanted to help Kate. She wanted to help Jen. She wanted to find a father for her baby. But she wouldn't put her unborn child in harm's way. Besides, she didn't agree with Kate about Mark being a louse. Her friends didn't know she'd dated him when she came to visit her mother two years ago—he'd treated her just fine and they'd parted on friendly terms.

Maybe she should just go home. What had she been thinking? She couldn't date another man while carrying Jared's baby. She hesitated in the doorway, but realized it would be rude to just walk out without at least having a drink with the guy. A man with a scruffy beard, and even scruffier jeans motioned to her from a small table in the back corner of the bar. He looked fierce. She felt her heartbeat quicken. With each step toward the man, her heart protested. She didn't want to be here. As much as she hated to admit it, she still loved Jared. She'd wanted desperately to turn her emotions off and learn to care for someone else but her heart didn't have a shut-off valve.

"Keith Alexander?" she asked. *Please let him say no.*

"Yeah?"

Looks and manners. How could a girl get so lucky? This had been a huge mistake. She'd promised Kate she'd help her, so she'd just think of this date as more of an interview. Maybe he'd turn out to be a big teddy bear—a big teddy bear with bad manners, she realized as he stared at her chest instead of her face. Just great.

Rebecca crossed her arms, feeling vulnerable. "S-so, this bar has great atmosphere."

"Long as it has booze, baby, I couldn't care less." He laughed and the raspy sound of his vocal cords scratching together made her want to flinch. "What drink do you want? Whiskey?"

"I'll just have a ginger ale."

"You're kidding?" His mouth dropped open. Then he frowned, shrugged, and hollered at the waitress loud enough to turn several heads. "Yo, we need a ginger ale over here. Pronto."

Rebecca sank down in her chair a little. Several women smirked at her and a few others smiled sympathetically. The sooner her drink got here and she could "test" this man, the better. Even with his rejection of her and the baby, this man was making Jared look like Mr. Perfect. Of course, Mr. Perfect didn't want them, so it hardly mattered.

"What do you do, Keith?" Since she was here, she was going to make the best of things.

"Ride my bike, hang out in bars, stuff."

"I meant for a living."

"Huh?" His gaze dropped to her chest again. "I don't have no job."

"Oh." She smiled at the waitress as the woman set a glass of bubbling ginger ale on the table.

"Do you make good money?" he asked. "I'm looking for a woman who can support me in the style I want to become accustomed to."

His laughter irritated the heck out of her. That scratchiness made her want to run screaming from the room. She lifted the cup of ginger ale. Oh, but this test was going to be sweet.

"I'm a nurse." As she finished the words, she threw the entire glass of ginger ale in his face. Although it was apparent her motion could hardly have been an accident, she placed her fingers to her lips. "Oops."

Keith jumped to his feet and shook his big head and Rebecca realized how large he was. If he did have a temper, her little test could have some severe consequences. She scooted her chair closer to the wall, prepared to run if necessary to protect her child. What was she doing? She didn't need to deal with this type of craziness. She should be focused on building a better life for her and her baby—a life without Jared or any man.

"Why'd you do that?" he screamed, glowering at her.

"Sorry." She swallowed. He'd failed test number one. Apparently he did have a bad temper.

He kicked his chair over and pounded his fist on the table. "I hope you don't think I'm paying for that drink."

"I've got it." Rebecca scooted out of her seat and grabbed her purse. She was going to get out of here—the sooner the better.

Keith grabbed her by the waist as she started to scoot past and leaned toward her. "The least you can do is give me a little kiss after throwing a drink in my face."

Droplets of sticky ginger ale dripped from his beard. Rebecca shuddered and shook her head but he didn't give her a chance to protest. He placed his lips on hers. His whiskers scratched the sensitive skin on her face. He tasted like stale tobacco and whiskey. She gagged, pushed him away, and started for the door. Two steps later, she stopped. Jared stood just in front of her, his eyes as dark as coal.

"Jared?" What was he doing here? He'd said they were through. He'd said—he thought—oh, God.

"Your mother said I'd find you here."

What had her mother been thinking? She'd known Rebecca was on a date. But Rebecca realized that her mother probably didn't realize this was the father of her child. What a mess.

"I see you didn't waste any time replacing me. Now I know why you dumped me." He turned and left the bar.

Rebecca threw some money at the waitress and chased after him. "What do you mean *I* dumped you?"

It was the other way around and he knew it!

Jared spun around to face her. Only the rapid rise and fall of his chest showed his anger. "On the phone, Rebecca. Couldn't you have waited until I was back in the country? Two weeks and I would have been home anyway. You at least owed me a face-to-face break up."

She'd just spent a week crying, worrying, and learning how to face life as a single mother. How dare Jared waltz in and act as though he hadn't done anything wrong? He was the one who'd said "we're through." She remembered the words clearly, because they'd sizzled into her brain with the pain of a branding iron. She stomped her foot.

"You are the one who broke up with me. And you know what, Jared? I think maybe you did me a favor. You aren't the man I thought you were. How you can just walk away from your responsibilities is beyond me. So what if I was on a date? You dumped me, remember? Now, I'm going home. Have a nice life."

She'd jumped in her car and made it halfway up State Street before the tears started. Her vision became cloudy and the streetlights took on an extra glow from the sheen of tears misting her sight. She'd just handled that entire situation in the worst way possible. What if Jared had changed his mind? What if he'd realized his mistake?

She shook her head. It didn't matter. He'd dumped her when she'd needed his love and reassurance most. She didn't want to spend her life with someone who wouldn't be there when she needed him. He would turn out to be just like her father and her child wouldn't be able to count on him. No, she was finished with Jared, and he could play the jealous, jilted lover all he wanted but they both knew the truth about who had dumped who.

On the other side of the bar, Mark had laughed when Rebecca threw her drink in Keith's face. Running true to form, she'd just performed the first test. It was just as Jennifer had said. The girls were in for a big surprise, because every man they dated was tipped off to what they were doing and they would all react badly to the tests.

"Mark?" Betty Tyler stood by his table, looking ridiculously out of place in her black slacks and button-down sweater.

"Mrs. Tyler." He stood and pulled a chair out for her. "Thank you for agreeing to meet with me."

"Anything for my future son-in-law. Please, call me 'Mom.' "

Mark smiled. Jennifer's mother really was a generous and sweet woman. He'd always liked her and never more than at this moment. Too bad her older daughter hadn't inherited some of her charm and gracefulness.

"Mom, then." He motioned the waitress over. "Let me buy you a drink."

"Amaretto Sour."

"Done," he said and placed her order. He shouldn't feel hesitant, but he wasn't sure how to start. Even though Kate was a thorn in his side, she was Betty's daughter. He could hardly say anything too negative about her. He'd have to rethink his approach a bit. The goal was to stop Kate in her tracks on several levels and to make sure the wedding went ahead as planned.

"What did you want to talk to me about, Mark?" She laid her hand on his arm. "You aren't having second thoughts are you?"

"No, no. Never. I'm crazy about Jennifer."

"Good." The relief in her voice was obvious. Jen said her mother desperately wanted grandchildren. She'd probably thought he was about to snatch her dreams away. "After last year, I just want Jen to be happy."

"It's just that I'm not so sure Jen's as crazy about me as I am about her." Here we go, old pal. Lay it on thick and get your point across.

"Jennifer loves you, Mark."

"Then why did she agree to that silly wager with her sister and Kate's friends?"

His words had their intended impact. Betty frowned. "What wager?"

"Oh, I thought you knew." He'd known darn good and well she didn't know. "I don't want to cause trouble. Forget I said anything."

The waitress set the mild drink in front of Betty. She picked it up, tossed the cherry aside and downed the drink in one long swallow. "Another," she told the waitress.

Mark fought to keep from laughing at her reaction.

"Tell me about the wager, Mark. I'll put a stop to this nonsense."

Mark leaned back and smiled. Life was so sweet. *Let's see you stop the wedding now that Mommy is onto you, Kate Tyler.*

★ ★ ★ ★ ★

Sarah hadn't been on a blind date in ten years and she had no intention of going on a blind date now. She knew a few of the basic tests in the diaries well and used them often on her dates, but she hadn't remembered all eight of them. Since she had no desire to get involved with another man now or possibly ever, her goal wasn't really to find the perfect man—as if that creature existed—she simply wanted to find a man who would pass seven tests. It didn't really matter if he was eight or eighty.

Oh, honey, Daniel did a number on you. The lilting sound of Aunt Mary's voice ricocheted inside her skull. She wasn't sure if it was the memory of Aunt Mary actually saying the words or her aunt sending a message to her. She shrugged. It hardly mattered. Her aunt was completely accurate—Daniel had done a number on her but she was working through it. Wasn't she?

There were two bars in this rinky-dink town worth meeting men in, and she planned to hit both of them tonight. If the pickings were thin, then she'd drive into Indianapolis and expand the hunt a bit. As was usually the case, since she wasn't interested in seriously finding a man, it seemed that every man in the room was interested in her the moment she walked in. Men were such fickle, backwards creatures. If she'd wanted to find her soul mate, they would have run as fast as they could from her. Well, that was fine. She'd use their penchant for wanting what they didn't think they could have to help her best friend.

She'd admit that she'd taken the time to look her best this evening, borrowing Kate's little black dress that showed more cleavage on Sarah because she had more there to show. It fit her curves nicely and hit mid-thigh, which was a good length for her, elongating her legs and making her look taller than her five foot four inches. The three-inch heels she'd added to the ensemble created a sexy look according to Kate, who had given her two thumbs up before she'd left.

Test number one involved drinks. Since there were ten men at the bar, she could choose anything from the preppied-up nerd to the dressed-way-down stud. She nodded and, reaching around the first man, tipped his drink into his lap. She continued down the line of men, dumping drink after drink in their laps, stopping only when she'd wet every lap.

She turned and surveyed the line of men, who instead of admiring her now glared at her. Ouch. Her gaze slid from one set of eyes to the next until she found one man at the end of the bar who grinned at her. She sidled up to the roughest-looking man in the bunch and linked her arm through his.

"Buy you a drink?" she offered. It was the least she could do, considering that she'd dumped his all over him.

"Strawberry Daiquiri," he said.

Sarah frowned. That was a girl's drink, wasn't it? She'd never known a man to order such a fru-fru drink. She signaled the bartender and ordered a daiquiri and a Coke and rum. A daiquiri? She shook her head, trying to get the thought out of her skull. What a man drank was not one of the tests, as far as she could remember, but maybe it should have been. Real men didn't drink sissy drinks. They drank stiff, hard liquor that grew hair on your chest. Sometimes they didn't drink at all. But they sure didn't have beach drinks.

"What's yer name?" He leaned closer and she pulled back a bit.

Whoa, cowboy. He wasn't even drunk and he acted punchy. "Name's Lola. I'll bet you're a Butch or maybe Duke."

The man frowned. "No. Gaylord."

"Gaylord?" The bartender set her drink in front of her so

she downed it in one long swallow. Maybe if she drank it fast enough, he'd turn into a Duke, or a Butch. At this point, she'd even take a William or John—anything but Gaylord.

"Where are you from, Lola?"

She choked and covered it with a cough. Well, if he had to be Gaylord, she certainly couldn't be Lola. That was a name for a Butch or a Duke. "I lied. My name isn't Lola."

"It isn't?" He frowned, looking confused and a bit frightened.

Uh-oh. She'd better rein in her free spirit or she was going to scare him off. She'd seen that "deer in headlights" look more than once before. Men typically had one of three reactions to her; love her, hate her, or run for your life!

"No. My name is—" What name went with Gaylord? She sure wasn't going to give him her real name. He might try to track her down or something. Besides, what was the fun in giving him a name like Sarah? No, tonight, she would be . . . "Geneviere."

Where had that come from? She waited for his reaction and wasn't disappointed. He grabbed his pretty, pink umbrellaed drink and backed away slowly. She watched him with some amusement. Perhaps he figured she was like a rabid animal and if he moved slowly she wouldn't attack.

"Where are you going, Gaylord?" She followed him.

Terror lit a fire in his eyes and under his feet. He began to back up in double-time, tripped over the leg of a chair, and knocked the man sitting in that chair flat out on the floor. Gaylord didn't seem concerned about the man, but tried to protect his showy cocktail instead. He held it far out in front of him but he couldn't keep both his balance and the drink upright. As the fruity concoction sloshed out of the glass and over his clothes, his feet kept moving. The floor became slick from the frozen drink and Gaylord's legs moved in cartoon character style a moment before they flew up in the air and he came down directly on top of the man he'd already knocked onto the floor.

"Get off me, you freak," the man shouted.

Gaylord seemed more concerned about his clothes, now stained pink from the drink, and flopped over on his stomach. He gazed into the man's eyes for a moment as realization dawned on them both that one lay on top of the other. Sarah threw her hand over her mouth as the first punch was thrown, then turned and fled the bar.

When she got back to her aunt's house, she picked up the phone and called Kate.

"How did it go?" Kate asked.

Sarah winced. "Let's just say that I don't think I'm allowed in that bar anymore."

But she'd figure out another way to find the perfect man and help her friend. Perhaps she should try the grocery store. One of her friends had once told her that was a great place to meet a man. She wondered if in the place of a spilled drink she could substitute pushing a man into a freezer case or spilling a gallon of milk on him.

She'd made a lot of mistakes in the past few months, Becca reminded herself as she walked into the *Daily Reporter*. Guilt weighed heavily on her because she hadn't talked to Mark before agreeing to Kate's crazy plan. It wasn't the first time she'd gotten involved in one of Kate's or Sarah's plans and regretted it. Their passion for living tended to draw her into the excitement of the moment; consequences were sorted out later. But she was no longer thirteen and that was hardly an excuse.

She owed Mark an apology and she intended to give it to him and then go see Kate and let her know that she wouldn't be part of this scheme any longer. Her friend might be upset with her but Kate would understand.

The receptionist didn't glance up until Becca cleared her throat for the third time. The woman sighed and placed the cap on the fingernail polish, blowing on her still wet nails. "Can I help you?"

"I'm here to see Mark Jackson."

The woman frowned and looked her up and down. It wasn't a look that Rebecca got often from other women. She didn't dress provocatively and didn't usually threaten women like this one, but apparently today it was different. And why did the woman feel she had a right to feel threatened? A niggle of doubt entered her mind and she wondered if perhaps Kate and Sarah were right about Mark.

"Is he expecting you?" The blonde woman uncapped her nail polish again and began to reapply the brassy color to the index finger on her right hand.

"He'll see me." She gave the receptionist her name and waited. The woman finally sighed and gingerly picked up the phone. "Rebecca Winters to see you. Really?"

She hung up the phone and glared at it for a moment before turning back to her nail polish with a sigh while she waved her hand toward the offices along the back wall. "Back there."

"Thank you." Geez. How rude could you be? She made her way to the office with Mark's name on the brass plate. She knocked lightly.

"Come in, Becca." Mark greeted her at the door and walked her to a chair. "What can I do for you?"

"I've come to apologize." She sank into the deep cushion in the leather chair and clasped her hands, shame filling her.

"For going along with Kate's plan?"

"So you know about that?"

Mark nodded. "I know what you girls are doing. Jen told me. I have to admit I didn't understand your participation in it; I thought we parted on good terms."

"We did. I don't know how I get into these things. I should know better at my age—"

"It's okay, Becca. Kate always was persuasive. She won't succeed, you know."

"I wouldn't bet on that. She's pretty determined." Becca didn't agree with Kate, but out of instinct felt she had to defend her. "She's just worried about her sister. The situation with Billy really tore her apart last year."

Mark nodded as though he understood. "I'm sorry as hell about that, but I can't let her ruin the best thing that's ever come into my life."

"You really love Jen, don't you?" Becca asked, watching him carefully. She needed to know for her own peace of mind that he would make Jen a good husband. If she was going to go against her best friend and refuse to help with the wager, then she needed to have a firm conviction that this man was right for Jen.

"I love her more than my own life." Mark laid his hand on his heart. He met her gaze without flinching, emotion shining out of his eyes.

Becca nodded, satisfied. "Then there's only one thing left for me to do."

Ten

"Katherine Elaine Tyler, how could you?" Her mother's eyes shone with the tears that had left fresh tracks down her cheeks.

"I told you, Mom. Mark isn't good enough for Jennifer. He'll break her heart." How had her mother found out about their bet? She had her suspicions and his name was Mark.

"That's for Jennifer to decide, Kate." She crossed her arms and scowled at Kate with the same expression that had made her squirm as a twelve-year-old.

Unfortunately, the glower still worked. Kate shifted in her chair. "The same way she decided about Billy? She isn't exactly the best judge of character. Mark's a liar and a cheat." He'd been a liar and a cheat in high school. From what Kate had heard, he was still a liar and a cheat. "A zebra might be able to paint himself white, but eventually the paint will wash off and he'll show his stripes."

"I think that you are letting your own disappointment color your vision." Her mother's jaw was clenched in a straight line. She was obviously furious over their wager to find the perfect man and end the wedding. "Mark made a mistake when he was a child, Kate. Give him a chance."

Maybe her mother was right. Maybe she was being too hard on Mark. She really didn't know him, other than what she'd heard from others. Perhaps she should give him a chance to prove that he was a changed man. She just didn't believe it was possible for someone to change themselves that much.

"And how dare you use my grandmother's tests in such a manner?" Betty's voice cracked. "She meant those tests to be used to help her family find men who were of the highest caliber, not for some ridiculous bet."

"I'm sorry, Mom. It was the only standard we could agree on." Kate wished the floor would just open up and swallow her. Or better yet, maybe a wormhole would open up and transport her back to New Orleans and she could forget about this wedding and the crazy wager.

"Well, I want you to stop this nonsense. Jennifer loves Mark. Do you really want to destroy your sister's happiness?"

The words cut deep under Kate's skin. Of course she didn't want Jen to be unhappy. She'd gone crazy when she'd found out Billy had kidnapped Jen after her sister finally broke things off with him. He'd stalked Jen for months, terrorizing her, shadowing her every move. His letters and phone calls had grown more and more threatening until the day he'd finally done what he'd promised and snatched her sister. Now Jen's life was safe but her future happiness was threatened. She was trying to save her sister from a miserable marriage. How could her own mother think she was doing anything other than that?

"Jen's happiness is *all* I'm worried about."

"Then give her your blessing, attend the wedding, smile, and wish her luck."

Maybe she should just give up. When she'd left New Orleans to come home and save Jen from marrying Mark, she'd never dreamed it would be this hard. Could she do that? Could she just stand back while Jen married Mark? Could she throw her baby sister to a wolf in sheep's clothing?

★ ★ ★ ★ ★

The argument with her mother had left a bitter taste in Kate's mouth. She wasn't prejudging Mark. Was she? So what if she was? But she knew that she truly hadn't given Mark a chance. When she'd gone to lunch with Jennifer, all she'd had in mind was how she could force him to show his true colors. She winced, not liking herself very much at the moment. She was a rotten sister. She hadn't even listened when Jennifer had tried to explain why she cared so much for Mark.

Well, she was going to make up for it now. Her sister's bedroom door was closed tightly, but Kate knew she was inside from the rustling she could hear on this side of the door. Even though they were sharing a room, she didn't feel like she could just barge in on her sister. She raised her fist and rapped her knuckles lightly on the door, smiling as she remembered a ten-year-old Jen taping a huge sign on her door that had read, "Knock!!! This means YOU, Kate."

"Come in." Jen's voice sounded muffled through the wood of the door.

Kate took a deep breath and turned the knob. Here goes everything. Clothes were strewn across the bed, armchair, along the dresser top, and on the floor.

"Did your closet explode?" She laughed.

Jen glanced up, a look of panic entering her eyes. She shrugged and folded a short black skirt and placed it in a suitcase. Kate realized she was choosing her wardrobe for her honeymoon. Had she put that touch of sadness on her sister's face? Guilt backed up in her throat. She tried to swallow it down but it was stuck.

"I'm just trying to decide what to pack for . . ." Jen trailed off and glanced away.

"For your honeymoon," Kate finished for her.

"Yes." Jen added a pale blue top to the skirt already in the suitcase.

"Need some help?" God this was hard. She still believed Mark was completely wrong for Jen, but she was willing to give him a chance. To really give him a chance and not just think of ways to prove that he was a jerk. Just because her sister made one wrong choice didn't mean *all* her choices were wrong.

"Seriously? Does this mean you finally approve?" The hope in Jen's eyes almost caused Kate to tear up.

She bit her lip. "It means that I'm willing to concede that maybe I wasn't exactly open to getting to know Mark as an adult. I am not agreeing to call off our wager yet, but I will agree to meet with him one more time and really give him a chance before I form an opinion."

"Oh, Kate." Jen jumped to her feet and threw her arms around Kate's neck. "Thank you so much. He usually goes to the country club on Tuesdays for a round of golf. You can probably catch him if you leave right now."

"Oh, now? I mean, I wasn't planning—"

"Why wait? I know you're going to see how perfect we are for each other once you talk with him. Go." Jen laughed and danced around the room in a circle, dodging clothes that still lay scattered across the pale pink carpet.

Kate took a deep breath and nodded her head. Okay, she would go find Mark, have a nice chat with him. *God, give me strength to not be judgmental.* But she was worried that God didn't have enough time or angels to cover her request at the moment. After all, there were important things going on in the world. Far more important than a simple hometown wedding in central Indiana.

Kate's hand was on the front door when the bell rang, so she yanked it open.

"Kate!" Rebecca's hand flew to her chest.

"Sorry. Didn't mean to scare you. I was getting ready to go out." Kate laughed at Becca's round-mouthed expression. "How are you feeling?"

"Fine." Rebecca waved her hand. "Well, physically, fine."

"Good. Come in for a sec. I was headed to the country club." Kate put one hand on her hip and flipped her hair with the other hand, putting an East Coast accent on the words "country club."

"Why?" Becca followed Kate into the parlor and they sat on her mother's dainty Victorian style armchairs. Betty Tyler was one of the few women in town who still kept a formal calling parlor for visitors. Kate had always rather liked the concept. The rest of the house could be a pit, but this room looked neat and clean and perfect. Not that her mother's house was ever messy, but if it had been no one would ever know.

"I agreed to go meet with Mark and try to give him a chance to prove me wrong." Kate hoped he could prove her wrong, but she had serious doubts. "The last thing I want is to make my sister unhappy. She and my mother are both upset at my refusal to even give Mark a chance. They both say he has changed. So, I'm going to try to have an open mind and we'll see."

"Does this mean the wager is off?" Rebecca asked.

"Not exactly. Maybe more on hold."

"I'm so relieved." Becca let out a long breath that she'd apparently been holding for a while.

"Relieved?"

"I have a problem. Jared is in town. He saw me on a date last night and he's furious."

Kate wondered if Becca realized that she'd taken to rubbing her stomach lately. She smiled at her friend's maternal instincts.

"What right does he have to be furious, Becca? He dumped you."

"That's what I said but he says *I* dumped him. I'm so confused, Kate. I don't know exactly what I should do but I do know that he took the time and trouble to follow me all the way to Greenfield and to track me down. He *is* the baby's father."

"And you still love him, don't you?" Kate knew Becca better than she knew her own sister, something else which she should probably feel guilty about. Becca had always worn her heart on her sleeve. She knew that more than anything, her friend wanted a stable home life for this child and that meant having a father around.

"I do."

"Well, he could have just been shocked when you phoned him, Becca." She took Rebecca's hand and patted it. "Maybe he didn't know how to respond. You should talk to him."

"You know, it's strange, Kate. I was coming here to tell you that I can't help with the wager. Jared was livid and I don't want to ruin any chance I have of at least discussing things with him. Even if he doesn't want me, he's still this baby's father."

"Absolutely. You need to work things out with Jared, Becca. That should be your first priority."

Becca swallowed and then looked at Kate with tear-filled eyes. "There's more, Kate."

"More?" Panic fluttered through her at Becca's expression. "Is the baby okay?"

"The baby is fine. I—" She stopped and placed her hands up to her eyes, rocking slightly. "I don't even know how to tell you."

"Just tell me, Becca. Since when do we keep secrets from

one another?" Becca's behavior was so out of character that Kate felt extremely off-kilter.

"That's just it. I kept a big secret from you and Sarah. Huge."

"Jared—I know. It's okay." Becca had already explained that she hadn't wanted to confess her love for Jared when it was so new.

"No, there's another one." Becca took a shaky breath. "Two years ago when I came home to visit my mother, I dated Mark."

"What?" Kate leaned back away from Becca. The room spun for a moment and she felt as though Becca had smacked her across the face. Becca had dated Mark? Why?

"I knew you'd be hurt," Becca cried. "That's why I didn't tell you. I never would have told you."

Kate shook her head, trying to clear her vision. Becca and Mark? Was that even possible? But looking at her friend's miserable expression, she knew Becca spoke the truth.

"Is this why you kept sticking up for him?" She tried to tamp down the hurt and anger rumbling inside her. Becca'd already been in the hospital once with this baby. She'd never forgive herself if she lost her temper and Becca grew so upset that she wound up back in the hospital or lost the baby. She closed her eyes and counted to ten. When that didn't work, she imagined a calm lake on a peaceful day. Graceful, weeping willows swept the bright green grass around her imaginary lake. She took several deep breaths and opened her eyes.

"I'm so sorry, Kate. He isn't such a bad guy. He was good to me. We parted friends." A stream of tears rivered down Becca's face as though they wouldn't stop until they reached the ocean. "Can you ever forgive me?"

How couldn't she forgive Becca? Besides, she'd already

agreed to give Mark a second chance. She'd take this as a sign that her decision to do so had been the right one.

"It's okay, I understand. Have you told Sarah?"

"Not yet, but we're meeting for lunch later. I'll tell her then. You know, I went to see Mark today and apologize for my behavior. At the same time, you were deciding to give Mark a second chance. It's almost like fate."

Or a sign from God that she was finally doing the right thing. But then why did she have this intensely uncomfortable, heavy feeling in the pit of her stomach?

How many cantaloupes could you squeeze before the management at the grocery store became suspicious? Sarah glanced at a produce stocker, realized he was male and at least twenty-one and threw him what she thought was a come-hither smile. He'd do just as well as anyone else for the tests.

"Hello." She waved at him.

His face flushed with instant redness and he looked over his shoulder as though to make sure she meant him. Then he turned and disappeared into the back room. She considered following him for a moment but didn't really have time to chase him. She still had to find a man to pass test number one.

The manager glared at her from the customer service booth, so she moved further into the store. She figured that Granny's tests were meant to see basic temperament and manners. For example, the test for opening the door could also be conducted if she needed to reach something on a tall shelf. A man who stopped and helped was a gentleman and passed the test. She shrugged. Close enough anyway.

She had exactly twenty minutes before she was due to meet Rebecca for lunch. She'd better hurry. On the cereal aisle, she stopped. Two men with shopping carts crowded the small aisle. No wedding bands on their fingers and no girl-friends in sight gave her the green light she sought. Test number two—manners.

She sauntered down the aisle between the two carts, smiling at each man. When she reached the middle of the aisle, she stepped onto the bottom shelf and reached for a box of cereal on the uppermost shelf at the top of the pile. At only five feet four inches, it was impossible for her to reach the top box. She glanced at the men who both watched her, one with a slight smile and the other with a frown.

She gave a little hop to try to reach that top box, but without any real intention of success. *Okay, boys. I can use your help anytime.* She peeked toward the two carts. Both men still watched her but didn't make a move to help. Irritation flooded through her. Didn't mothers teach their sons man-ners these days? What was the world coming to when a lady had to climb onto shelves and hop around like an idiot to get a box of cocoa crispies? Okay, maybe "lady" was stretching it a bit in her case, but neither one of them offered to help.

Well, that was just fine. She wasn't a helpless damsel in distress and she hated these outdated tests anyway. She would get the cereal and she'd do it without a man's assis-tance. She curled her toes into the metal shelf and bent her knees, preparing for a giant leap. A moment before her feet left the metal ledge, she realized that an entire row of the same cereal sat at eye level. Too late to worry about an easier target at this point, she was already in flight. Her hand reached out and grabbed the top box and she gave a small cry of victory. Her feet landed on the tile floor and she held the box up in triumph. *Take that you Neanderthals.* A soft rattle above her head caught her attention the second before all the boxes on the top shelf came tumbling down, hitting her on the top of the head. The force of fifteen boxes of cereal raining down on her sent her sprawling onto her back. She came up sputtering, buried in a pile of Cocoa Puffs.

The two men had disappeared. At least she was alone in her humiliation. She pushed to her feet and brushed her clothes off just as the store manager came running.

"Are you okay, ma'am?" He grabbed the boxes and began to stack them to the side out of the main traffic route.

"Nothing hurt but my pride," she said as she left the store with her head held high.

Kate drove slowly up the long, tree-lined drive that led to the country club. An empty field stretched out to her right and a walking trail, mostly hidden by trees, curled to the left. The parking lot seemed fairly busy even for a weekday. She hoped she hadn't missed Mark while she'd been talking to Rebecca. Jen would be so disappointed and somehow she thought she'd probably disappointed her sister enough lately.

She had no idea what kind of car he drove, so she parked the rental car and made her way to the Pro Shop. "Hi, Mike." She remembered the pro shop manager from days long ago when her father had played golf every weekend. The man had been a young boy back then and working as a caddy, but his carrot top shock of hair and wide grin made him easily recognizable even with a few years of added maturity etched onto his face. She noticed his freckles still crawled over his nose and ended high on his cheekbones.

"What can I do for ya?" he asked.

"I'm looking for Mark Jackson." She couldn't disappoint Jen, who she knew would be home waiting to hear about her opinion of Mark. She'd have to track him down if he wasn't here. Somehow she suspected he wouldn't be anxious to see her, so it might not be easy to find him, even in a small town.

"He was in a while ago. I'd say he's probably finished with the course or pretty close to it. You might just want to hang out up here and see if you can spot him."

"Thanks." She walked back outside.

The closely cropped green grass rolled across the sprawling golf course, and was sprinkled with a few players in the distance. A small lake with a fountain spray made the scene picturesque. Not much had changed since she was a child and some of the tension she'd felt since returning home eased from her shoulders. It was nice to see that something was the same. Everything else had changed around her child-hood home. There was a comfort in familiarness and this place offered that.

She wondered if Daddy still played golf here. He'd never taken a cart but always walked, carrying his own clubs, and claiming it was excellent exercise. Her mother had gone with him one time, failed miserably at the sport, and decided golf wasn't for her. She smiled. Her father'd taught her some of the most important lessons of her young life while golfing this course. She'd walk alongside him, his hand on top of her head, and he'd tell her stories of his youth and relate those stories to any given situation she was dealing with. She could sure use one of her father's stories at the moment.

Spotting Mark's unmistakable swagger and closely cropped dark head, she started to raise her hand to wave at him. But when a woman appeared at his side and wrapped her arm through his, she lowered her hand and stepped back into the shadows of the overhang.

Open mind, Kate. Maybe she's just a friend. The woman's long, blonde hair fell in practiced waves down the length of her back. Her slacks were tight and showed off her slim curves; tiny waist accentuated by a thin, tightly cinched brown belt. She didn't just have her arm hooked through

Mark's, but she hugged it tightly, looking up at him in near hero-worship. Kate gagged. She was going to be sick.

Of course she knew she'd been right about Mark, but having the evidence slap her squarely in the face was another thing. How could he do this to Jennifer? Right in front of everyone, too. He didn't even have the decency to drive to town and have an affair where she wouldn't hear about it.

Slow down, Kate. You promised Jennifer you'd give him the benefit of the doubt. Okay, she could be wrong. The girl could be his—her mind hit a brick wall. She could be his friend from college, his best friend's wife, or his secretary.

They stopped just in front of Kate and she held her breath, knowing that if Mark glanced up he would spot her hiding there in the shadows. He'd assume she was spying on him. Truly she hadn't been. She'd come here with the best of intentions. Maybe the other woman was a family friend.

The blonde raised on her tiptoes and planted a kiss on Mark's mouth. He didn't push her away. Kate's lips tightened. And so it begins. Already he was cheating on Jen and their wedding was less than a week away. Give her blessing for this marriage? There was no way that would ever happen.

As a matter of fact, Mr. Jackson had just given her even more reason to do everything in her power to keep that man from marrying her sister. There was no way she was going to sit idly by and let him break Jen's gentle heart. Her sister had been through enough already.

But what was she going to tell Jen when she returned home? Her sister would be waiting, wanting to know her opinion of Mark. Would she even believe Kate about another woman at this point? Or would she think that Kate was making it up to try to stop the wedding? No, maybe it was better if Jen heard about this from someone else. She already had the means to stop or at least postpone the wedding. The wager was still on. She had made it clear she wasn't calling it off. She'd simply tell Jen that her opinion of Mark remained unchanged; that all bets were on. And then, she would make sure she found someone who could pass the tests. In fact, it wouldn't be hard at all to prove that there were men out there who were better than that snake.

Eleven

"So, what did you think of Mark?"

Kate had to turn away from the hope shining out of her sister's eyes, so she busied herself pulling a cheesecake from the fridge. Her mother had covered the dessert with fresh blueberries and strawberries, but Kate didn't really have an appetite. She just needed to figure out what to say to her sister.

"Kate?" Jen's voice was low.

"I'm sorry, Jen." She met her sister's gaze and noticed the barely contained veil of tears. The last thing she wanted was to hurt her sister but she was going to be hurt no matter what Kate did. If she gave her blessing and watched her sister marry that liar and cheat, then Jen would suffer even more than if she was a little upset that her sister didn't like her fiancé.

"Did you really give him a chance, Kate? Or did you pre-judge him?"

"I didn't prejudge him. As a matter of fact, I did my best to give him the benefit of the doubt, but the evidence was over-whelming." She took a deep breath. "I am more determined than ever to convince you to postpone this wedding."

Jen shook her head in disbelief. "I don't understand it. How could you talk to him and decide you don't like him? He's charming."

"Sometimes there is more than meets the eye, Jennifer. I love you. I'm your big sister. It's my job to protect you."

Jen jumped to her feet. "Well, I love him and I'm going to marry him. You can come to the wedding or not, that is your choice. But I won't hear another word against Mark."

"We have an agreement," Kate pointed out, hating herself more than Jen could possibly hate her. She sliced a piece of the cake and laid it on a small, china dessert plate with fili-greed silver along the edges.

"You're serious?" Jen asked. "You actually plan to test some men and try to stop my wedding?"

"I'm afraid so. I do have your best interests at heart, if that helps."

"It doesn't." Jen ran from the room and up the staircase. Kate heard the muffled slam of her bedroom door.

That hadn't gone well. She scraped the cheesecake into the garbage disposal and flipped the switch. How could she eat when her life was falling apart? It was becoming very clear to her that Mark Jackson had worked things so that she was bound to lose even if she won. She leaned her hands on the stainless steel kitchen sink, wishing she could follow the cheesecake down the drain and hide out there for a while.

A face appeared for a second in the kitchen window. Kate turned quickly toward it, knowing she wasn't imagining things this time, but there wasn't anyone there. She shivered and backed away from the window. What was wrong with her? Of course there wasn't anyone there. Her emotions were out of whack, that was all. She should talk to her father. He always gave good advice. He'd know what she should do.

She headed for the garage, knowing that her father was likely to be in there working on his hotrod. The rev of a heavy duty engine confirmed her suspicions. She knocked on the open door, but her father didn't hear the sound over the throb of the car turning over.

When the engine noises died down, she walked closer to the car. "Daddy?"

"Hey, punkin. What are you up to?" The words were familiar; she'd heard them over and over throughout her childhood; but his appearance had altered drastically. He'd become a senior citizen in the last few years and the change struck her again.

"I was hoping you could offer me some advice," she said.

"I can try." Her father slid out from behind the wheel and moved back to the engine of the sporty car. "Hand me that wrench."

She grabbed the tool he requested and handed it to him, the motion familiar and soothing. "Jen is angry at me because I won't call off this bet. I gave Mark a chance, Daddy."

"Did you?" He looked at her for a moment and Kate wondered if he could see through her skin down to her very soul.

She shifted uncomfortably from foot to foot. She *had* given Mark the benefit of the doubt. "Yes. All I got was proof that I'm right."

"Mark's a good boy," her father said.

"I don't think so."

"Honey, I love both you girls. You have to do what you think is right. But I've never seen your sister happier. It's nice to see her happy after last year."

Kate agreed. She couldn't bear to see her sister unhappy again. But she knew in her heart that Mark Jackson would bring nothing good to Jen's life. She sighed.

"You'll work it out, honey. You're a smart girl. Always were." Her father winked at her.

She hoped he was right, because right now she didn't know if her plan was smart or stupid. It didn't matter if Jen was angry. She knew what she had to do. She straightened. It was her job to protect her baby sister. It had always been her job. Just because it was tougher than normal and emotionally draining didn't mean she could opt out. She would stop this wedding one way or another.

Tuesday evening—only three days until the rehearsal dinner and four days until the wedding. Kate glanced at her watch. Already her date was fifteen minutes late. Maybe it had been insane to plan back-to-back dates tonight, but she was desperate. Not only did she have to find men to date and who could pass some of the tests, she had to find a man who would pass seven of the eight tests and pass them by Friday evening, so she could get Jen to call off the wedding. Saturday would be too late to inform invited guests that the wedding was postponed. No, it had to be by Friday.

"Kate Tyler, you are just as pretty as you were in high school." Jerry Dillon arrived with a big smile but no apology for being late.

Ian was rarely late for anything. Kate gritted her teeth. *Ian also fired you, you moron. Forget him.* She plastered on a smile. "So good to see you again, Jerry. Have a seat."

When they'd graduated from high school, Jerry had left on a football scholarship. Even all these years later, his muscles showed that he worked out regularly. He wore polished, brown leather boots and denims that looked like they'd been ironed. One lock of his sandy blonde hair fell on his forehead and his hazel eyes twinkled with good humor. His wide smile reminded her of a boy who always had a joke and laughed often.

"I have to say I was pretty surprised when you called me. I'm not much for dates, but I have to admit I was curious to see what you'd pull."

"Excuse me?" What did he mean? Did he know about the tests? But that was impossible. She shook her head. "I'm just glad to see you again. Want to order a drink?"

"Ah, the drink. Sure. Why not?"

Jerry was acting very strange. Kate stared at him for a moment, wondering if he'd always been so eccentric. She remembered him as a down-to-earth, big brother type. His sister, Eloise, was the town's biggest snoot, but whatever gene she'd inherited seemed to have skipped him. She shrugged. Whatever. As long as he passed her tests, he could act as nutty as he wanted. She had no intention of getting married to him. She just wanted to stop that dreaded wedding.

"Vodka," Jerry told the waitress. Then he winked at her. "Has less fumes than other alcohol."

Okay. Was he a lush? Maybe that was the problem—he was already rip-roaring drunk. Kate made a mental note not to let him drive if they went anywhere else together. She had no desire to wind up wrapped around a tree.

"So, do you like New Orleans?" he asked, while they waited for their drinks.

"Love it. I've been working as a haunted history tour guide but I want to start my own business." Some day. For now, Ian had pretty much ended that dream. Oh, well. She'd find another job when she returned home and she'd save up some money again and eventually she'd have her own tour guide business. It would just take a little longer. Okay, a lot longer.

"I hurt my knee second football season in college and came back home. Now, I work at a local factory and have a small farm just east of town."

"Really? You always did seem like a cowboy to me." She grinned, relaxing a bit. This was actually going pretty well. She felt none of the physical attraction toward Jerry that she did for Ian, but that wasn't a requirement for winning the wager.

The waitress arrived with Jerry's drink and set it on a napkin in front of him. He didn't pick it up but slid it across the table toward Kate. Strange. She blinked but didn't comment. Maybe he wanted her to taste it or something. Anyway, if it was closer, she'd be able to spill it on him a bit easier without being obvious.

"Looks great." She made a motion to pass it back to him but intentionally over calculated and the glass landed in his lap.

Jerry burst out laughing. "Kate, you are such a riot. You always were."

"You aren't mad?" *Please let him say no.*

"No."

She relaxed. Test number one—passed. Test number two up next. She smiled. Jerry was the type to open doors without having to be given a hint. Test two would be a cinch.

Jerry was easy to get along with. He always had been. That was probably why they'd been such good friends in high school. She wished for a moment that she hadn't made another date, but she had to exercise all her options. She had exactly forty-five more minutes to spend with Jerry and she'd like to at least get to test number two.

"Would you walk me to my car?" she asked.

"Certainly."

As they approached the front door, she hesitated for a moment. Please open the door. Please. This is an easy test, Jerry. Right on cue, he reached out and opened the door for her. She relaxed. This was her perfect example and her key to stopping Jen's wedding. She was certain of it.

"This was so much fun. Can we meet again while I'm in town?" she asked. Please let him say yes.

"Anytime, darlin'. When?"

"Tomorrow? Lunch?" If she was lucky, she could get in lunch with Jerry and another date in the evening. More chances to stop the wedding. Failing wasn't an option—she wouldn't even consider it.

"Thanks, Jerry. I appreciate this more than you know." Mark handed Jerry a hundred bucks. It was a small price to keep Kate occupied and ensure she couldn't stop their wedding. A moment of indecision almost singed his fingers where he held the money, but he loved Jen too much to risk losing her.

"I feel bad taking money, Mark. Kate is just as sweet as always. I'd probably hang out with her anyway."

"Just remember that you can only pass six of the eight tests. You still have the list I gave you?" Jen hadn't suspected a thing when he'd asked her to let him in on the tests. He'd been a little surprised to discover that she'd tried out a few of them on him, but then his sense of humor kicked in and he'd realized that if he hadn't passed most of them, he wouldn't be engaged to her now.

God, I'm crazy about that woman. No, he wouldn't let Jen's sister ruin things. She was being completely stubborn about their wedding. Why couldn't she accept that he'd changed? Why couldn't she just be happy for them? Was she already a bitter dried-up old hag? It was a shame. She was an attractive woman. He was certain she could have been happily married herself if she wanted. A vague sense of unease poked him in the gut. What would future holidays and family events be like when his sister-in-law despised him? What would that do to Jen? But it wasn't enough of a deterrent to make him want to call off the wedding. Thank God she lived in Louisiana. At least he wouldn't have to see her very often.

"I have the list. I think she's already done the first two." Jerry laughed. "I mean, I know she did the first test. My wet lap proves it. But I always open doors for ladies, so I'm assuming I passed that one."

"Good man. When are you seeing her again?"

"Tomorrow for lunch."

Mark whistled. "The lady doesn't waste any time. Maybe you'll fall in love and elope—that would get her out of my hair for a while."

"No chance of that, friend. She's great, but there's no chemistry there, ya know? She's like my sister."

"Well, just as long as you keep her busy until Saturday, I'll be more than happy. Since she's moving so fast, if you can stall her on any of the tests, I'd greatly appreciate it."

"Will do my best." Jerry looped his thumbs in the buckle bands of his jeans.

"You're coming to the bachelor party tomorrow night?"

"I wouldn't miss it."

"See you there." Mark's wallet was a hundred dollars leaner, but his heart was lighter at the thought of Kate being kept busy on a "wild goose chase" while he finished planning his wedding.

Test # 3: Mention the children you'll someday have together. This will chase off any commitment-phobes.

Jerry was late—*again.* Kate glanced at her watch in irritation. She always arrived early everywhere, even when she didn't want to. The one thing in this world that she couldn't stand was waiting. Oh, she could understand that everyone ran late sometimes, but this was the second date in a row that Jerry hadn't arrived at the appointed time. It was like a smack in the face as far as she was concerned. It showed that he didn't have enough respect for her to bother to be on time.

If she didn't need him to pass the tests and help her stop this wedding, she'd get up and walk out. He was already thirty minutes late. She sighed and ordered another cup of coffee. At the forty-five-minute mark, she grabbed her purse, prepared to leave just as Jerry walked in.

"Hey, babe," he said.

No apology for being late, she noted. She lifted a brow. Maybe he had more of Eloise's tendencies than she'd realized.

"I'm late. I know. I'm always late though. Don't take it personally."

Kate forced a smile past her gritted teeth. She couldn't afford to blow this opportunity. At the moment, Jerry represented her best chance to win the bet. Time to put her plan into action. She didn't have a moment to waste and if Jerry was going to fail a test, then she might as well get it over with now.

Most men didn't want to talk about commitment after going out for months, much less on the second date.

"Do you want a family, Jerry?" she asked.

He didn't even flinch. "Sure. I'm ready to get married and settle down. I've been looking for the right woman is all."

Kate frowned. Something didn't add up with this scenario. She'd never met a man who would answer her question that way on the second date. Of course, Jerry wasn't just any man. He was far from typical. He definitely had an eccentric streak. Maybe that explained his unusual reaction. Or maybe she hadn't been clear enough about what she meant.

"So, what kind of children do you think we'd have?" There. She sat back. That should scare him.

He flushed a bit but didn't stutter or jump up and bolt from the table. "Hopefully little girls with your good looks and my charm. And boys with my strength and your sense of punctuality."

"Okay." Kate found herself at a loss for words. Of all the responses she'd expected, that hadn't been it. She tilted her head and looked at Jerry. Too bad she didn't feel any physical connection to him whatsoever, because he might just be the one man in the country who could pass the tests without even trying.

She should be thrilled. If he kept passing, she'd have her "perfect" man well before Friday. Three down, four to go. Did she really want this? She knew Jen would be devastated but wasn't it better for her to be distressed now than in five years when she'd invested love, time, and possibly children into a marriage that would ultimately end badly?

Perhaps it was time to test Jerry on the jealousy factor. She had a date this evening at Blue Moon Rising. How could she get him there?

"I hear they are having a great band at Blue Moon Rising tonight," she said.

"Really? What kind of band?"

What kind of music do you like? She took a wild guess. "Country."

"What time?"

"Seven, I think."

"I might try to go."

Okay, now she couldn't be obvious about what she was doing. She'd be there with another date, testing him. She wanted Jerry to think it was a coincidence. She couldn't take a chance that Jen would question her and think that she'd cheated in any way.

"Oh, well, it will probably be crowded and stuff. Might not be a good idea."

"Hmmm."

Shoot. It was impossible to tell if he'd taken the bait. She'd just have to go on to the bar and hope he showed up. Even more important, she hoped he passed test number four.

Ian felt a bit out of place as he pulled his small sports car into the driveway of the two-story house on the corner. So this was where Kate had grown up. The bright flowers on the front porch and the brightly painted numbers on the mailbox spoke volumes about Kate's parents and their love for their home. He imagined growing up here had been wonderful.

Two blonde girls whizzed their bikes down the sidewalk, the spokes glistening in the quickly waning summer sun. He could almost picture Kate, Rebecca, and Sarah as young girls, riding their bikes through town.

Making his way up the porch steps, he hesitated before knocking on the door. She'd already brought someone else home with her. She would have introduced him to her parents. What would they think when he showed up looking for Kate? Maybe he was mistaken. Maybe she'd come home alone. But she'd made it clear that she was bringing someone with her. There could be little doubt about it. He only hoped it wasn't too late to attempt to win her heart.

Raising his hand, he knocked quickly. Footsteps sounded on the other side of the door and a rosy-cheeked woman greeted him with a smile. "If you have a delivery for the wedding—"

"Oh, no, ma'am." Great. She thought he was a delivery boy. "I'm here to see Kate."

"Kate?" The woman's brows knit together and then she smiled slowly. "I see."

Maybe all wasn't lost. Kate's mother seemed happy to see him. Perhaps her parents didn't like the man she'd brought home. In that case, she would be very excited to see another man come calling for Kate. A swift surge of hope kicked to life inside him. Kate felt something for him. Maybe it wasn't love just yet, but he believed it would be one day if she opened herself to him.

"I'm Ian Fields." He held out his hand.

"Betty Tyler." She took his hand and held it in both of hers, gazing deep into his eyes.

Ian shifted uncomfortably, wondering if the woman could reach into his brain and pick out his thoughts.

"You're Kate's boss," she said. "C'mon in. Kate isn't here. I apologize for thinking you had a delivery. We're in the last stages of Jen's wedding."

Her words were soothing and stinging at the same time. So Kate had come home for her sister's wedding, but she hadn't invited him and hadn't told him about it. He wondered if Kate had told her mother that he'd fired her just before she left Louisiana. But Betty had spoken as though he were still Kate's boss, so apparently not. That was good. He needed to let Kate know that no matter what happened between the two of them, she still had her job as long as she wanted it. She'd had time off due her. He'd allowed his emotions to overrule his better sense when he'd given her that ultimatum.

The house smelled of cinnamon and freshly baked bread. Betty led him to a small parlor where pictures of two dark-headed imps lined the walls and lay scattered across the small side tables, mixed in with a few black and white photographs. A younger Kate, with two front teeth missing, smiled at him from the coffee table. He picked up the framed picture.

"Kate was seven in that picture. Always trying to watch out for her baby sister, Jennifer." She pointed at a similar picture on another table of another toothless child who resembled Kate. "She's still trying to protect her I guess, even if she is sometimes misguided."

Ian wondered what family dynamics he'd just walked into when Kate's mother sighed deeply.

"Mrs. Tyler . . ." He felt an urgent need to track down Kate and let her know how he felt. The sooner the better.

"Oh, call me Betty, please. Would you like some cookies? I just finished baking some snicker doodles. They're Kate's favorite."

"Betty, I really need to find Kate."

"I'd say. Anyone who would drive all the way up from New Orleans must have some pretty serious business to discuss with my daughter. I mean, if it was something minor, you could have just phoned."

Her eyes sparkled with deep intelligence and Ian realized there was quite a bit more to this woman than what appeared on the surface. He imagined that Kate got her strength from her mother. The woman might put on an outward façade of being Betty homemaker but inside she was filled with years of wisdom.

"Kate is at Blue Moon Rising. She left about ten minutes before you got here."

Just his luck. Betty Tyler gave him directions to the small bar where she said the locals hung out.

"Is there a hotel near there I can check into?" he asked.

"Nonsense. You'll stay here." She waved her hand as though the topic didn't even merit discussion. "Kate is rooming with Jennifer, so you can sleep in her old room."

"Oh, I don't think—"

"That's right. Don't think about it. Just stay." She shooed him out the front door. "Go find my daughter. You didn't drive all this way to talk to me."

Ian was tempted. Staying at Kate's house would also give

him another edge over the competition. Unless, the other man was staying there too. He stopped halfway down the front steps, the thought just occurring to him. Surely Betty wouldn't be that cruel?

Twelve

Todd Singer—what had ever possessed her to agree to a date with him? He'd been an idiot in grade school; he'd been even worse in high school; and time hadn't helped matters.

He'd failed test number one with flying colors and test number two before they even got through the front door. Two strikes and you're out, buddy. There was no point in continuing the date except that Kate needed his help to perform test number four on Jerry. She hoped that Jerry passed this test as well. The clock was ticking, she was running out of time.

"I see a hot chick. This date is going nowhere. I'm outta here." Todd made a move to stand, but Kate grabbed his arm. She was going to hate herself for this tomorrow—normally she would tell a guy like Todd exactly what she thought of him—but she needed his help and there wasn't time to line up another test for Jerry.

"Have a seat, slick. You might get lucky here if you play your cards right." Kate refrained from laughing at the thought. Todd Singer get lucky with her? Not in this lifetime. But he had to think there was a possibility, at least until Jerry arrived. As usual, Jerry was running late.

She cringed when Todd didn't sit down on the other side of the table but pulled a chair up alongside hers and ran his hand along her inner thigh. His fingernails were long and rough against the tender skin on her leg. Ewww. She couldn't help the slight shudder that coursed through her body. *You'd better get here fast, Jerry, before I punch this creep.*

"Maybe we should leave right now." He'd leaned over and whispered the words in her ear, his breath hot and moist.

If he breathed on her neck one more time, she was going to be sick. The smell of whatever aftershave he'd slathered onto his clothes and skin was just discernable under the smell of hard liquor. Argh!

She pulled away and glanced toward the door, hoping to see Jerry. He was already thirty minutes late. *Any time, Jerry.* Instead, she met Ian Fields's gaze.

"Ian?" What was he doing here? She shook her head to try to clear the hallucination, but instead of disappearing he began to move toward their table. The air crackled around him and his eyes snapped with hurt mixed with anger.

"It's Todd, sweet thing. T-O-D—"

Ian arrived at their table at the same moment that Kate realized he couldn't possibly be a hallucination. Boy was she going to have something to write in the diaries this week! She'd been fully prepared for Jerry's potential anger over finding her out with another man. She hadn't been prepared to deal with Ian's.

"Is this him?" he asked, glowering at Todd.

"Ian, I know this sounds clichéd, but it's not what you think."

"Oh, it's what you think, dude. And then some." Todd put his hand back on her thigh and she saw Ian's face turn three different shades of red, one bordering on purple. She'd never seen Ian's face turn that color, but it didn't seem like a positive sign. She suspected Ian had just failed test number four.

She pried Todd's fingers from her leg and slung his hand back toward him. "You aren't helping, Todd."

"Oh, now you remember my name, 'cause earlier you were calling me some prissy name. Ian."

Ian's palms landed on the table top and he leaned in close to Todd. "Unless you want to lose a few teeth, you'd better get lost, partner."

"Ian!" She'd never considered testing Ian while they'd been dating, but over the last few days, she'd begun to see the wisdom of her great-grandmother's little tests for finding a compatible man. There could be no doubt now. He'd just failed the jealousy test miserably.

"Kate, don't do this. Walk away from this man." Ian's deep, dark gaze pleaded with her.

It was almost her undoing. She closed her eyes and brought Jen's face to the forefront of her thoughts. She'd never forget the time when they were six and eight and she hadn't been there to protect Jen from some girls who were bullying her. They'd sent Jen home with a bloody nose and years later so had Billy James. Well, what Mark would do to her was far worse than a bloody nose and there was no way she was going to let her baby sister marry him. Her feelings for Ian would have to be dealt with later.

"Can we just talk later, Ian?"

"No. You have to decide now. Leave with me or stay here with him."

Was he really giving her *another* ultimatum? Her stomach dropped to her toes. Hadn't he learned a lesson the last time? Just like before, she had no choice. She had to put her sister first, especially after she'd seen Mark with another woman. Why was life so unfair? She didn't want to lose Ian.

Todd leaned forward and grabbed her drink. "Here, allow me, Kate." He stood and dumped the contents over Ian's head.

She'd only taken one sip of the Long Island Iced Tea and

what remained now dripped down Ian's face and onto his once white shirt. The good news was that this evening couldn't possibly get worse.

"What's going on?" Jerry appeared at Ian's elbow, his usual smile plastered on his face.

No. This could not be happening. She knew better than to think that things couldn't get worse. The second you thought things were as bad as possible—fate twisted and turned and threw some more logs on the fire.

"You out on a date with one of these jokers, Kate?" Jerry pointed at Ian and Todd.

Good enough. He hadn't thrown any punches. He'd just passed test number four. She grabbed her purse and stood.

"Not anymore. Let's get out of here."

"Just a minute!" Todd grabbed her arm.

"Let go, Todd."

"Kate?" Ian said.

She could have walked away if his voice hadn't cracked just the tiniest bit at the very end of her name. She doubted anyone else had noticed but she knew how strong and steady he spoke. She'd memorized the cadence of those soothing tones that made her feel safe and loved. The crack in that constantness spoke louder than words ever could have.

She turned back to Ian. "Ian, there is a lot going on here. I can't explain at the moment. Can you just trust me?"

"With him?" He nodded toward Jerry, his fists clenching and unclenching by his side.

Apparently his size and bulk scared Jerry because he flinched a bit and held up his hands. "Whoa, I'm out of this. Mark didn't say anything about a jealous boyfriend."

"Mark?" Kate spun around and pointed a finger at Jerry's nose. "Mark Jackson?"

Jerry shrugged.

"Yeah, we're all onto your little game," Todd said, apparently tired of being ignored. "Our buddy Mark tipped us off to your crazy, female bet. You won't get any man to pass your little tests. Not in this town."

Jerry shook his head at Todd. Kate stared at him, feeling a bit hurt. Although she wasn't romantically interested in Jerry, it had been nice to think that he might be just a little interested in her. Her ego, which had been shattered when Ian had fired her, had been soothed a bit.

"Kate, what in the world is going on?" Ian ran his hands through his hair, his anger apparently gone under the mass confusion raining down on them all.

"I made a bet with my sister that I could find a man better than Mark without any trouble. I don't want her to marry him. He's a cheat and a liar."

"I see." Ian's frown told her he had more to say but was holding back.

"What?"

"Well, I guess I just don't understand why you'd drive all the way up here to try to ruin your sister's happiness. Seems to me like it would be better to just stay back in 'Nawlins."

"You don't understand." Her voice had risen and several heads in the bar turned her way. She took a deep breath and tried to speak softer. "He has her fooled."

Didn't anyone in the world understand the gravity of the situation but her? Was she going completely insane? Being completely unreasonable? Perhaps she was but the fact that Mark had actually tipped off every man in town told her that he was hiding something. Why else would he be this desperate?

"Is this the guy who you came to town with?" He motioned toward Jerry.

"What?" She blinked. She should have told him she wasn't

leaving town with another man. Had he been worrying about it since she'd left? "I brought Sarah and Rebecca to town with me, Ian."

"Oh." He didn't quite meet her gaze. "I actually just came to town to offer you your job back."

"I'll have to think about that." Could she still work with him after everything that had happened? She wasn't even sure she wanted to date him, much less see him everyday at work.

"Fair enough."

"So, I guess our date is off?" Jerry laughed.

"You're real funny, Jerry." She punched him on the arm. "If you knew all about the bet, why didn't you throw a fit over the spilled drink like all the other men did? Why string me along?"

A dull red flush rose up Jerry's neck and settled across his cheekbones. "Mark paid me."

Kate's vision narrowed. Mark *paid* him?

"Mark is your sister's fiancé?" Ian asked.

Kate nodded her head, unable to speak. She stared at Jerry. She wanted—no, she *expected*—an explanation.

"I'm sorry, darling. You know I am crazy over you," Jerry said.

Kate saw Ian clench his fists and his color turn a bit redder. Just terrific. He probably thought she and Jerry were an item. Kate gritted her teeth so tightly together that she'd probably need major dental work. Apparently Ian knew about her sister's wedding since he knew Jen had a fiancé. Why he was still acting like an insane, jealous idiot, she wasn't sure. Right now, she was more concerned about Mark and his sneak attack. "What exactly did Mark pay you to do, Jerry?"

"String you along until Friday but only pass six tests."

"I see. And the other men in town?"

"All know about the tests and your wager with Jen."

Kate wanted to lie down on the floor and wail. The rehearsal was two days away, no man in town was going to play along with their tests, and her sister was doomed to life with a cheater. She should just tell Jen what she'd seen at the golf course. The last thing she wanted was to hurt her sister with that type of news but she couldn't let her marry Mark without sharing the information.

Jen would either hate her or not believe her but somehow she knew her sister wouldn't thank her for the news.

Two days after seeing Becca in that bar, and Jared wasn't sure why he didn't just leave town, except that he still needed to gather his thoughts. He'd thought Rebecca was honest and straightforward but she'd just twisted that hallucination into tiny pieces and thrown them into the air. How could she claim that it was he who dumped her? He'd heard her words clearly—they were etched into the broken pieces of his heart.

"That's it, we're through."

He'd never forget her words or the finality in her voice. For her to pretend that it hadn't happened felt like a punch in the gut. He couldn't shake the image of her kissing the scraggly man in the bar. What a woman with Becca's panache saw in a man with such obvious lack of refinement or basic manners was beyond him. Maybe that's what she wanted— someone who would treat her badly.

He frowned even as the thought entered his head, knowing that it didn't describe Becca. They'd only been seeing one another for six months. What did he really know about this woman? *Only that you want to spend the rest of your life with her.* He was lonely, that was all. He'd spent so many years focusing on medical school, and then building his career, that he'd been unable to establish a lasting relationship with a woman. The myth about women wanting to marry doctors might be true in theory but in practice the long hours and on-call days often equaled ticked-off girlfriends who broke up with him after a few weeks.

But with Becca it was more than just the fact that she'd been willing to date him. From the moment he'd looked into her bright blue eyes, he'd felt a connection. It was as though a string ran from her soul to his and joined them together even when they were apart. He sighed and pulled into the parking space at the hotel. He really should just keep driving until he was out of this flat state where everything looked like a never-ending corn field. Something held him back.

He entered the lobby of the hotel and headed straight for the bar area. Rarely did he drink. Most of the time, he was on call and he'd never risk even the slightest impairment when he might be called in to tend to a patient. But he wasn't on call this evening and suspected if he didn't unwind just a little that he was never going to get any sleep.

One other man sat in the bar. He looked almost as frustrated and out of sorts as Jared, so he didn't bother to speak to him, simply nodded his head and addressed the bartender.

"Whiskey, straight up."

The bartender whistled. "Another one, huh? Must be tough out there these days. I sure am glad I'm married. Dating isn't what it used to be."

Jared wondered when bartenders had gotten so chatty. Bars sure weren't what *they* used to be. There had been a day when you could go into a bar and order whiskey without anyone trying to figure out what was wrong in your love life. Of course, he hadn't been in a bar for around ten years.

"Good evening." The other man nodded as he sipped from his tumbler.

The bartender sat Jared's whiskey in front of him, so he

lifted it in a salute to the other man. "May your love life be better than mine."

The other man gave a short, solemn laugh. "Not likely, my friend. I drove all the way up here from New Orleans to try to resuscitate my love life and all I found was my girlfriend out with not one, but two other men."

Jared whistled. Maybe his new friend did have it worse. "Here is a coincidence for you—my girlfriend, who I found with another man as well, lives in New Orleans."

"Her name wouldn't be Rebecca or Sarah would it?" the other man asked.

"R-Rebecca." *Please, God, tell me she hasn't been out with him too.* Jared swallowed. Was Rebecca the other man's girlfriend he'd spoken of only moments before?

The man held out his hand. "Ian Fields. I'm dating—*was* dating—Becca's friend Kate."

Jared let out a slow breath, realizing that every muscle in his body was still tensed. He wasn't sure how he would have reacted if Ian had said that he too was dating Becca. "Jared Wells."

He lifted his own tumbler of whiskey but the smell almost gagged him. Okay, maybe drinking away his pain wouldn't work since he couldn't really tolerate the taste of whiskey. He set the glass back down, untouched.

"I'm crazy about Becca," Jared admitted. "God help me. I don't want to be. But I still am."

"Yeah. I feel your pain, buddy." Ian pushed the tumbler away. "I'd really love to get drunk right now, but I'm not in my twenties anymore. I just don't have the taste for drowning my troubles."

"Me either." What was he going to do about Rebecca? She insisted that he'd broken things off with her but they both knew it had been the other way around. Maybe she'd realized breaking up with him was a mistake and just couldn't admit her blunder.

Should he allow her to save face and pretend that she hadn't broken things off? Maybe he should go back to her mother's home and see if he could track her down. He'd flown across several countries to get to Indiana. The least he could do was try to work things out. His cell phone rang loudly into the silence of the bar, where both men sat deep in their own thoughts. The caller identification showed Rebecca's last name paired with another woman's first name. He assumed she was calling from her mother's house.

"That's Becca. I'm going to go take the call." He slapped Ian on the back. "Good luck. To hear Becca talk about her, this Kate is gold."

"Good luck to you too." Ian looked as dejected as Jared felt.

He hesitated for a split second, wondering if he should offer the other man an ear for a bit longer but then turned and walked into the hall, hitting the answer button on his phone.

"Jared?" Becca sounded nervous.

"Hi, Becca." Waves of astonishment wound through him. He hadn't expected her to phone.

"Can we talk? I-I'll meet you anywhere."

"Why don't I just come to your mother's house?"

"Okay. I'll see you when you get here." She hung up the phone with the soft sounds of her voice still echoing in his ear.

Jared pushed a button to end the still open connection and replaced the cell phone in his pocket. His stomach tightened with uncertainty. What if she just wanted to see him to confirm that she no longer wished to see him? He'd asked for a face-to-face break-up. Perhaps Becca planned to give him what he'd requested.

★ ★ ★ ★ ★

They all thought they'd gotten rid of him. They were so smug and sure of themselves. He'd show every one of them, and soon. He waited in the shadows, watching the large, two-story house. Jennifer's bedroom light flickered on around nine o'clock. He watched as her outline appeared on the other side of the blinds.

A year ago, he'd made one little mistake and she'd forsaken him, forgetting her promises. Jezebel! She'd moved on to another man. He'd decided long ago that if he couldn't have her, no one could have her. The court order kept him away for a while but a piece of paper couldn't truly keep two souls apart. That piece of paper couldn't hurt him once they were both dead.

His heart ached as he watched her shadowed movements on the other side of the window. Only a few hundred feet separated them, but he knew he must wait for the perfect moment. He couldn't afford to make another mistake like the last time and allow her to escape. He wouldn't go to jail. No, the timing had to be perfect.

Once he had her alone, he'd be able to convince her that dying together was the only solution—the only way their love would ever be accepted. She loved Shakespeare, so surely she'd see the similarities between their story and *Romeo and Juliet*. If she didn't agree, maybe she'd change her mind after they passed over into eternity together.

He blew a kiss toward her window. "Parting is such sweet sorrow, my love. Let us say goodnight 'til it be 'morrow."

Thirteen

Rebecca still wasn't sure what happened. What had Jared meant when he said that she'd been the one to dump him? Did he mean because she got pregnant? That it was entirely her fault? The last time she'd checked, it still took two to create a baby.

If it wasn't for her child, she'd probably walk away from Jared and never look back. As much as she'd loved him—still loved him—his rejection had cut deep into the very essence of her soul. Jared's rejection touched the chord that had lain dormant since the day her father walked out the door. She'd finally opened herself to loving a man, trusting a man, and he'd deserted her too. Maybe it was something she lacked. Jared wasn't like her father, she knew that just as surely as she knew she still loved him with every fiber of her being. So, the problem must be with her or with something she lacked. But she knew that thought was utterly ridiculous. Her head understood that. Her heart just ached.

She closed her eyes and let out a low breath, vowing to remain calm. All the stress and turmoil rumbling through her body couldn't be good for the baby. If Jared truly didn't want to see her anymore, then why had he followed her all the way here? It couldn't have been easy tracking her down. Why would he go to all that trouble? Unless—what if she'd misunderstood? Their phone connection had been terrible.

She shook her head. "No, I very clearly heard him say that we were through."

There hadn't been any static when he'd uttered those words. His meaning had been blatantly clear. Obviously, he'd had a change of heart or perhaps he was just curious about whether or not she would seek support. Maybe he'd decided he wanted the baby but not her.

She hadn't really thought some of these issues out herself yet. Part of her wanted to be completely independent and not ask him for anything but the truth was that this was his child and he should share not just the financial investment but the emotional as well. As much as she wanted to tell him to get lost, she knew that she would have to sit down and discuss these concerns. There were so many things to work out. Would he want visitation? Her heart jumped. What if he wanted custody?

Hand shaking, she'd finally picked up the phone and punched in Jared's cell phone number. She'd vowed never to dial that number again after the way their last call had ended, but she didn't have a choice. He didn't know her mother's telephone number and they had to work some things out. There was a child involved whose future emotional needs had to be considered. Now he was on his way here and she didn't even know how to start the conversation they needed to have.

Sarah found it amazing that eleven years could pass and nothing change. Other than the new strip malls and fast food restaurants, Greenfield was frozen in time. The large clock tower perched at the center of town, watching over its citizens while often offering the incorrect time.

She squinted up at the limestone building. She stood on the sidewalk leading up to the front entrance of the building that housed a couple of courtrooms and countless county offices. The statue of James Whitcomb Riley stood center stage, a Mona Lisa-type smirk on his lips.

Year after year, she'd marched alongside the other school-children and placed flowers at the base of this very statue. By the end of the parade, the base would be filled completely with a wide variety of flowers—some store-bought, some hand-picked from home gardens. She loved Riley's work and thought it was a beautiful tribute to a poet who had brought so much joy to children's lives.

". . . and the goblins'll get ya if'n you don't watch out," she whispered to the statue.

Funny how his words rang true even after all these years. When you weren't paying attention, bad things could happen. Like what had happened with Daniel. Well, she'd learned her lesson. She wasn't likely to fall in love again any-time soon and she certainly wouldn't *trust* another man.

She completely understood Kate's desire to protect Jen. She still remembered Kate's panic when she'd thought Billy might harm her sister. And it was Kate's shoulder she'd cried on after Daniel's maliciousness. Her friend knew the effect a man's duplicity could have on a woman. Kate didn't want her sister to suffer a broken heart and potential financial ruin. When Kate had phoned and said she'd seen Mark kiss a blonde woman, it only firmed Sarah's resolve to help Kate save Jen. She'd do the same thing as her friend if she had a sister.

A woman walked past and stared at Sarah for a moment. The woman shook her head, as though she just couldn't com-prehend why a grown woman would stand in front of a statue, and walked into the courthouse.

This town never changed. Sarah sighed. In New Orleans, people didn't lurk around corners and watch your every move. If she wanted to stand and stare at a building or statue for an hour, others in the city barely took notice. Of course, the big city did have its drawbacks, such as a higher crime rate. She'd had about all she could take of this town, though. If it wasn't for Kate and Aunt Mary, she'd head back home tonight.

However, she was here for a reason, and she had business inside that courthouse with a certain blonde clerk who liked golf courses. She intended to get some sort of proof of Mark's infidelity—preferably a confession from the lady herself.

A warning shiver skittered up her spine and she turned and looked at the old bank building across the street with the unique architectural curve on the corner. Something wasn't quite right, but she couldn't put her finger on it. Still, she'd learned to trust her instincts and she didn't think the shiver boded well for Kate. A sinister force blew into town with a heaviness you could almost taste. Sarah frowned and hurried into the building, wanting to put some distance between herself and the sensation so she could gather her scattered thoughts.

The interior of the building was warm from the summer heat outside; any attempt to cool the room escaped into the huge center that rose to the top of the building. The foyer offered balconies on three floors and a view all the way to the top of the courthouse. The wide marble staircase encased with detailed wood rails beckoned. Sarah stood for a moment and admired the historical beauty of the building. The style was small town, Victorian Indiana. The details were flawless and breathtaking. You just didn't see architecture like this anymore. Instead, new buildings were often bland and impersonal. Many hands had poured hours and hours of love into this building and it showed more than a hundred years later.

She trailed her fingers up the highly polished, dark wood of the handrail, wondering what kind of wood it was. Hickory maybe, or perhaps mahogany. As her hand brushed up the rail, she picked up sensations from decades of people passing through the building. Some of the impressions were happy, others desperate, a few deeply sorrowful. She snatched her hand away. She knew better than to touch something like that in a public place. If Kate was there, she would have stopped her. She'd always admired and understood Sarah's unique gifts even when no one else had and even though she didn't fully understand. That was why she owed her friend this help.

According to Aunt Mary, the blonde woman worked in records on the second floor. She went to the office her aunt had described. Aunt Mary had her sources and Sarah didn't bother to ask where she'd gotten the information. She was as likely to hear that the answer had come from the spirit world as to hear that it had come from a local busybody.

"Excuse me?" She knocked lightly on the door.

The woman's blonde head bobbed up. Sarah studied her features, wondering if it was the same woman Kate had seen kiss Mark and knowing in her heart that it was. Classic features made her almost beautiful. She reminded Sarah of the type of woman you might see in a Miss America pageant— wholesome and classic.

"Hello. Can I help you?" Her voice was soft, like the tinkle of little Christmas bells.

Sarah blinked, sensing a warmth and caring coming from the woman that she wouldn't have expected. If she was having an affair with Mark, then she wasn't aware that he was getting married Saturday. Sarah could sense that she was genuine just from her voice and looking into her gentle, pale blue eyes.

"I hope you can help. You see—" *Are you having an affair with Mark Jackson?* Sarah laughed. No, probably not a good idea to just blurt it. "This is awkward."

The woman smiled. "Have a seat. Maybe that will help."

"Thank you." Sarah sat in the chair opposite the woman's desk. "I'm best friends with Kate Tyler."

"Oh, Tyler—she's Jen's sister?" The pale blue eyes never glanced away.

Sarah frowned. If the woman knew about Jen, how could she be so calm over having an affair with Mark? And why did she seem so warm and kind? Something wasn't adding up correctly. Was this the sense of dread she'd felt outside? No, she knew it wasn't. That hadn't been related to this woman. She hadn't felt such an intense fear since she was sixteen and Billy James had tried to rape her one night while she'd walked home with him. She rubbed her arms to remove the chill. He hadn't succeeded and she, Kate, and Becca had tracked him down the next day and set him straight.

"Kate is Jen's sister."

"I can't wait to meet Kate," she admitted. "Mark tells me that she absolutely loathes him and wants to stop the wedding. I figure any woman who can worry Mark this much must be really strong. I admire that."

Sarah coughed to cover her surprise. "So, you know about the wedding?"

"Know about it? I'm one of Jen's bridesmaids."

Well, well. What a tangled web she was unraveling. So the mistress was a bridesmaid in Jennifer's wedding. How did Mark think that was going to work?

"I'm confused," Sarah admitted.

"Over what?"

"Kate saw you kissing Mark at the golf course."

"So?" The woman stared at her: not flinching, not blinking.

Under the stacks of files on the edge of the woman's desk, Sarah's gaze caught a half-buried name plate. She leaned forward to get a better look. Tabitha Jackson. *Jackson!* Was she related to Mark?

"Kate thought Mark was having an affair."

Tabitha fell back in her chair laughing. "We wondered why she never showed up at the golf course like Jen said she would. I'm his cousin. I just moved here from California last year. An affair. That's really funny."

"Not really." Sarah couldn't quite bring herself to smile. Kate thought that Mark was kissing another woman and she was going to tell Jen. And Sarah suspected that Mark had set the entire thing up to trap Kate in just this manner.

"What's wrong?"

"Kate is going to tell Jennifer." And play right into Mark's hands.

"Oh, no. I hope Jen doesn't get upset. Maybe she'll realize the blonde was me."

Sarah jumped to her feet. "I'd better go. I need to tell Kate before she says anything."

"It was nice meeting you," Tabitha called after her. "I'll see you at the wedding."

Sarah raced across the slick marble floor and down the stairs. She had to stop Kate before she said anything to Jen. Their sisterly relationship had been damaged enough by Mark Jackson.

"Jared." Rebecca felt relief that he stood on her mother's doorstep. She wasn't sure if he'd come after their earlier argument at Blue Moon Rising. That emotion was followed by shame at her simple upbringing. Her mother had never had much money and the tiny apartment above the hardware store wasn't in the best shape anymore. Actually, it had never been in the best shape. Her mother had done the best she could—adding homey touches such as a colorful throw slung over the back of the couch.

"I'm glad you called, Becca." Although his hands were in his pockets, she sensed that they were probably clenched with frustration and nerves.

Well, he deserved to be nervous. He had dumped her when she'd needed him most and then arrived and acted like a jealous idiot. Granted, she had been out with another man, and his jealousy showed that he at least cared.

"I thought we should talk." She pulled the door open wider and walked to the couch, leaving him to follow. Her legs felt as though they were made of sawdust.

Jared closed the door after entering and sat on the couch next to her. "Who was that man you were out with?"

"It was so stupid, Jared. I'm embarrassed at my part in it really. Kate doesn't want her sister to wed the man she's marrying this weekend. I don't know why I went along with them. I actually think that Mark is a decent guy and would be good to Jen. They came up with this bet that if Kate, Sarah, or I could find the perfect man by Friday, then Jennifer would call off the wedding. There were tests he had to pass. I didn't even know that guy."

"Well, I guess that explains why you threw a drink in his face. When I saw him grab and kiss you, I assumed it was a lover's tiff."

"No. It was test number one. Spill a drink on him to see if he has a bad temper."

"Did he?"

"Of course. He was a jerk."

"So there's no other man?"

"No other man." As much as she'd love to provide her child with the white picket fence atmosphere, she didn't think she would be able to think about loving someone else for a very long time. He hadn't said a word about the baby.

He opened his mouth as though he wanted to say something and then closed it again. Becca groaned. Enough of this! If he wasn't going to speak, she was. And she planned to make it very clear that she had no intention of being a burden on him.

"Look, Jared. I can appreciate the fact that you were shocked by my call—"

"That's an understatement," he interrupted.

Becca glared at him. Okay, he wasn't going to make this easy. "As I was saying, I don't expect anything out of you. I just thought you had a right to know. But your reaction told me that you aren't ready for this."

"I don't understand." Jared frowned.

Becca moved a little further away from him on the couch. His nearness would be her undoing. Even though he'd dumped her when she'd needed him most, she felt the heat of their attraction wrapping tendrils around her heart. He must care for her a little or he wouldn't have been so upset over finding her out with Keith. She still didn't want to feel this magnetism between them right now.

"I don't expect anything from you. If you want to be involved, that's fine. If not, that's fine."

"Becca, *you* are the one who dumped *me*. Quit trying to act as though the ball is in my court."

She'd dumped him? Was he crazy? Surely he didn't really believe she'd told him she was pregnant and broken off their relationship in the same breath? She'd have to be completely insane to do such a thing.

"I did not!" she cried.

"I know what I heard." Jared's jaw clenched and Becca realized that he wasn't putting on a show. He truly believed she had dumped him.

"Jared, are you serious? What do you think I said when I called you?"

"You said, 'That's it. We're through.' " His mouth turned down at the corners.

Suddenly, the heaviness that had settled into the very core of her being lifted as she realized a bad cell phone connection had caused all the trouble. Becca laughed.

"It really isn't funny, Becca. It felt like you sucker-punched me. I wasn't expecting that."

"I did not say that we were through." Hope fluttered to life right alongside the child growing in her womb. "This is like one of those commercials about bad cell phone reception."

"What did you say then?" he asked.

"I said that the stick turned blue."

He stared at her for several long moments, not speaking. She knew the moment that understanding budded in his mind though, because his eyes lit up and then he shook his head.

"And I said we were through." He moved closer and enclosed her in his arms. "Oh, Becca. I'm so sorry. Can you forgive me?"

"There's nothing to forgive, Jared. It was a misunderstanding. But I want you to know that I don't expect anything from you."

"Becca—"

"No, hear me out. My father deserted my mother and me. Just walked out one day and never came back. I grew up without a daddy. I always swore I'd never allow my children to live like that."

"Becca, I would never do that," he protested.

"Jared, I know that or I never would have fallen in love with you. But you have to understand that worse than not having a father there was knowing him and then having him reject me. Do you understand?"

He stroked her hair and brushed gentle kisses across her eyelids as though he could take her pain away. "I could kick myself for lashing out when I thought you were calling things off between us. If I'd only been kinder, then maybe this craziness of the last week never would have happened."

"I love you, Jared. I want you in this child's life. But only if you plan to stay in his or her life for the long haul."

"Of course—"

"I don't mean that you have to stay with me, love me, or anything like that. But this child is innocent. Once you come into this child's life, you have to stay, even if it's as a weekend father. I won't accept anything less for my child, so be very sure before you commit." She stared deeply into his eyes, trying to make sure he understood very clearly that she was serious.

He took her face between his two large hands and planted a kiss on her lips. "I love you, Becca. I was going to ask you to marry me when I got back from my mission trip."

"You were?" Was he just saying this because of the baby?

"I'm crazy about you. I want to grow old with you. Let's get married right away. The baby will just come a little sooner than expected."

"And the wedding too."

"Yes, but I didn't want a long engagement anyway. I don't want to be apart from you ever again. This past week has just about killed me." He choked the words out as he pulled her tighter into his arms and tucked her up against his heart.

"Me too," she admitted.

"So, we're okay?" He pulled back and gazed into her eyes. His vulnerability shone out of his eyes like two naked beacons of light and she realized how hurt he'd been when he'd thought she'd broken off their relationship.

"We're great. All three of us," she said, and brought his hand to her still flat stomach.

"When we get home, I want to propose to you formally."

"You don't have to do that—"

"No, I want to do it right, Becca. I had this romantic getaway on a steamboat planned. I think we should still go, if you're feeling up to it. We'll have the captain marry us."

"Sounds divine." Had she really just used the word divine in a sentence? She was losing it.

In the last ten minutes, she'd gone from doubting she could raise this child on her own to being the future Mrs. Jared Wells. She chewed on her bottom lip. There was still the problem of Jen's wedding this Saturday.

"What's wrong, darling?" Jared asked.

"I'm worried about Kate. I don't know how she's going to stop Jennifer's wedding without doing something drastic. There's so little time left. I basically just deserted her and Sarah by saying I wouldn't help. I never do that to my friends. I can't help but feel she's making a horrible mistake. I should be there to at least counsel her."

"So, go figure out how you can help her. If this guy is so horrible, maybe you should stop the wedding. Just remember that things aren't always as they appear. Look at what happened to us."

Becca felt a shiver travel up her spine. His words were almost prophetic. She'd never accepted that Mark was a liar and a cheat. When she'd dated him, he'd been kind and they'd developed a good friendship. She just needed to help Kate discover what a great guy Mark could be. And now that she knew she still had Jared's love, it would be easy to focus on helping her friend.

Fourteen

"Kate, I'm so glad you suggested we do this. It's been a long time since I hung out at the park, much less fed the ducks." Jen threw a small piece of bread out into the creek and several ducks quacked their way toward it, one bobbing his head under the surface in a dramatic capture of the morsel. His feathered rear end wiggled in the air and Jen laughed at his antics.

"I wanted somewhere that we could talk privately. Without interruption." So she could break her baby sister's heart. She still didn't know how she was going to tell Jen that she'd seen Mark with another woman but she knew that she had to. She couldn't stand by and let Jen marry Mark when she had this information. It had nothing to do with whether or not she liked the man—she didn't—it had to do with making sure her sister had all the information she needed to decide whether or not she wanted to marry him.

"I'm just so glad that you wanted to spend some time with me before the wedding. It means a lot to me. I know that you are having a hard time over the fact that I'm marrying Mark. Just the fact that you are trying—" Jen brushed a tear away. "That means the world to me, Sis."

Kate swallowed. Her sister knew just how to say the right thing at the wrong time and stab the knife of guilt into her heart and give it a good hard twist. It was pretty hard to tell your sister that her fiancé was cheating anyway, but the fact that she so opposed this wedding made it even harder. Would Jen even believe her?

At this time of day, this end of the park was deserted. Most of the children had opted for the newer, fancier playground on the southeast end of the park. A vague feeling of unease settled between her shoulder blades. She glanced toward a set of large maple trees across the creek. She rubbed her arms. It felt as though they were being watched, but that was crazy. Her nerves were just on edge from the situation with Mark and the blonde.

"Let's go sit on the swings." She motioned toward a small set of tire swings that rested just to the south of where they fed the ducks.

"Just like when we were kids," Jen said, as she skipped over to the swings.

Her sister thought this outing was a fun event. The truth was that it was anything but fun and unfortunately she was going to have to point that out. She only hoped that Jen could forgive her one day, but she feared that their relationship would be destroyed forever. Was she really willing to risk her sister hating her? She didn't have a choice. Even if Jen hated her, at least she wouldn't be blindsided by Mark's betrayal.

The swings creaked as they pushed them to and fro in slow circles. Jen smiled and it seemed as though every tooth in her mouth appeared. "Only one more day until the rehearsal dinner. Did you find Mr. Perfect?"

Jen knew darn good and well that she hadn't. "Not yet."

"Give it up, Kate. He doesn't exist. Don't you get it? That was Granny's point."

"I get it that your fiancé sabotaged me." Mark had tipped off every single man in town and probably the married ones as well. The test had been flawed.

"What do you mean?" Jen's smile faded and she planted her feet on the ground, stilling her swing.

"Mark told every man in town what we were up to. Our tests went nowhere."

Jen shook her head. "Mark wouldn't do that."

"Well, he did. And then he paid Jerry Dillon to keep me 'busy' until the rehearsal dinner but not to pass more than six of the tests." She lifted her brow. That was the kind of man that her sister was marrying—a jerk.

"Kate, you misunderstood something. Mark wouldn't be that underhanded. And if he was, then you drove him to it." Jen crossed her arms over her chest and jutted her chin out.

"What? You are actually going to blame me for his sneakiness?"

"You haven't given him a chance. You were supposed to go talk to him and you blew him off. You never even saw him." Jen's voice had risen to a shrill pitch.

Okay, there came a point where she had to stop sparing her sister's feelings and worry more about her future. She refused to let Mark make her look like the guilty party when he was the one doing something wrong.

"Oh, I saw him, Jen."

"Don't lie to me, Kate. Mark said he never spoke to you on Tuesday. What possible reason would he have to lie?"

"I didn't say that I spoke to him. I said I saw him. There was no need to speak to him after what I saw." Kate pushed her toe into the dirt patch under the swing. The patch had been rubbed bare by hundreds of pairs of feet kicking off to get the swing spinning in crazy circles. She wished she could spin fast enough to escape her sister's hurt expression.

"What do you mean?"

176

"He was with a blonde. A beautiful blonde."

"So? She was probably a friend." But the panic on Jen's face showed that she wasn't as certain as she tried to sound.

"And Mark usually kisses his friends?"

"He kissed her?" Jen's voice deflated and her shoulders hunched over. "He actually kissed a blonde woman?"

"I'm sorry, Jen. I didn't want to tell you." Kate jumped up from the swing and rushed over to her sister but Jen pushed her away.

"If you really saw this, why would you keep it from me? Didn't you think this was something I needed to know before my wedding? God, Kate. What is wrong with you? You are all chatty when I don't need to hear things and then when I do you clam up."

"I should just go home." Hopefully Jen would be reasonable enough to call off the wedding.

"You aren't staying for my wedding?" Two fat tears fell from Jen's eyes.

"The wedding is still on? I thought—" Kate bit her lip. This was one of those times Jen had spoken of—she needed to shut up. Whether or not Jen married Mark was her sister's decision.

"I'm so confused." Jen rose to her feet and took Kate's hand. "Do you have any idea how long it took me to get over what Billy did? I still have nightmares you know. I think I see him—lurking everywhere."

Kate frowned. She thought she'd seen Billy once too. Maybe it wasn't a nightmare. What if Billy was back? But even Billy James wouldn't be that stupid.

"Come with me, Kate."

Where did her sister want to go? Maybe she wanted to leave town, get away from everyone and everything. They could go to the East Coast. Maybe visit D.C. Just get away from it all so Jen could think things out and they could reconnect as sisters.

"Where are we going?"

"To Mark's office. He should still be there. It's only two o'clock."

"What?" Kate yanked her hand out of Jen's. "Why are you going there?"

"Because I want to confront him and I want you there to back me up. I need to know why he thought it was okay to date another woman the week of our wedding."

"I don't think that's a good idea, Jen." Hadn't her sister been hurt enough? What if Mark told her she wasn't enough for him? Or hurt her with some other insensitive words?

"No. I need to know for sure. What if it's a misunderstanding?" Jen gave a funny, half-laugh. "I sound ridiculous don't I? But I'll always wonder. There's more at stake than you realize."

"I understand. Of course I'll go with you." And if Mark Jackson caused even a smidgeon more pain in her sister, she'd strangle him with her bare hands.

Kate passed another tissue to Jen, so her sister could dab away fresh tears. She shifted uncomfortably in the passenger seat of Jen's car and wished she hadn't been the one to tell her sister about Mark and the blonde.

"Maybe I should drive." Jen's tears might blind her to oncoming traffic.

"I-I'm fine," Jen wailed and blew her nose into the tissue. She slung the tissue into the back seat and took another from Kate's outstretched hand.

If she didn't love Jen so much, she'd just walk away from this whole drama. Ian was furious with her and according to her mother he'd been invited to stay at their house but hadn't appeared last night. He'd probably headed back to New Orleans. She hated that things hadn't been worked out between them; hated that he thought she'd been seeing not one but two other men behind his back. She sighed. She didn't have time to worry about her own love life at the moment. She needed to focus on her sister.

"What are you going to say to him, Jen?"

Her sister swerved around a turning car and sniffled. "I don't know. I guess I'm going to ask him to explain it to me. I want to know why he'd do this. I thought he loved me."

Jen's words were more of a plea. Kate couldn't detect any hint of anger in her sister's voice. She frowned. That was probably a bad sign. Shouldn't Jen be furious over Mark's duplicity? Not only had he sabotaged Kate's plan but he'd cheated. If Jen married him in spite of his sneakiness and lying, she was done. She would walk away and know that she'd done all she could possibly do to help her sister. If Jen didn't want to be helped, then it was Jen's problem. She'd have to deal with the consequences of marrying the man.

"Just don't let him talk circles around the issue, Jen. He's good at that." She was going to have a hard time keeping her mouth shut and letting Jen handle the situation. But she had to bite her tongue. It wasn't her place to break up with Mark. It was Jen's.

"How would you know, Kate? You don't really know Mark. Not the way that I do." Jen swiped at a fresh batch of tears.

"You've only been dating him a couple of months, Jen. I doubt you really know him either."

Jen opened her mouth but all that came out was a series of long sobs. She grabbed several more tissues and pulled them to her face.

"Are you okay, Jen? Maybe we should go have a cup of

coffee and let you calm down before you confront him." Jen had always been very sensitive. Her feelings were easily hurt. Kate worried that her sister wasn't emotionally strong enough to handle a harsh rejection if Mark chose to get nasty. She was still frail from the turmoil that psycho Billy had put her through. Her sister deserved to find love, get married, and have a family—just not with Mark Jackson.

"He leaves the office in twenty minutes. There isn't time to have coffee." Jen pulled her car into a parking space in front of the newspaper building.

Kate followed her sister, admiring the sleek lines of the metal and glass on the building. The tiny lawn on either side of the entrance was neatly manicured. It looked as though someone had gotten down on their hands and knees and cut the grass with scissors. The trimness reminded her of the golf course where she'd seen Mark kiss the blonde and strengthened her resolve to stand behind Jen while she confronted the snake.

Jen's hand shook as she reached out and opened the door. Kate winced. Poor Jen. Maybe she would have been better off remaining oblivious. Perhaps if Kate had stayed in New Orleans, Jen would have married Mark and remained unaware of his straying ways. No, her sister would have found out eventually, and she might not have been here to lend emotional support.

She placed her arm around Jen's shoulders as they walked across the tiles in the foyer and made their way to a small office toward the back of the building. "It's okay, Jen. I'm here for you."

"Thanks." Jen sniffled again but her tears seemed to have dried up.

She saw her sister straighten her shoulders and stand a little taller. Perhaps Jen was stronger than she'd suspected.

Surviving a madman who was intent on keeping you for himself through all eternity must have matured her more quickly than an average twenty-seven-year-old. Her baby sister was grown up. It was an amazing transformation and one that she'd just realized. She had to admit that she'd often pictured Jen as a cute seven-year-old who needed protecting from bullies. But just as Kate was no longer the same person she'd been back then, Jen had grown too. Their roles had changed. Now, it was her job to support her sister. To be there while her sister protected herself.

Jen moved toward the secretary's desk and cleared her throat to catch the woman's attention.

"Jen! How wonderful to see you." The woman stood and gave Jen a quick hug. "I can't wait to see how beautiful you look on Saturday."

Jen smiled at the woman but Kate knew that it wasn't her sister's usual brilliant beaming smile. "Is Mark in his office?"

"Sure. Go on in, honey. He'll be glad to see you."

Somehow Kate doubted he would be glad to see them once he realized the purpose behind their visit. Mark stood when he saw them enter and moved to Jen's side. When she didn't step into his outstretched arms, he frowned and glared at Kate. Kate shrugged. This wasn't her fault—well, okay, she'd spilled the beans—but it wasn't her fault that he was a cheat. He'd made that decision all on his own.

"What's wrong?" he asked. "Please tell me you aren't calling off the wedding, Jen."

"I'm confused, Mark." Jen bit her lip and Kate saw moisture on the tips of her lashes. She knew her sister worked hard not to break down and cry. "I thought you loved me."

"I'm crazy about you." He made a move to take her in his arms again but Jen stepped away.

Kate should have felt a sense of elation over the situation.

Mark had tried to stop her at every turn. There should have been some victory in finally getting her sister to see the light. Instead, she felt a deep pain in the center of her chest. It wasn't fun to see Jen in so much emotional torture. Jen loved Mark—that was obvious. Breaking off the wedding was the hardest thing her sister would ever do. Kate felt as low as the throw rug in front of Mark's sleek, modern desk.

"What did you do now?" he hissed at Kate.

"What did *I* do? Maybe you should ask what *you* did." The lying, cheating—argh! She wanted to punch him, so she turned toward the windows and crossed her arms, trying to still her temper.

"Okay, what did I supposedly do?"

Oh, he was good. A real con artist. Innocent until proven guilty.

"Remember how Kate was supposed to try to get to know you better on Tuesday?" Jen asked.

Mark nodded.

"Well, she saw you with a blonde woman." Jen swallowed, the muscles in her throat working overtime. "She saw you kiss her."

Mark shook his head and then a slow smile spread out across his features. He threw his head back and laughed.

What was his problem? Surely he didn't think this situation was amusing? He'd just been caught in the act. Couldn't he at least show a little remorse? Kate glanced at Jen, worried about her sister's emotional state, especially in the face of such blatant disregard for her feelings.

Jen stared at Mark, a soft smile on her face. Kate blinked. *Oh, Jen, please don't fall for his games.*

"Do you know who the blonde was?" Mark asked Kate.

"Your latest floozie?" She hated him. She hated his smirky smile and she hated his arrogant attitude. The only person she hated more than Mark Jackson at the moment was Billy James and it was a close call.

"No." He turned back to Jen and she allowed him to hold her hands this time.

The movement showed a solidarity that she didn't care to witness. Kate flinched.

"It was Tabitha, Jen."

"Tabitha?" Jen's smile slowly reappeared. "Really?"

"Of course. I wouldn't cheat on you. Kate just jumped to conclusions as always."

"Oh, Mark. I'm so sorry I doubted you." Jen threw herself into his arms and kissed him on the lips.

What had just happened here? Kate stared at Mark. He'd known she was coming to the golf course to try to talk to him. Had he set her up? His smirk over Jen's shoulder as he hugged her sister close told her that he had planned the entire thing. Fury bubbled through her veins.

"See, Kate. You were wrong about Mark. Again." Jen tossed the words over her shoulder.

Kate couldn't tell whether or not Jen was angry but *she* sure as hell was. "What about his efforts to sabotage our bet?"

Jen pulled back a little. "Did you do that, Mark?"

He grinned sheepishly, a dull red flush coloring his face. "Can you blame me? She was determined to stop our wedding. I didn't want to lose you. I was just hedging my bets."

Jen laughed and flung her arms around Mark's neck. "I can't wait to be Mrs. Jackson."

"Me either." Mark gave Jen another kiss.

"I'm going to be sick," Kate said, wishing she could keep her mouth shut.

Jen pulled away from Mark and turned to Kate. Her eyes shot with the sparks of fury Kate had hoped to see from her when she'd thought Mark was cheating on her. Sure she wanted Jen to have a backbone, but not against her!

"If you care about me at all, you will stop this nonsense, Kate." Jen put her hands on her hips. "Just accept that this wedding will go on as planned. There is no way you can find Mr. Perfect in two days."

"So, you admit that I still have two days?" She would find Mr. Perfect or at the very least she'd find some proof that Mark Jackson was a louse. If Ian was still in town, he could probably pass most of Granny's stupid tests. Okay, so he'd already failed one, but surely he could pass the other seven. After all, he was a pretty terrific man.

"Well, I guess you have until the wedding." Jen frowned. "But there isn't much you can do in that time frame."

"I have just under forty-eight hours. I hate to break up the love fest, but can I have a ride home? I have a lot to do."

Jen tossed the keys to her. "Take my car. Mark will see me home."

"See you at the rehearsal dinner," Mark called after her.

If there *was* a rehearsal dinner. If she had anything to say about it, there wouldn't be. She'd gone too far to turn back now. She was going to stop that good-for-nothing scoundrel one way or another.

"Jen, why didn't you tell Kate the bet was off?" Mark asked.

A frown furrowed his brow, and Jen stood on tiptoe and placed a soft kiss there to help smooth it away. Mark had been so patient through this entire situation. It was a good thing he loved her. Many men wouldn't put up with her sister's antics.

"Don't worry. She won't find a perfect man."

Mark pulled away and walked to his window, his back to her. "What if she does? Will you cancel the wedding?"

"She won't find him." She followed him to the window and wrapped her arms around his waist from behind. She laid her head in the hollow of his back. She couldn't wait to be his wife. She loved her job but ever since she'd been a little girl what she'd really wanted was what her mother and father had—a happy marriage, and a couple of children. Was there any job more important than raising a productive, happy adult?

Mark gently pulled her arms away and turned around to face her, holding her hands in his. "Jen, I'm worried. I'm terrified that Kate is going to ruin the best thing I've ever had. I love you."

Jen swallowed several times. Why couldn't her sister see what a wonderful man Mark was? Often, he wore his heart on his sleeve, at least with her. She knew he was concerned that her sister would stop this wedding.

"Kate's always been protective but after Billy kidnapped me—" she stopped for a moment, unable to continue. The terror of that time was still fresh and raw. She'd thought she'd never see her family again. Billy's intention was to kill them both so they could spend eternity together. He'd been the last person she'd ever want to spend eternity with. She'd escaped through a bathroom window at a truck stop and begged a driver for help. She could still feel the sharp knife he'd held to her throat when he'd snatched her off the sidewalk in front of her own home.

"It's okay, sweetheart. I'm not going to let anything like that happen to you ever again. It's over." He stroked his hand over her hair. "I just hope Kate doesn't ruin our wedding."

"She only has two days, Mark. I didn't call the bet off because my big sister needs to learn a very important lesson."

"What lesson is that?"

"You can't stop fate or true love."

Mark smiled and leaned down to place a kiss on her lips. She felt her toes curl as his lips touched hers. That was the feeling that made her fall in love with him. The rest of the world faded into nothing and she felt every inch of his passion right down to her little toe.

"I just hope she learns her lesson before she causes any more trouble."

"That's doubtful with my sister, Mark. She's extremely stubborn. Some people have to get their feet kicked out from under them before they get the point."

Sarah's car was parked haphazardly in front of Kate's parents' house as though she'd been in a rush and hadn't had time to bother with proper parallel basics. Kate grinned. Her plan would require Sarah's help. She could really use Rebecca too, but knew that her friend was dealing with a lot at the moment and didn't want to bother her. On Friday night after the dinner, she'd fill her in on everything that had happened. They had decided to have their diary date after the dinner and turn it into a slumber party, just like when they were kids.

If she wasn't able to stop the wedding, it would be a nice distraction and it would get her out of the house so that she wouldn't have to listen to her mother and Jen making plans for the big day. It seemed that all her mother did was make favors and decorations for this wedding. She wondered if the woman even slept these days.

Several boxes trailed along the left wall of the entry. Kate winced. Wedding gifts. If the wedding was called off at this point, Jen was going to have a lot of work to do just tying up loose ends. She wondered if her sister would truly call off the wedding or was bluffing and hoping that Kate wouldn't be able to find Mr. Perfect.

She followed the smell of chocolate and the rumble of voices into the kitchen. Her mother had two dozen plastic molds lined up along the counters. She shook the small plastic bottle of melted chocolate and filled in each mold.

Sarah sat on a bar stool and poked out air bubbles with a toothpick. "Your mom put me to work," she said when she saw Kate.

"She always did." When they'd been kids, Sarah often could be found in her kitchen helping with a sink load of dishes or peeling some sort of vegetable.

"Sarah is one of the family. I always put family to work." Betty patted Sarah on the arm as she passed on her way to the molds on the other end of the counter.

"Thanks," Sarah said. Kate noticed a sheen of tears in her friend's eyes. She knew Sarah didn't remember her parents; she'd been too young when they died. But often, she'd seen that look of longing on both Sarah and Becca's faces when they'd been at her home. It reminded her again how lucky she was to have both her parents. She gave her mom a quick hug, before turning back to her friend.

"Nice parking job out front, Sarah," Kate teased.

"I need to chat with you."

Betty stopped pouring chocolate and watched the girls with interest. "This isn't about stopping the wedding is it? I thought you girls had given that up."

"It isn't about the wedding," Sarah said.

"Good." Betty nodded approvingly. "You girls go chat. Sarah, don't forget about the rehearsal dinner on Friday. You girls aren't planning on missing it for your diary meeting are you?"

That was a thought. If Kate thought she could get out of it without hurting her family, she certainly wouldn't attend the rehearsal or the dinner. But that wasn't an option. If she couldn't find the proof, she'd attend and she'd paste a smile on her face. She'd hurt her sister enough. The look on Jen's face this afternoon when she'd told her about the blonde had been painful to watch.

"It's a beautiful day. Let's go outside," Kate suggested.

They made their way into the back yard. A white picket fence separated the yard from the neighbor's. The old freestanding bench swing glittered from a fresh coat of white paint. Other than that, it was the same as it had been while they were growing up. Out of habit, the two girls made their way to the bench.

"I'm glad I caught you, Kate. I tracked down our blonde. Tabitha Jackson. She's Mark's cousin. There's no affair there."

"I know. I told Jen this afternoon and went with her while she confronted Mark." She wished Sarah had caught her a couple of hours ago.

Sarah's hand flitted to her mouth. "Oh, no."

"Yes. Jen is furious with me and I look like I'm trying to cause trouble."

"I'm so sorry, Kate." Sarah put an arm around her shoulders. "Jen has to know you only care about her."

"I'm not so sure." Kate dug her toe into the dirt and shoved the swing into motion. "The worst part was his smug smile. He set me up. I'm sure of it. Just like he sabotaged our dates. He knew I was coming and he intentionally gave his cousin a quick kiss, knowing I'd jump to conclusions."

"Do you think he's that underhanded?"

"Yes! I do. I'm just so furious. Then on top of everything, I'm dealing with Ian being here—if he still is."

"So, what are you going to do? Go to the wedding, smile, and bite your tongue?" Sarah asked.

"I've got two days. I am going to hope Ian shows back up. And I'm going to use him to prove Mr. Perfect does exist."

"Ian? Perfect?" Sarah raised her brows. "I mean, he's wonderful, but he's not perfect. What man is?"

"It's my only option, Sarah."

"It's okay, honey. Everything will work out just as it is supposed to, you'll see."

"I need to ask you for a favor. It's a little underhanded."

Sarah smiled her wide smile. "Then you've come to the right girl."

Kate laughed. "I should have known you'd be interested. I want you to talk to others in town. See if you can dig up anything on Mark. I don't believe people change as much as he claims to have changed. He has a bit of a reputation as a bad boy. Find out why. Find out who he's dumped. Why they broke up."

Sarah's smile slipped.

"I know it's asking a lot, Sarah. I remember how the people in this town used to treat you. If I wasn't desperate, I wouldn't ask . . ."

"I'll do it."

"And I'll try to find Ian and start testing him. Maybe between the two of us, we can come up with something in the next thirty-six hours."

"I'm sure we can, but will Jen forgive you when we do?" Sarah's question hung in the air. Kate didn't know but she'd gone too far to turn back now.

Shudders racked Sarah's body. Kate rubbed her own arms, suddenly chilled despite the eighty-degree weather.

"There. Did you feel that too, Kate?" Sarah looked at her friend with wide eyes. "That isn't good."

"Does it have to do with Mark?" Kate asked, half hopeful.

Sarah shook her head. "I wish it did. Something I can't quite put my finger on—a sixth sense. Just be careful."

Kate nodded, feeling as though someone watched them. It was a feeling she'd become accustomed to since returning home. Perhaps it was just the neighborhood busybodies. Some inner instinct told her that wasn't it at all. She rubbed her arms again, wishing the sensation away.

Sarah and Kate sat in the back yard swing. Billy watched them from behind the cover of a large bush on the opposite side of the street. He knew the homeowners wouldn't catch him and give up his position, because he'd made certain they couldn't when he'd slit their throats as they slept.

The two girls' heads were close together as though they plotted. He remembered what they'd done when he'd tried to make love to Sarah in high school. Oh, she'd pretended to not want him, but he'd known better. He'd seen her watching him with that strange look on her face; had seen the shivers that racked her body whenever he drew close; had seen her rub away goose bumps more than once when he'd passed. She'd wanted him, but then she'd gotten scared. The three of them had tracked him down after school the day after he'd tried to make love to Sarah unsuccessfully.

"Stay away from Sarah." Kate poked her finger in his chest.

Billy rubbed the spot, which stung as though he'd received a vaccination.

"Leave me alone, Billy James, or I'll call the police." Sarah glared at him and he wondered what happened to the shivers she usually had when he was around.

"She won't have to call the police. I'll beat you to a pulp." Kate wasn't a big girl but he'd believed her. Her eyes snapped with fierce anger.

"And I'll help her," Rebecca added.

Billy tucked his head and ran from them. He didn't know what Sarah told them, but he'd get even with them all one day.

Coming back to the present, he watched the two girls rise from the swing and go back inside the house. He wasn't sixteen anymore and he wasn't scared of a gaggle of women. If they got in his way, he'd kill them. Jen was his now—not theirs. And he would be with her forevermore.

Fifteen

"I think we should just tell her, Jen." Mark collapsed onto the brown leather sofa in the living room of his small apartment and pulled her down onto his lap.

"No. I don't want her to think I am marrying you for any reason other than love."

"She's your sister." He pulled her head to his shoulder and felt some of the tension leave her body. "She loves you."

"That's right and she should support my decision."

"To be fair to her, she is just trying to protect you." Mark winced. He couldn't believe he'd just defended the woman who was trying to destroy his relationship with Jennifer.

"She's stubborn and single-minded." Jen sat up and looked into his eyes.

"Reminds me of someone else I know," Mark laughed.

"It isn't funny."

"Not really, but she'll come around eventually. She just has to get over my sordid past."

"But your past isn't all that sordid," Jen protested.

"I know that. You know that. Kate doesn't know that. I think if you would tell her—"

"No. She knows that I've succeeded at other things. I finished college and am pursuing my dream of teaching. I lived on my own for several years before I came back here. The only reason I'm living with Mom and Dad is because that whole Billy incident happened before I could get my own place here and everyone is scared of me living alone. Why can't she accept that I can be a success at choosing a husband?"

"Part of her concern is how fast we jumped into this wedding, Jen. If she knew the reason, maybe she would understand."

"I think it'd just give her more ammunition to use against us, Mark. I don't want her to know just yet."

"It's your decision. I just want us to be married and I don't want your day ruined because your sister is unhappy."

"If Kate doesn't want to see us get married, she doesn't have to attend the wedding."

Her words were strong but Mark felt the tremor that ran through her body. He knew that she wanted her big sister's approval and that Kate's resolve to keep her from marrying him was tearing Jen in two directions. He hugged her closer and hoped that Kate would have a change of heart before Saturday. If she didn't, he might just tell her their secret himself.

Ian knew he couldn't hide out in this hotel room forever. Sooner or later he'd have to face Kate and find out if she'd forgiven him for thinking she was coming to town with another man. He should have known it was Sarah or Rebecca traveling with her. Those three were closer than most sisters he knew.

She'd seemed awfully chummy with Jerry, even if it was just to try to stop the wedding as she'd claimed. He wondered if she had deeper feelings for the other man than she'd admitted. While it was true that he was the one who'd given her an ultimatum and fired her, he'd thought it would take her longer than two seconds to find someone new.

"We never talked about being exclusive." He slammed his

fist into the palm of his right hand, cursing himself for not making it clear that he didn't want to date other people.

He and Kate had just been getting to a point in their relationship where they felt comfortable with one another. He'd never been one for fancy words of love and sappy sentiments. His lack of flowery words had cost him relationships in the past but this time was different. He was crazy about Kate. In fact, if he hadn't been so out of his mind with jealousy, he never would have made the mistake of firing her.

What if she wouldn't come back to Ghost Hunters Tours? The thought of going to work for the next fifty years and not seeing Kate's beautiful face and expressive eyes was like a swift kick in Ian's chest. He took a shaky breath.

"You've got it bad, my boy," he said. And he wasn't even sure if Kate had any feelings for him whatsoever. "But I'm going to find out."

He grabbed the keys to his car and headed out the door. There had been two main choices of hotels in the small town; and he'd chosen to stay at Motel 8. Ignoring the fast food places that dotted State Road 9, he followed the road until it turned into a two-lane street with nineteenth century houses gracing either side. He made a right onto North Street and pulled up in front of Kate's childhood home.

The two-story house reminded him of the home he'd grown up in as a child on a farm in Iowa. His mother would love Kate, if she ever had the chance to meet her. Kate was comfortable in the big city but she also had a good dose of small town, Midwestern values.

He knocked on the door and was surprised when Betty opened it rather quickly.

"Mrs. Tyler." He nodded politely.

"Now stop that. I told you to call me Betty. You come on

in. I thought you were the delivery man again. The packages have been flowing nonstop."

"That's good for Jennifer and her intended. They'll have all they need to set up their house." Ian followed Kate's mother into the kitchen, which still smelled of fresh-baked cookies and lingering traces of chocolate. Ian wondered if the kitchen in this house always smelled of cookies.

"I'm glad you're here, Ian. Maybe you can talk some sense into Kate." Betty measured out birdseed into small circles of tulle and then pulled the edges together and tied them with a pretty pale pink ribbon.

"If Kate is even talking to me," he admitted.

"Oh, it's like that." Betty waved him onto a bar stool and passed some circles of fabric and a bowl with birdseed. She handed him a spoon. "You put a good two spoonfuls into the center, and then tie it together."

He hadn't really planned to make up favors for a wedding, but he didn't mind helping. The task would keep him busy so his mind wasn't racing at such a chaotic speed. "Where is Kate?"

"Upstairs. She should be down any time. She's supposed to help me with these but I suspect she's too busy plotting how to interfere with her sister's wedding."

"Kate?" That didn't sound like Kate. She always talked about Jen with such affection. She'd said at Blue Moon Rising that Mark wasn't good enough for Jen.

"She hates Mark," Betty said with a frown. She tied the ribbon around the tulle with a bit more flourish than necessary.

"She may have mentioned something about it." He tried to tie the skinny little ribbon around the birdseed packet he'd just made but his fingers were too big.

"Here. You stuff and I'll tie." She took the packet and tied it neatly, placing it into a white, open-lidded box. "Maybe now that you are here, she'll forget all this stopping the wedding nonsense." Betty patted his hand.

"Not likely." Kate stood in the doorway.

Ian's breath caught in his throat. Her hair was pulled back in some sort of sleek bun thing, making her eyes stand out. Black slacks molded to her curves and her white, sleeveless sweater looked soft. He wanted to pull her into his arms and hold her close.

"Hello, Kate," he said.

"Ian." She moved to the counter and grabbed some fabric.

"Really, Kate, have you not accepted that your sister is getting married Saturday?" her mother asked. "I'm so worried, honey."

Kate sighed and Ian could tell from the slump of her shoulders that she was emotionally and physically exhausted. "It's okay, Mom. Jen and I are working it out."

"But you aren't. Can't you just trust your sister's judgment?"

Ian kept his mouth shut. He knew better than to get in the middle of a mother/daughter argument. His own mother and sister had taught him that lesson early in life.

"I wish I could, Mom. I think when it comes to Mark, she has blinders on."

"The same could be said for you, honey." Betty stopped mid-tie and stared into Kate's eyes.

Kate laid down the fabric and stared back at her mother for several long moments. "I'm going to take Ian out to dinner. I'll be home later."

Betty sighed long and deep. Ian felt her pain across the counter and knew that she didn't want either daughter disappointed or feeling bad. He swallowed. The love she felt for Kate shone out of her eyes. She reminded him of his own mother. He felt the stirrings of a long-forgotten homesickness.

"Be careful, kids." Betty didn't say anything else about the wedding or Kate's lack of support toward it.

"Thanks, Mom." Kate leaned over and kissed her mother on the cheek.

Ian saw Betty's face relax a little and she hugged Kate close. When she pulled back from Kate, she walked around the counter and gave him a quick hug. "The offer to stay here is still open. You shouldn't be in a hotel."

"Thank you, ma'am."

"So polite. Kate, this one is a keeper."

"Mother." Kate's face flushed bright red. "Shhh!"

Betty just laughed and went back to making her birdseed pouches. She hummed *The Wedding March* under her breath. Ian wondered if it was because of the wedding already planned or if she was trying to give him a hint.

Ian followed Kate out to his car. He opened her door for her and she grinned. Test number two passed. She hadn't even had to wait or hint. This evening was off to a promising start and it was a good thing because tomorrow night was the rehearsal dinner, the wedding early on Saturday. She'd have to speed things up and give him the seven remaining tests tonight.

Okay, that was crazy. Maybe tonight and tomorrow. *Sorry, Ian.* She didn't have a choice.

"Are you hungry?" he asked.

Perfect. In a restaurant, she could easily spill her drink on him. Hopefully he wouldn't catch on to what she was doing. "Famished."

"Where is the best place to eat in town?"

"*Brandywine Steakhouse*. It's a quaint little place right downtown but they have excellent food."

He nodded and followed her directions on where to turn and where to park. They probably could have walked the short distance but it wouldn't have afforded her the opportunity for him to pass one of the tests.

They were seated immediately as the dinner rush hadn't quite started. A basket of bread was placed on their table. "I wanted to talk about your job," Ian said and then took a healthy bite of his roll while waiting for her response.

Kate frowned. She didn't have time to waste on chit-chat about topics like her career. She was going to have to speed up the tests and that meant doing them out of order when the opportunity presented itself. She reached across the table and grabbed Ian's hand. Time for test number four; *mention the children you'll someday have together. This will chase off any commitment phobes.*

"When we have a son, I hope he has your eyes," she said. God, that sounded corny.

Ian choked on the piece of bread he'd just swallowed. He coughed spasmodically for several long minutes before he finally reached for his glass of water to wash the food down. Finally, he seemed to recover.

"What if it's a girl?" he asked.

Kate blinked. She wanted him to pass the tests but was a bit surprised at his words after his initial reaction. She bit her lip. Had he passed or not? He hadn't freaked out, so she'd take it as a good sign. Pass. Okay, maybe she was stretching things a bit but it was for Jen's own good.

"Never mind. We aren't even dating. I don't know what I was thinking," she said.

And they probably wouldn't be after the tests she had to go through over the course of a single date or two. Ian would think she was insane and decide she was more trouble than she was worth.

She closed her eyes. It was for her baby sister. The thought of the rest of her life without Ian made her want to curl up under the table and hibernate. She pushed the emotions aside. She couldn't let herself grow weak now. She needed to save Jen. After the smirk Mark had thrown at her over Jen's shoulder, she was more determined than ever to stop the wedding. He had something else up his sleeve. She wasn't sure what it was but it was something big and something that perhaps even Jen didn't know.

Ian's head spun from her abrupt about-face. What was going on with Kate? Usually she was steady and easy to get along with but over the last fifteen minutes or so she'd become a complete maniac. Perhaps it was the worry over her sister's wedding that was making her act so flaky.

"Kate, I'm here to ask you to come back to work at Ghost Hunters. I was wrong to fire you. Forgive me?"

She stared at him across the table for several long moments and then took her glass full of soda and tipped it right into his lap. Ian grabbed his napkin and dabbed at the dampness on his lap. What in the world was going on with Kate? It wasn't like her to act so—so—crazy.

"Okay, so you don't forgive me." He sighed.

Kate's face broke into a wide grin. She didn't have to rub it in that she was holding a grudge. He had never seen this side of Kate and he wasn't really enjoying what he was seeing. What was going on with her? He narrowed his eyes. Hadn't Jerry said something about tests? Was Kate *testing* him? No, they'd been dating for a while. If she planned to test him, she'd probably done so already.

"I forgive you," she said.

"Then why did you dump a drink in my lap?" He swiped at the dampness again.

She shrugged. "It was just something I needed to do."

"Well, I hope you feel better."

"Actually, I don't. I don't want steak. Let's go back to my house. I'll cook you some chicken."

There was an underlying urgency in her voice that troubled him. She'd been in a huge hurry to leave her house earlier and now she suddenly wanted to go back. "Kate, are you feeling okay?"

"Of course. C'mon. Let's go. Let's go."

"Okay." He informed the waitress that they were leaving and paid for their drinks, including the one that remained on his slacks. He threw in a good tip to lessen any sting from their abrupt departure.

He wasn't sure what was going on with Kate, but she certainly was acting out of character. He couldn't help but wonder what she'd do next. He hoped she didn't throw a chicken on him.

Sixteen

Test # 5—Invite him to dinner and then burn the food horribly. His reaction will tell you whether he can make the best of a bad situation.

Normally, Kate was an okay cook. It wasn't easy to intentionally burn food to a cinder but she was determined to do so. She'd opted to cook the chicken on the outdoor grill. Her mother still controlled every available inch of the counter space in the kitchen. Her mad dash to finish last-minute wedding goodies and add the small touches disturbed Kate, who hoped the wedding never got off the ground. She certainly didn't want her mother to pour hours and hours into a wedding that she planned to stop.

She lifted the lid of the grill. The chicken was a bit crisp but not quite burned enough to be inedible. She lowered the lid and forced herself to walk a few steps away. Ten more minutes and the food would be unsalvageable. She hoped Ian passed this test. He couldn't fail a single one. If he did, then she was sunk. He'd already failed the jealousy test.

The heady aroma of burnt chicken tickled her nostrils. She winced and approached the grill, opening the lid a final time.

"Dinner is served." She walked into the kitchen and set the plate of burnt chicken on the cool stove top. It was the only free spot in the entire kitchen, which was now covered with yards of pink and white ribbons that her mother fashioned into huge bows.

Kate shook her head. There were people you could pay to do that work, but maybe her parents were on a budget. She'd never really worried about it before. There'd always been enough while they were growing up, but now she wondered how financially stable her parents were.

"Mom, why didn't you just hire the florist to do that?" she whispered. "You've been working your fingers to the bone."

"And miss one little thing in my baby daughter's wedding? Not a chance. When she walks down the aisle and sees these bows on the ends of the pews, she'll know her mother made each and every one with love."

Kate cleared her throat. "That's so sweet, Mom." She hugged her mother.

Ian stared at the plate of black lumps. "Dinner?"

"I cooked them a little too long."

He laughed. "I think we should have stuck with the steak."

Was he making the best of a bad situation? Darn it. She wasn't sure. The tests were easy to apply but hard to evaluate. She wanted to be fair. She turned to her mother.

"What do you think, Mom? Is Ian making the most of a bad situation or not?"

Ian's smile faded and a scowl covered his face.

"Oh no you don't, Katherine Elaine Tyler. You are not going to pull me into your little schemes."

"Is that what you're doing, Kate? Are you testing me?" Ian's voice was so low she could barely hear it, but his eyes screamed in high-pitched anger. And deep under the anger was an intense hurt.

"Ian—"

"I don't want to hear it." He stood from the bar stool and

nodded to her mother. "Betty, thank you for your hospitality but I've lost my appetite."

He looked at Kate, shook his head and walked toward the front door. What had she done? She chased after him.

"Ian, wait."

He stopped with his hand on the front door knob. He stood ramrod straight, his back stiff.

"I'm sorry. I was just trying to—"

"Kate, you went way too far. I know exactly what you were doing. You used me to try to stop your sister's wedding. *Used* me!"

His words rained like small darts into her heart. He was right. She'd gone way too far. What had she been thinking? She could feel his disappointment and deep hurt, even though he still didn't face her. She placed a hand on his back. He stiffened and opened the door before turning to face her.

"I'm going home, Kate. I suggest you go to your sister's wedding and smile, before you hurt anyone else."

Ian closed the door behind him just as a deep sob erupted from low in Kate's abdomen. She'd lost him. He'd never forgive her for using him in such a way. What had she been thinking anyway? Of course no one could pass those ridiculous tests. She climbed the stairs to her room, feeling as though her feet had lead weights tied to them. It was pointless. There was no way to stop that vile wedding. But deep inside of her a spark flickered and she promised herself that she would find another way.

Sarah couldn't think of a better place to end her research than Mark's workplace. Her conversation with Eloise Dillon-Jones this afternoon had been quite revealing. She approached the receptionist and smiled.

"Can I help you?" the girl asked and then chewed on her gum.

It reminded Sarah of a cow chewing its cud and she wondered if anyone had ever bothered to teach the other woman manners or if she'd just chosen to ignore those lessons.

"I actually have a question for you. You're Tara right?" Eloise said Mark dated Tara before Jen and their affair had been red hot.

"Yes." The other woman narrowed her eyes to thin slits.

Sarah smiled. "Did you used to date Mark Jackson?"

"Are you writing a story or something?" Tara blew a large bubble and it popped loudly.

She barely resisted the urge to gaze at the ceiling in disgust. *This was a real winner you picked here, Mark.* She couldn't imagine he'd dated the woman for anything other than the way she looked.

"Not exactly. It's more like a wedding present." For Kate.

"Yes, I dated him." The phone rang on Tara's desk and she answered it, turning her back on Sarah without so much as a simple "excuse me."

"Gawd!" she screeched. "It's on the top shelf in the supply room. Yes it is. Yes it is. It is too. Yes it is."

Sarah tapped her foot and wondered if Mark realized the image the woman presented for the newspaper. Maybe he didn't care since he'd slept with her.

"Yes it *is!* Forget it, I'll have to come show you. Do I have to do everything?" She slammed the phone down and jumped from the desk. She didn't bother to let Sarah know if she'd be back or not.

Sarah leaned over the counter and looked at the computer screen. Nothing. A bunch of figures from ads or something. Glancing over her shoulder to make sure no one watched, she leaned further over the counter and rifled through a stack of papers in the outgoing tray. The third letter down was written on pink stationery and caught her eye.

My dearest Mark,

My love, I can't tell you how very happy I am to be carrying your child. I can't wait until we can be together forever.

The sound of rapidly approaching footsteps startled Sarah. She pushed the letter back into the stack and wiggled off the counter.

"What did you want again?" Tara asked, looking irritated.

"You're busy, I'll just leave you alone." Sarah walked for the front door and never glanced back.

"What did you find?" Kate phoned Sarah on Friday morning. A good night's rest hadn't made her feel much better but it had refreshed her. The rehearsal was at six o'clock tonight. She had exactly eight hours to come up with another plan.

"Are you okay? You don't sound good," Sarah said. "I'm picking up all kinds of angst from you, Kate."

Kate sighed. She loved that Sarah had a sixth sense where she and Becca were concerned. At the same time, she didn't want to talk about Ian.

"Things didn't go well with Ian, did they?"

"Stop that, Sarah. Don't read my mind." Kate clicked her tongue and changed the subject. "I was calling to talk about your research on our project."

"Okay, but you need to deal with this, Kate. It's not good to push things down under the surface. They tend to boil over when you do that."

"I know." She just couldn't think about Ian right now or she'd break down.

"I found a couple of interesting things. First, Mark was dating a girl right before he started seeing Jen. They broke up abruptly. She thinks he was seeing Jen and that's why he broke it off. No proof though."

"Well, we probably can't use that. I don't want to risk another false accusation."

"He was also dating another woman about a year before that. Her name is Tara and she works at the newspaper. I found a letter in her things addressed to 'My darling Mark' talking about carrying his child. But I couldn't finish the letter to make sure it had her signature or see when it might have been written."

"That's odd."

"I thought so." Sarah laughed. "Horrid girl. Very rude."

"Maybe she's more suited for him?"

"I wouldn't even wish this on Mark, Kate."

"That bad huh? There might be something there." Why had they broken up and had she been carrying or *was* she carrying his child? Had he cheated on Tara?

"Against my better judgment, I spoke to Eloise Dillon-Jones."

"How did that go?"

"She's as vile as ever."

Kate laughed. "No surprise there. What did she say?"

"That Mark slept with her a week ago."

"What?" Kate's pulse rate increased tenfold.

"Yep. Said that he and she have been on again off again for years, even when he has girlfriends—including Jen."

A vague gnawing feeling settled into her stomach. Disappointment? A part of her had been hoping that Mark was truly innocent and she'd been wrong about him. After seeing her sister with him when they'd visited his office, she knew that Jen loved him deeply. And she'd almost wondered if he cared for her as much as he was capable of after the tender way she'd seen him treat Jen. He'd been protective of her, which was something Kate could appreciate.

She felt disappointment but she wasn't shocked. She'd known Mark was a louse. Now she had the proof. This time, however, she wasn't going to take it to Jen. She couldn't bear to see that hurt look on her sister's face again. No, she was going directly to the devil himself and confront him. He could either tell Jen or not but she was going to see to it that he called off the wedding. She barely heard Sarah's final words.

"I'm not sure she was telling the truth, Kate. She isn't trustworthy."

She'd been surprised when Mark answered his office phone. Who worked on the day of their wedding rehearsal? She supposed it should be a point in his favor, since it showed that he was a hard worker and would probably support her sister and be a good financial partner, but it was hard for her to allow the charitable thought through. She had to force it through like a thick piece of yarn through a tiny needle's eye. He'd agreed to meet with her and here she was.

"Kate, I hope you've come to make peace." Mark motioned to the chair in front of his desk.

Kate took a seat. "Not exactly."

He lifted a brow and leaned forward slightly. "I can't wait to hear what you've come up with this time."

"That's hardly fair. You and I both know that you've cheated in the past. I'm just trying to protect Jen. If you love her the way you claim you love her, then you should understand."

"I haven't cheated. The worst thing I'm guilty of is dating around, but only one at a time."

She felt her jaw drop. He wasn't seriously going to sit right across from her and lie? Didn't cheat? He'd cheated on her in high school. And now, she had information that he'd cheated on Jen. Oh, he was a liar and she could not stand a liar. She was about to drop a bomb on him and she hoped it wiped that smug smile off his face.

"According to Eloise Dillon-Jones, you have." She let the words drip syllable by syllable from her lips.

Mark didn't respond for several long moments. Gotcha! Then he looked up. "Kate, the situation with Eloise is very much he said/she said. But that was ages ago."

"Ages ago? A week is ages?"

"A week? Are you crazy?" He jumped to his feet.

"Sarah spoke with Eloise yesterday and Eloise is prepared to tell Jen everything. I don't want my sister hurt again. I am asking you to call the wedding off. Postpone it. Tell her or don't tell her about Eloise. But don't try to marry my sister and have your honey on the side." Fury bubbled in her veins. She wouldn't let him play Jen for a fool. If Jen wouldn't protect herself, somebody had to do it.

"I don't suppose it would help to say that I'm innocent? That Eloise always has been and always will be a liar? She tries to wreck relationships to make herself feel better."

"No. I don't buy it." Was he serious? She snorted. *Checkmate, Mark Jackson. You won't be marrying my sister.*

"I'm not calling off the wedding," he said. His dark blue eyes glittered with suppressed anger.

"Excuse me?" How could he not call off the wedding? Didn't he realize that as soon as Jen knew what he'd done she would break things off with him?

"You heard me. I am marrying your sister. I haven't done

208

anything wrong and I really don't care if you believe me or not. At this point, I don't even care if you attend the wedding other than the fact that it will hurt Jen if you don't." He walked to his office door and held it open. "Good day."

Kate couldn't believe what had just happened. Had Mark Jackson really taken the best proof she'd had to date of his infidelity and turned the tables on her? He'd put her in a situation where she had to either tell her sister about Eloise or keep her mouth shut and let her sister walk into marriage with a monster.

Kate pulled into her parents' driveway feeling as though she just wanted to curl into her bed and sleep for a month. She was confused and didn't know what to do. If she made another accusation against Mark, she didn't think Jen would ever forgive her. But how could she stand by and let her sister marry Mark when he was having an affair with Eloise?

Her mother rushed out onto the porch and flagged her down. Lines of worry furrowed her normally smooth brow. Kate jumped from the car. The vague sense of unease that had stalked her since she'd returned home came back a hundred fold. Was it Jen? Had Billy come back?

"Mom, what's wrong?"

"Honey, Ian's been in an accident. A truck ran a red light and hit his car. He's at Hancock Memorial. Daddy heard it on the police scanner and recognized the car's description as Ian's. The hospital wouldn't give me any information over the phone."

Kate didn't wait to hear any more but jumped back into her car and tamped down her desire to drive ninety to the hospital. It wouldn't do any good to lose control of her car and get in an accident herself. Ian would be okay. He had to be okay. *Oh, God, what if he dies?* If he died, she'd never forgive herself for using him.

Suddenly, stopping her sister's wedding didn't seem like the most important thing in the entire world. If she lost Ian . . . her throat closed off until she could barely breathe. She skipped the new multi-level parking garage and opted for a space in the emergency lot.

After a quick sprint across the parking lot, she reached the reception area in the emergency room. "Ian Fields."

Her breathing was heavy from her dash. The nurse looked at her. "Are you family?"

She blinked. If she said no, they would turn her away without an update on his condition. That couldn't happen.

"What do I need to be to see him?" she asked.

"Fiancé?" the woman suggested.

"Okay. How is he?" Ian would probably be furious that she'd taken on the title of his fiancé without his knowledge—particularly after their last conversation. She didn't care. Right now she just wanted to see him and see that he was breathing. *Please, God, let him be okay. I love him so much.*

The depth of her emotions almost knocked her to her knees. She loved him but she'd probably lost him. He'd never forgive her for using him. What she'd done had been a slap in the face to someone like Ian who was always up-front and honest.

"He's stable. I won't be able to give you more information until the doctors are finished working on him." She pointed to a small waiting area behind Kate. "I'll call you when I know more."

Kate walked to a vinyl and metal chair and collapsed. In the corner, a small boy played with some blocks on a table and another woman, apparently his mother, sat nearby chewing her fingernails.

What if Ian were badly hurt? She wished she had the ability to kick herself in the butt for treating him the way she had. *I'm so sorry, Ian.* While she'd been preoccupied with ousting Mark, Ian had been lying in this hospital by himself. She wondered if she should try to track down his family but wanted to wait until she had more news. It wouldn't do any good to phone them and not be able to answer their questions about his condition. She didn't want to worry them unnecessarily.

"I love you so much, Ian," she whispered softly.

The little boy looked over at her and smiled. His two top teeth were missing. She smiled back.

"The tooth fairy has been to my house twice this week," he said.

"Cody, leave the lady alone," his mother said around her fingernail.

"He's fine. How old are you, Cody? About six?"

"Seven in October." He puffed his little chest out. "When I grow up, I'm going to work on machines just like my daddy."

His mother let out a muffled sob that sounded as though it had been held in for quite a while. Kate glanced at her nervously, not sure how the child was going to react. The little boy went to his mother's side and patted her on the shoulder. "It's okay, Mommy. I won't get hurt like Daddy did."

"Just keep praying for Daddy, Cody."

Kate thought that was pretty good advice.

"My husband was repairing a machine at a local plant and got caught. They won't tell me anything." The woman's eyes were wide with more than just fear—an edge of panic rested there.

Kate was familiar with the feeling. It came from realizing that you'd finally met your soul mate and he could be snatched from you so easily. In her case, even if he was physically okay, he might never want to speak to her again. In the woman's case, the physical aspect was the most threatening.

"My boyfriend was in a car accident. I don't know anything yet."

The woman nodded and then went back to biting her nails. Kate focused her attention internally and started to pray. A few minutes later, the squeak of the nurse's white shoes alerted them to her presence.

"Mrs. Andrews, your husband would like to see you." The nurse smiled.

"He's conscious?" The young mother jumped to her feet.

"Yes, ma'am."

The woman grabbed her handbag, stood, started for the hallway, and then looked back at her son.

The nurse waved her on. "Take him with you. Shh!"

Mother and son rushed happily down the hallway. Kate was relieved for them. The tick-tock of the clock on the wall seemed to move slowly as she waited to hear about Ian's condition. At five o'clock she picked up the phone to call her mother.

"Mom?" She knew her voice sounded shaky, but couldn't prevent the tremor. With each hour that passed, she grew more and more frightened that she'd never see Ian again.

"Honey, is Ian okay?" Her mother sounded rushed and Kate knew she was busy with getting ready for the rehearsal as well as worrying over Ian.

"I don't know anything. They keep saying they'll know soon." She paused. "I'm scared, Mom. After what I did—"

"Honey, it's okay. I tried to test your father and my little brother told him what I was doing. He was so furious that he didn't speak to me for two days. But he forgave me and look how happy we've been the past thirty-three years."

"Thanks, Mom. I'm worried I might miss this dinner."

"Jen understands. You do what you have to there. I called Sarah and Becca and let them know what was going on too. We're all praying for him."

"Thanks." Kate hung up the phone. The thought of missing the dinner stung. She'd hoped to shame Mark into calling things off with her mere presence but that was probably a crazy notion anyway.

She sank into one of the gaudy orange chairs but didn't have time to settle into misery before Sarah and Becca rushed through the sliding glass doors and sat down on either side of her. Sarah put her arm around Kate's shoulders and Becca held her right hand.

"He's going to be just fine, Kate."

She hoped Sarah was right. If she lost Ian, she didn't know how she would cope. Funny, how the thought of losing his love hadn't stung nearly as bad as it did now that she thought he might be gone from this world. Death was too final. She'd never have a chance to even apologize for what she'd done.

Seventeen

The nurse motioned for Kate to follow.

Becca squeezed her hand. "It's going to be fine. We'll be right here."

"You don't have to wait." Kate shook her head.

"We want to," Sarah said.

Kate didn't have time to argue with them. They should go home but right now she just wanted to see Ian and make sure he was breathing. She followed the nurse. They walked down a short hall, turned right, went through double doors and into an area with cordoned off rooms. Finally, the nurse pointed to a curtain. "He's in there."

Kate took a deep breath and pulled the edge of the curtain back. Ian's dark head contrasted sharply with the white pillow. His eyes were closed and he was hooked up to a blood pressure monitor that bleeped out a steady rhythm. She let out the breath she'd taken, when she realized that he wasn't hooked up to life support or any machines that would indicate he was in immediate danger of dying.

She sat in the chair next to his bed. His eyes opened and he stared at her. She scooted forward and brushed her fingers over his hair. He didn't knock her hand away. Either he was still dazed from the accident or he wasn't as furious with her as she'd thought.

She leaned her head on his arm, trying to contain the emotions that threatened to spill out onto her cheeks and drench him. He stroked her head with his other hand and she heard his voice as he croaked out a greeting.

"Am I in that bad of shape?"

"I don't know." She lifted her head, knowing that tears filled her eyes, refusing to let them fall. He was alive.

"My car?"

"Who cares about your stupid car?" she said. She'd been worried he would die and he was concerned about a car.

"I care."

"Right. Sorry. I don't know about your car. I've been here since about noon and don't even really know anything about your condition." Her words stopped abruptly as she struggled for composure. "All I know is that you're alive."

He winced as he moved his arm back to his side and she realized he was in more pain than he was letting on. Now that she'd gotten over the relief of finding him alive, she noticed the lines around his mouth that hadn't been there before and his paleness.

"Are you in pain?"

"I'm fine." He gritted the words through his teeth.

"Let me get a nurse."

He grabbed her arm as she stood to leave and then groaned from the effort. She sat back down quickly.

"Wait," he said.

"I was so worried about you."

He looked at her. "Were you really? You pretend like you care."

"Ian—" What could you say to someone you'd hurt as deeply as she'd hurt Ian?

"Save it, Kate. I heard how you really feel about me loud and clear."

She shook her head. No, he hadn't. She loved him. She'd

just made a mistake—a really, really big mistake.

"I think maybe you'd better leave," he said. "If I need the nurse, I'm capable of punching a button."

His words were like daggers shooting straight into her heart. She opened her mouth to protest, but the look on his face was set. She knew Ian well enough to know that any argument would fall on deaf ears. She'd ruined everything with her scheming. She stood again, but this time he didn't try to stop her. Early in their relationship, she'd learned that it was better to let Ian cool down and then try to talk to him. He was banged up a little but not in any real danger and she had to get to Jen's rehearsal. Already, she was going to be an hour late. Any chance she'd had of guilting Mark into confessing during the practice was shot. There would be food and conversation at the dinner. The wedding was at noon tomorrow. Time was quickly running out.

"I have to go to Jen's rehearsal dinner." For a moment, she looked at him, happy that he was alive. Maybe she should just stay here whether he wanted her to or not. He wasn't in any condition to prevent her from staying. But she suspected it would cause him stress and he needed to rest. "I'll be back tomorrow."

"Don't bother."

But she would. What kind of person would she be if she deserted him? Even if she didn't care for him, she wouldn't have done that. "I'll be back," she whispered as she left the room.

Ian closed his eyes as the waves of pain washed over him from head to toe. He didn't remember being blindsided by the pickup truck they'd said had hit him. All he remembered was cold blackness, muffled voices, and waking up to see Kate's angelic face filled with concern.

When she'd rested her head on his arm and then raised her face and looked at him with tear-filled eyes, he'd almost broken down and begged her to marry him. But she didn't care about him and the sooner he accepted that fact the better off he'd be. He'd already tried to force one woman to love him and look how that had turned out. Angela hadn't cared about him in the end and neither would Kate. He refused to repeat the same mistake over and over. Kate and Angela might be different in every way, but that didn't mean both couldn't break his heart.

His ribs hurt like hell and his head felt like a million tiny ice picks chunked away at his skull. The fact that Kate hadn't argued much about leaving but had been more intent on getting to her sister's rehearsal hurt. If she'd been the one in the accident, he would have refused to leave her side. But then, he loved her. She didn't return the sentiment.

You told her to leave, you fool. She knew him well enough to know that arguing was pointless. She had said she'd return tomorrow, but he wasn't sure she'd bother. He'd come here with the intention of keeping her love for himself but the truth was that he'd never had her love and never would. As soon as he was able, he was going home.

When Kate arrived at the church, the entire wedding party was already in place and Mark and Jen faced each other, hands bound together, staring into one another's eyes. Kate forced down the bile and slid into a seat a little way back from the rest of those there.

So much for guilting Mark into confessing. Sarah and Becca had been invited to attend the dinner and had rushed home to change after spending the afternoon at the hospital with her while she'd waited to make sure Ian was okay. Really, there was no reason for her to be here at this point other than the fact that her sister had begged her to come to the rehearsal.

Mark had effectively foiled her plan to take her news to him and stop the wedding. She narrowed her eyes as she watched him throw a cocky smile toward her parents and them respond with warmth. Was this what holidays would be like if he and Jen married? She'd be an outsider watching the festivities go on around her while he soaked up the love and warmth of her family like some kind of vampire.

She straightened her back and gave herself a mental kick in the rear. *That sounded jealous, Kate. Cut it out. Remember your purpose.* Her purpose wasn't just to give Mark a hard way to go or be difficult. She wanted to protect her sister. But it was almost too late.

"Kate." Jen waved from the altar. "You made it."

Mark glared at her as though daring her to say anything. Kate bit her tongue to keep from shouting what she knew and wiping that cocky look off his features. That would only hurt Jen and she didn't want to hurt her sister.

"How is Ian, honey?" her mother asked.

"He's going to be okay." As she'd left, she'd confirmed with the nurse that Ian was in a bit of pain, mainly from broken ribs, but was going to be okay if she left to come to the rehearsal.

"Maybe we'll be here for your wedding soon." Jen smiled and stood on tiptoe to give Mark a quick kiss.

Kate squirmed. Did her sister have to look so happy? All her innocent dreams would be crushed when Mark violated her trust. A spark of hate flared to life inside her as she watched Mark gently take her sister's hand and slip an imaginary ring on her finger. He put on a good show, she'd give him that. But his heart was as black as the devil's.

Her father slipped down the aisle and sat down on the pew

next to her. Kate scooted over a bit to make more room for him. "How you doin', kiddo?" He patted her shoulder.

"Okay, Dad." She forced a smile.

"Funny, you look like someone forced you to chew glass and then swallow."

"Is it that obvious?" She really was trying to contain her emotions but she felt so strongly that Jen was making the biggest mistake of her life that she wasn't sure how to hide her feelings. She still wanted to stop the wedding and would jump at any chance to do so. But she didn't want to break her sister's heart in the process—not for a lost cause.

"Probably not to everyone, but this is your old dad you're talking to."

"He isn't right for her."

"Did you know that your Uncle Matt beat me up the week before I married your mother?" He chuckled. "Broke two ribs and gave me a black eye."

"Dad! You never told me that." Kate couldn't believe it. Uncle Matt?

Her father nodded. "Seems he'd heard I had a reputation for being with a lot of ladies and didn't think I was good enough for his sister."

Kate couldn't believe it. The idea of Uncle Matt beating up her father didn't sit well. There was no way Dad had been a ladies' man either. It wasn't his nature. He was too quiet and reserved.

"Guess what?" Her father pointed at Mark and Jennifer. "I married your mom anyway and we've been blissfully happy for over thirty years."

"It's different, Dad." She couldn't look at Mark and Jennifer as they shared their practice kiss for when they'd be pronounced man and wife. "You weren't actually a ladies' man."

"Honey, it isn't different. Matt refused to speak to me the first two years your mother and I were married. It broke Betty's heart. I'd hold her while she cried herself to sleep after holiday dinners. Do you really want to do that to your sister?"

No. She didn't. Her father was a wise man but Mark had fooled him just as he'd fooled everyone else around them. Well, she wasn't gullible and she knew that Mark was a fraud.

"I won't nag." He hugged her close. "I love both you girls. Just don't make things too hard on yourself. Jen will marry Mark no matter what you do. You might as well try to accept it. The sooner you do, the happier we'll all be." Her father moved back to the front of the church, leaving her to think over what he'd said about accepting the marriage.

Well, she wouldn't accept it until she had to. Until the last "I do" was said and they were officially married, she still had time. Anything could happen between now and tomorrow. The hairs on the back of her neck rose and she glanced over her shoulder toward the darkened doorway of the church. A shadow crept across the doorway. She frowned and started to say something to the wedding party but didn't want them to think she was just trying to stall the rehearsal. She shrugged and moved toward the back of the room. Enough of these cat and mouse games. Someone was spying on her and she wanted to know who it was.

The voices in the sanctuary faded into nothing as she moved out into the pitch black foyer. A large circle of classrooms and offices circled the main worship room itself. The distant clang of someone bumping into what sounded like a trash can came from that darkened circular hallway.

She followed the noise, creeping down the hallway as quietly as possible. If Mark had paid one of his friends to spy on her, she wanted to know and she wanted to know this minute. She stopped just on this side of an open doorway, listening for any additional sounds. Her heart thundered so loudly in her ears that for several long moments it was all she could hear. Slowly, the gentle rasp of her breathing replaced that sound. She held her breath for a moment and the breathing continued.

Run! She knew she should listen to her instincts and take off back toward the lights and people, but her curiosity won out and she stood her ground. The breathing grew louder and she realized the man moved closer. Could he see her? She couldn't see anything. The blackness was nearly complete. Hazy outlines of doorways and walls were all her naked eye could recognize.

The scent of unwashed hair filled her nostrils and she barely kept from gagging. It certainly wasn't Jerry following her—he was the cleanest cowboy she'd ever met. A skitter of unease that she'd ignored previously skipped up her spine. Fear clogged her throat. What had she been thinking to chase an unknown shadow through the darkness?

"Back off, Kate, or die." The words reached her ears. She strained to hear them, wondering who the voice belonged to before the words themselves registered on her brain. Her feet felt as though they were glued to the floor. She wanted desperately to run but didn't know which way to go in the disorientation of the darkness.

"Kate?" Her father's voice called to her from behind her. She felt the breeze of the man's body as he moved toward her.

Stumbling backwards, she found her footing and raced down the hallway toward her father's voice. When she arrived back at the doors to the sanctuary, she glanced over her shoulder and saw the outline of a man standing just inside the shadows, stalking her. Her heart leapt back into her throat and she stumbled down the aisle.

"What is it now, Kate?" Mark snapped.

"I-I think someone is out there. In the hallway," she said. Okay, it sounded crazy and she could hardly tell them she'd gone off following some unknown spy because she thought Mark had paid someone.

"How convenient." Mark glared at her.

Jen whispered something in his ear and he seemed to calm down.

"Can we please just finish this rehearsal?" he asked.

"Of course." Kate moved closer to the wedding party and took a seat behind her parents. She'd clearly heard her father's voice calling her but how had he gotten back into the sanctuary and into his seat when she'd been running in high gear toward him? It wasn't possible. She glanced back over her shoulder but the doorway remained clear this time—no shadows and no hairs standing on end.

She knew she hadn't imagined the incident, but perhaps she'd blown it out of proportion. More than likely Mark *had* paid someone and he'd been afraid of being discovered, so he had threatened her in order to scare her. Well, Mark would pay for that, just like he'd pay for every other rotten trick he'd pulled on her. You couldn't do dirty, rotten things and not have them come back to bite you on the butt.

Rebecca and Sarah were already at the restaurant when the wedding party arrived for dinner. Kate couldn't remember being more relieved to see them. Normally she felt comfortable in her own skin and with her own family. Mark's presence had brought a strange air to the entire group and she'd stood on the outside circle for most of the actual rehearsal. His friends obviously knew she didn't approve and she suspected that Jen's friends did as well. Her mother was irritated at them both for not being able to get past the situation and enjoy the moment and her father was worried. Kate definitely felt the cold shoulder from Mark, not that she cared what he thought.

"You holding up okay?" Sarah asked. She looped her arm through Kate's right arm.

Becca took the other side and looped her arm through Kate's left arm. "We're here for you."

"It was horrible. I'm getting the cold shoulder from half the wedding party and the other half keeps looking at me like I'm insane. My mother keeps looking at Jen, looking at me, and then shaking her head and clucking her tongue. I wish this week was over." She gave a short, barky laugh. She didn't mention the incident with the unseen man. It only made her sound crazy, and even though she knew that Sarah and Becca would believe her, neither of them needed anything else to worry about right now.

"We didn't have time to talk after you saw Ian at the hospital. I was just relieved to hear he was okay. Did you two work things out?" Sarah asked.

She shook her head. "No. He won't hardly talk to me. He told me to leave."

"Ouch." Rebecca squeezed her arm. "What is he so upset about?"

"Our Kate tried the tests out on Ian as a last-ditch effort to prove he was Mr. Perfect."

"I take it that the tests backfired?" Becca said.

They entered the restaurant behind the rest of the wedding party and were promptly seated at a table as far away from Mark and Jen as was possible in the banquet room with the fireplace. It was too warm this time of year for the fireplace to be in use but it lent a nice ambience to the room.

"I tried to do too many at once. He caught on to what I was doing. He's furious. And he should be. I can't believe I used him in that way."

"What about Jen and Mark? Any luck at all?" Becca frowned. "I feel so out of the loop. Like I've deserted you."

"No, Becca. You needed to focus on Jared. I'm glad you two have worked things out."

"Me too." Becca smiled dreamily and Kate felt a small flash of envy. She was happy for her friend but she'd love to have the opportunity to smile dreamily over Ian.

"Sarah found out that Mark slept with Eloise just last week, but we have no proof and he isn't admitting it. I don't want to take another accusation to Jen after the last time."

"Her again?" Becca frowned. "Are you certain?"

"Jen has a right to know." Sarah threw a glare toward Mark.

"I can't tell her," Kate said.

"Then Sarah should." Becca picked up a fork as a server set a salad in front of her and speared a leaf of lettuce. Then she pointed the speared leaf at Sarah. "The sooner the better."

"Why me?"

"Because you talked to Eloise." Becca popped the end of the fork into her mouth and chewed with satisfaction. "If you think she's so trustworthy, you should speak up."

"You don't have to do that, Sarah. She's my sister. I should tell her."

Mark's hearty laugh sounded from the main table at the front of the room. He stretched his neck and looked back at their table and then leaned over and whispered something to one of his groomsmen who chuckled. Swift hot fury that had bubbled just below the surface erupted.

"Did you see that?" she asked Sarah and Becca.

"Jerk." Sarah reached down and pulled out her purse. "I didn't want to use this but I think this is the time."

"What is it?" Kate tried to peek into Sarah's purse.

Sarah pulled a plastic Ken doll with black hair out of her purse and set it on the table. Its face was set in a grimace and its tiny eyes sunken into its skull, as though years ago some child had lit a match to its features and melted them into something unrecognizable. It had no clothes and a missing arm.

"That is so ugly." Becca laughed.

"It's ugly to represent the ugliness Mark has on the inside." She laid it on the table. "The gypsy woman gave it to me before we left. It's a voodoo doll."

Kate laughed. "Are you serious?"

"Let's use it." Sarah pulled out a bobby pin and twisted it into a spear.

Kate stopped her. "Wait. What if it really works? I mean, I don't believe in that stuff, but what if it does?"

Sarah laughed. "I was kidding. It wouldn't work. I got it at a garage sale earlier today. Talked them down to twenty-five cents, baby! You know I don't really mess with black magic of any kind. Just trying to lighten the atmosphere a little."

"In that case . . ." Kate took her fingers and flicked the doll in the head. Half hopeful, she glanced at Mark but he had no reaction.

"It won't work, Kate," Sarah smiled.

"I know. Just wishing."

"I thought it would be a fun release of all that negative energy. You take your frustration out on this cheap little doll and then maybe you can approach the situation without all that pent-up anger and see a clear solution that will work."

"You're a good friend, Sarah."

Sarah fluffed her hair. "I know. Now squish the dolly's head."

Kate laughed and felt some of the tension leave her body.

A few moments later the best man stood and clinked his glass with a fork.

"I'd like to start the toasts and then I thought we could go around the room and each of us say a few words to Mark and Jen. Mark, I've known you since college and this is the first time I've seen you this happy. May you and Jen have many happy years together free of interference or heartache." He glanced at Kate as he said the interference part.

He passed the fork to the next groomsman. "Mark and Jen, you two make a great couple, and don't let anyone ever tell you differently." He too glanced at Kate.

Sarah leaned over and whispered, "This isn't a round of toasts. It's a bash Kate fest."

Her father stood. "I like to tell the story of how my brother-in-law beat me up the week before I married Jen's mother. He didn't think I was good enough for her and here we are thirty-three years later." Everyone laughed. "But seriously, Matt and I are the best of friends now and I'm glad I took the time to get to know him because his friendship has meant the world to me." He looked over and winked at Kate.

Thanks, Dad. She mouthed the words at him.

"Oh, my turn?" Her mother giggled nervously. "I'll just be relieved when this wedding is over. It's been stressful to say the least. I love you Jen. You'll always be my baby and I can't wait to be a grandmother."

Kate glanced heavenward, praying for a silent tongue. When the fork came to their table, Sarah grabbed it and stood.

"Jen has seemed more like a friend over the years than Kate's baby sister." She glared at Mark. "You'd better take care of her, Mark, or the three of us will hunt you down."

Everyone laughed except Mark and his groomsmen. Kate

knew Sarah meant what she said. She handed Kate the fork. "You're on, Kate."

She stood. What did you say when you didn't want to ruin your sister's big day, didn't want to disappoint your parents, but couldn't stand the groom? She cleared her throat.

"I don't think it's any secret that I've been opposed to this wedding."

"Amen," the best man shouted.

Sarah shushed him and he quieted.

"Growing up, Jen was my best friend. I love her and as her big sister it is my job to protect her. I let her down once and I will never let her down again. I'll probably be protecting you when we're eighty and eighty-two, Jen."

Her sister smiled. "I love you too, Kate."

"Mark and I had a long talk this afternoon." She looked at him and he glanced away. She saw him tug at his shirt collar. Good, he was nervous. Too bad she had no idea what she was going to say next.

Eighteen

Jen's eyes filled with tears. Indecision ripped at Kate. Were the tears because she thought Kate had finally accepted Mark or were they because she knew that something was about to be revealed? Kate took a deep breath.

"Hang in there," Sarah said quietly. The words gave her strength.

"I believe that Mark should be the one to share the topic of that conversation with my sister."

Jen leaned over and said, "What did you talk about, Mark?"

Mark shook his head, his gaze locked with Kate's. It was a battle of wills and Kate truly didn't feel capable of winning this round. Mark would probably not tell Jen what they'd discussed and more than likely they'd get married anyway tomorrow. It was too late. There was nothing more she could do.

"Jen, I love you. And because I love you, I'm going to just shut up and I'm going to try very hard to let you make your own decisions."

Jen nodded and then whispered something else to Mark.

"Kate?" Sarah looked shocked. Kate knew it wasn't like her to back down but she felt torn in so many different directions.

"I'm fine, Sarah. I just don't have any fight left in me."

"That isn't the Kate I know. You're just tired."

Kate shrugged. "Maybe." Tired of hitting brick walls everywhere she turned.

Becca stood. "Jen, we love you. You are an honorary diary girl—you know what I mean—and you're welcome to join us any time that you need a break from your rowdy new husband."

Jen laughed and saluted Becca. Kate choked down one bite of salad. She was worried about Ian, who lay in pain all alone in that hospital room. What if he was hurting and couldn't get to the button to tell the nurse? What if he needed something? She needed to leave and get back to the hospital.

On top of that, Mark had won. But it wasn't Kate who had lost. She looked toward the main table where her sister giggled at something Mark said as he kissed her on the forehead. No, the real loser was Jen.

Kate couldn't sit still and watch Jen and Mark smooch one more time. She laid her fork down and threw her napkin on the table. "I'm going to the ladies' room. I'll be back."

"Are you okay?" Sarah set her own fork down. "Want us to go with you?"

"No. I just need to get away for a minute. I want to freshen up and then I'm going back to visit Ian, if they'll let me." Kate couldn't believe it but she was about ready to cry again. She rarely cried but all of a sudden she was just a big ball of sobs. She had to get it under control.

The ladies' room was located in the back right corner of the restaurant. It was a single room with four stalls. People already occupied two of the stalls, so she chose the one closest to the back wall. The lock slid quietly into place.

Luckily, the stalls were the kind that set each section off into a separate room. She didn't even have to look at the feet of the other women in the bathroom. She could just stand silently and try to compose herself before she had to go back out and face the firing squad. She took slow, deep breaths.

"Can you believe it? I was so shocked when I found out." A woman's voice carried through the door and Kate recognized it as one of the bridesmaids who'd toasted Jen and Mark.

"Are you sure she's pregnant?" another woman asked.

Kate stopped breathing. Who was pregnant?

"Yes. I always knew Mark was a stud but getting married while knocking someone up all in a matter of a couple of months—I'm impressed."

The women giggled, their footsteps trailing away and the door clicking closed behind them. Kate sat down on the toilet seat. Mark had gotten someone pregnant—probably Eloise. The woman had been telling the truth. How was that for proof? Oh, Jen. What a mess. She'd just promised her sister to stay out of things. But this was worse than even she'd thought. Not only would Jen's life be affected but so would the unborn child's. How could Mark marry Jen and not even tell her about this?

Well, it didn't matter what she'd promised—she wasn't going to just shut up and let her sister make such a huge mistake without speaking up. She left the stall, and bumped into Jen.

"You heard them?" Jen asked.

Maybe she should just walk away. Let Jen make her own mistakes. But she couldn't. "What are you going to do now, Jen?"

"Do? Marry Mark of course. I love him."

Kate couldn't believe love was *this* blind. "Another woman is carrying his child!"

Jen laughed. "Don't be ridiculous—"

She stopped talking as the back stall of the bathroom squeaked slowly open. Kate frowned. She'd thought both women had left already. She saw Jen's blue eyes widen with alarm and glanced over her shoulder. Billy James stood two steps behind her—holding a gun.

"A rose by any other name would still be Jen," he said. He waved the gun toward Kate's head. She stepped in front of her sister.

"I'll shoot you, Kate."

"No, Billy. Don't do that." Jen pushed Kate to the side. "I'll go with you. I've been waiting for you."

Suddenly Mark and their petty arguments seemed very juvenile. Everything clicked into place—the strange feeling of being watched, the shadow in the church—Billy James had been stalking her sister again. Only this time, she didn't think he'd give Jen a chance to get away. If he still planned to commit a murder/suicide, he'd be successful. She couldn't let him leave this room with her sister.

She stepped back in front of Jen. "Leave her alone, Billy."

"Shut up, Kate. What are you doing? He'll kill you." Jen tried to move back in front of her again but Kate braced herself.

"No, he'll kill you. That's been his goal all along."

"I've waited. I've bided my time. Our families have kept us apart, my love. But if we cannot be together in life, then let us be together in death."

"He loves Shakespeare," Jen whispered. "Remember that."

"Jen?" Three quick pounds hit the outside of the ladies' room door. Mark's voice was muffled through the thickness but Kate had never been so happy to hear anything. He was an amateur bad boy compared to Billy.

"Who is that?" Billy demanded.

"Are you that demented?" Kate asked loudly, hoping Mark would hear her. "She's getting married tomorrow, you freak."

Billy threw his hands over his ears, still holding the gun but obviously in less control than he'd been a moment ago. "Make her stop, Jen. I'm not a *freak!* Don't call me that."

Kate blinked. Obviously she'd touched a sore spot. She wasn't sure if that was good or bad but her goal at the moment was to save Jen. Her mind raced with a million possibilities. If he didn't have a gun, she'd rush him and tell Jen to run for it, but with a gun anything could happen and none of it good.

"Billy, it's okay. I've been waiting for you." Jen's voice seemed to soothe Billy. He lowered his hands. "We'll run away together. We can go to Vegas and get married."

He shook his head. "No. It's too late for that. There are too many people against us; out to capture us; the only way out is through the veil that separates the living and the dead."

Dammit, Mark. Couldn't he tell things weren't okay in here? What was he doing? If he cared for her sister at all, he'd charge in here and rescue Jen from this madman.

"Put the gun down, Billy," she shouted.

"Stop yelling." Billy raised the gun and pointed it at Kate's chest. "Do you think I don't know what you're doing? I'm crazy. I'm not stupid. Not stupid!"

Kate glared at him. When he was enraged, would his aim be off? Maybe if she made him angry enough—she opened her mouth but Jen interrupted.

"She's sorry, Billy. She's just jealous because she knows I'll have an eternal love and she won't."

"Jealous." Billy nodded and lowered the gun.

She glanced at the window above Billy's head, realizing he'd probably come in through the high, narrow opening and hid in the stall just waiting for an opportunity to try to snatch Jen. There could be no doubt that his intent was to murder her sister. He'd said one too many things about dying and living eternally. She couldn't allow that to happen. If she had to, she'd give up her own life to save Jen's but she'd rather figure out a way to get them both out of this mess. But it was her job to protect her sister, and she would make the ultimate sacrifice when the time arrived.

The window already stood wide open, but she barely kept from showing her shock when Mark's head appeared in the opening. He took stock of the situation and then pulled back abruptly. Billy glanced over his shoulder.

"What are you looking at?" he demanded.

"Is that how you came in?" Kate quickly covered her blunder. "You'll have to take Jen out that way too. It's too risky to go through the restaurant."

"She's right." Apparently, Jen had seen Mark's brief appearance in the window as well. If they could talk Billy into crawling back through that window, he'd be a sitting duck as his head came out and his body hung into the room.

A plan began to form in Kate's mind. "Maybe you should go first and make sure that the coast is clear and then Jen can follow. I'll cover for you two lovebirds here."

Billy frowned. "You wouldn't help me. You hate me."

"Not as much as she hates Mark." Jen squeezed Kate's hand.

"That's right. Everyone in town knows how much I hate him. Ask anyone."

Her single-minded pursuit of stopping this wedding might have finally paid off. Kate waited for Billy's reaction. If he'd been spying on them, then he had to know that she didn't like Mark. It wasn't a secret.

"You do hate him, all right." Billy smirked.

Kate wondered how much of this Mark could hear outside the window. If he could understand what their plan entailed, then they could pull off capturing Billy and saving Jen from his intentions.

"So, you and Jen go and be happy forever. I'll know you are two bright stars shining down on me. I'll wait in here as long as I can and stall Mark."

"And I'll go first to make sure the coast is clear."

Kate didn't raise her voice this time, not wanting to tip Billy off to their plan. "You go first," she said in her regular voice.

She hoped to God that Mark could hear her. She and Jen glanced at one another as Billy started for the stall he'd hidden in.

"Here, we'll give you a boost," Jen offered. "Then Kate can help me."

Billy hoisted himself up to the open window and poked his head out. The loud shout of several men sounded outside and they saw Billy raise his right arm.

Kate nodded at Jen and they each grabbed a foot. "Now!"

They gave his legs a mighty shove and hurled him through the window, into the waiting arms of the Greenfield Police Department.

"Thank God everyone is okay." Her mother patted her heart. "I don't think I can take anymore excitement today."

Kate pulled Jen off to the side of the room. "Jen, honey, are you okay with this other woman carrying Mark's child? Are you sure you want this wedding tomorrow?"

"I know all about the woman Mark got pregnant, Kate." Jen's face was three different shades of red.

"Y-you do?" Kate's words tumbled over one another. "And you're marrying him anyway."

"I'm the woman he got pregnant."

Kate felt as though someone had grabbed her ankles and yanked her down onto the floor. Jen was pregnant? She took a step away as though she could escape the news. It wasn't true. It couldn't be true.

"Are you the only one who is pregnant?" Kate asked.

"I can't believe you'd actually ask that," Mark said, coming up behind them. "I think you'd better leave, Kate. Jen and I will be married tomorrow and there's not a thing you or anyone else can do to stop that."

Sarah and Becca came to her side, handed her a purse, and ushered her out the front door. Confusion fogged her brain. Everything she'd thought was right seemed somehow upside down. What was truth and what was assumption? This had been one hell of a day.

The ritual of writing in the diary was a balm to Kate's bruised heart. She scratched her entry across the page with quick strokes, dotting her I's and crossing her T's with more finesse than was necessary. Rebecca's bedroom was exactly as it had been when they were children. A simple wood dresser painted a bright white matched the twin bed in the northeast corner of the room. Becca's mom had painted tiny yellow daisies across the drawers with a green vine wrapping throughout. A large daisy rested on the headboard.

She knew that Becca often felt ashamed of her simple up-bringing, but the hours of love that her mother had put into decorating this room seemed to Kate to be worth more than money. The quilt thrown over the bed was made from scraps of old clothing that Becca had worn as a small child, but the panels with the bright yellow, embroidered daisies were from material Becca's mom had saved pennies for until she could afford to buy a yard of pale pink, her daughter's favorite color. Kate had gone with Becca's mother the day she'd bought the material and the woman's pride at being able to give her daughter something special had shone on her face. She remembered thinking that Becca might not have a father but was very lucky to have such a wonderful mother.

She swallowed. If she'd shown her own sister a smidgeon of the support and love that Becca's mother had shown on that day in the fabric store, then she wouldn't be in the mess she was in right now. If she'd shown Ian any love or support, he wouldn't have refused to see her twenty minutes ago.

When Kate was finished she set the diary in her lap but didn't kiss the page. "I really blew it with my sister, didn't I?"

"How were you supposed to know? I blame myself." Sarah reached over and grabbed Kate's tube of lipstick. She took the cap off and twisted it up so the purple color peaked over the edge of the sleeve. She handed the lipstick to Kate.

Kate held the makeup but didn't attempt to put it on. "Why would you blame yourself? I'm the big mouth who screwed up."

"Because I told you about the letter and about Eloise. If you hadn't known about that, then you wouldn't have assumed someone besides Jen was prego."

"Let's just say we've all made mistakes this past week." Rebecca's lips turned down at the corners.

"What mistakes did you make?" Sarah asked.

"I was so involved with Jared that I deserted my best friends. I kept secrets instead of telling you guys I dated Mark two years ago. I feel terrible. I let Kate down."

"Oh, stop it." Kate finally put the lipstick on but it wasn't with her usual excitement at the ritual. "You are both wonderful friends. But sometimes we are going to have other things going on in our lives."

"But we agreed to always be there for each other."

Rebecca took the journal Kate had just kissed but didn't write in it just yet.

"We are there for each other. You guys are here tonight and I probably need you more than I ever have."

"Can you believe he disinvited you to the wedding?" Sarah said. Fury glittered in her lovely green eyes. "Well, *I* wasn't disinvited. I'll just bring you as a guest."

"No. I'm not going." Jen didn't want her there. She hadn't protested when Mark had asked her not to attend. She wouldn't do anything else to hurt her sister. She'd done enough damage to last a lifetime. In fact, she doubted she'd even be welcome on holidays.

"Then we'll stay with you." Rebecca picked up the ink pen. "Okay, I have a few things to write."

She jotted several sentences. Kate closed her eyes and listened to the sound of her childhood friend scribbling in their journal. She'd known that by trying to point out Mark's flaws she risked losing everything. Especially after seeing Jen and Mark in his office and the strength of her sister's love for the man, she should have known that nothing she could say would have an impact. Almost losing her sister to Billy a second time had made her realize how petty and insignificant her protests about Mark really were. But before she'd had a chance to explore her newfound outlook, she'd opened her big mouth and stuck her size eight right back in there.

"I'm going to call the hospital and check on Ian while you finish writing," Kate said as Becca handed Sarah the journal.

She moved to the bedside table and dialed the hospital. The nurse was the same one who'd suggested she pose as Ian's fiancée earlier in the evening.

"He's resting comfortably, honey."

"Did he—" she twisted the phone cord. "Did he ask for anyone?"

"He's sedated from the pain killers. He'll probably sleep right through until morning."

In other words, he hadn't asked for her. She sighed. At least he was okay. "Thank you," she said and hung up the phone.

"Is he okay?" Sarah placed the journal in the center of their circle.

Kate settled back onto the floor. "Resting comfortably."

"He didn't ask for you though?" Becca sighed. "I'm sorry, Kate. Men can be so stubborn."

Kate nodded but knew that just like with her sister, Ian being angry with her was entirely her fault. Why did she have such a penchant for screwing up her life? She picked up the journal. "Want to read them out loud this week?"

"Let's." Sarah snatched it from her hands. "Me first."

"Okay." Kate laughed.

"Dear Lipstick Diary." She paused and cleared her throat. "This week I ran into my old school nemesis Eloise Dillon."

Sarah had a flair for the dramatic. Kate had often felt she should have tried acting.

"I can remember thinking Eloise was bigger than life," she read. "I was terrified of her. But she's just a very bitter woman. The three of us shot her down in two minutes flat. It was very freeing." Sarah marked the page with the satin ribbon and passed it to Becca.

"I'm so glad you finally feel like you're out from under that cloud, Sarah. You never deserved how they treated you."

"I know. Thanks to you and Becca I always knew that. But it still hurt. It doesn't hurt so much anymore."

"I wish I could get out from under the Eloise cloud. I feel like she hurt me as a teen and now she's going to hurt Jen even more." Kate frowned. And there wasn't a thing she could do about it, so she might as well not be a party pooper. "Becca's turn."

"Dear Lipstick Diary," Becca began. "This week, for the first in twenty-one years, I let my best friends down. It didn't end well."

Becca already had a near miss with a miscarriage. The past week should have never happened anyway. She'd made enough errors in judgment to last a lifetime. And while she was still a little irked at Becca's deception over dating Mark, it wasn't worth causing anymore stress to her friend.

"Don't feel bad, Becca. It wouldn't have mattered anyway. Jen is pregnant. In her mind, that means that she has to marry Mark."

"In this day and age?" Becca snorted, but Kate knew she'd struggled with this issue herself. She also knew how relieved Becca was that Jared wanted to be a part of the baby's life.

"Remember what a small town this is. Traditions are important here. Jen wants to be married. Nothing will change her mind."

"You're right. Thanks, Kate. I feel better."

"Your turn, Kate." Sarah passed the journal to her.

Kate cleared her throat. She'd written two lines. "I wish I knew how to keep my mouth shut. I wish Ian and Jen would both forgive me."

"They will, Kate." Sarah jumped to her feet. "Give it time. This party has grown way too serious. You know what we need?"

Kate laughed as her friend pushed a button on the CD player and Aretha Franklin crooned a song about respect. "What do we need, Sarah?"

"We need to dance." She pulled Kate and Becca to their feet. "C'mon girls. We need some R-E-S-P-E-C-T."

Kate and Becca joined Sarah in romping around the room. The vibrations of the music sang through Kate's body as she gave herself over to the moment, forgetting for a second all her troubles and just having fun with her two friends. This was really what the Friday night diary dates were all about—being with two people who understood her and who knew how to have fun.

But even as she laughed, she worried deep inside over what tomorrow would bring.

Nineteen

The sun came up early and shone through the sheer curtains over the window, landing on Kate's face. She groaned and tried to pull the covers over her head but it was pointless. She and Sarah had decided to leave Becca's at about two in the morning so they could all get a good night's sleep.

She glanced at the bedside clock, which read seven A.M. "Too early." She went ahead and swung her legs out of bed and threw on a robe. She'd have to hunt down some coffee and try to wake up.

Her mother was already in the kitchen and the smell of freshly brewed coffee drew Kate to her side. She whizzed around the room at a pace Kate hadn't seen many twenty-year-olds keep up with.

"There's so much to do today." Her mother mumbled the words to herself and then realized Kate was in the room. She smiled at her eldest child. "Good morning, darling."

"Is it?" She'd just remembered what today was. Jen's wedding. All the excitement and hustle and bustle of a wedding had already started and she wasn't going to be a part of it.

"Jen thinks it is." Her mother patted her hand. "Honey, sometimes you have to just admit that you're wrong and move on."

"Wrong?" Kate sipped the coffee. It scalded her tongue, numbing her taste buds. "I'm not wrong."

"I think you are. Matt was wrong about your daddy. You are wrong about Mark."

"Eloise Dillon-Jones said—"

"Oh, and she is such a reliable source after all. I never did understand that girl, but she gets some kind of kick out of trying to make other women feel bad. I don't think you can trust her word."

Kate set her coffee down. Her mother was right. Why did she automatically believe Eloise over Mark? Eloise wasn't trustworthy. She never had been. Not that Mark was trustworthy either. She'd been up for fifteen minutes and already her head pounded from the many thoughts tumbling around. She did know that she and Jen were both still alive and well today thanks in large part to Mark Jackson. Perhaps it was time to finally admit defeat and try to make amends.

"So you think I should apologize to Jen?" She owed her sister an apology and then she needed to head home. It could take weeks to track down another job, because she was pretty sure that Ian didn't want to ever see her again.

"No." Betty pulled out a small cake topper couple in tux and wedding gown, both with dark hair. "I think you should apologize to Mark."

"To Mark?" No way. Okay, well she needed to really, but the thought brought a bitter taste to her lips. It should be easy to admit her mistakes but it wasn't.

"Do you want to go to the wedding, Kate?"

"Of course." But she'd been disinvited. Would an apology really change anything?

"Then apologize to Mark."

Kate sighed. She hated it when there was something she didn't want to do and her mother was so right. Didn't her mom realize how hard it would be to apologize to that man?

"Be the bigger person, honey."

"Okay. Where do I find him?"

"He's in the garage with Daddy. Stopped by about thirty minutes ago to chat with us about the situation with you. Seems Jen is pretty upset you aren't going to be at the wedding."

"She is?" Today was Jen's day. She'd done so much to hurt her sister in the last week—really if Jen had done half of what she'd done and it was her wedding, she'd be furious. She was going to make it up to her sister. She would bite her tongue, grit her teeth, apologize to Mark, and beg if need be to attend the wedding. At least he wasn't Billy. "I'll go talk to him."

"Just be polite," her mother said as she headed toward the garage.

"Katie." Her father motioned her over. "I was just chatting with Mark about your Uncle Matt."

Great. Now she was Uncle Matt. That wasn't exactly flattering, but she supposed she deserved the analogy. "Daddy, I need to talk to Mark."

Her father looked uncertain for a moment but Mark nodded so he wiped his hands on a rag and headed for the kitchen. "I'd better go wash my hands or your mother'll have a fit."

"Mark—"

"Kate—"

They both stopped. Okay, apparently they both had a lot to say.

"You first," she said.

"Look, I know you don't think much of me but I do love Jen. She's upset about last night. She wants you at the wedding."

"I'd like to be there."

"She said you put yourself between her and the gun." His

eyes glistened with something that looked similar to tears. "Thank you for that."

"She's my baby sister." What was the big deal? Any big sister would do the same to protect her younger sibling. It was part of the job.

"You're welcome at the wedding. But I want your blessing before you come." Mark's words were like a dash of cold water.

"Blessing?" She could apologize. She could even grovel but she wasn't sure she could grant her blessing just yet. Couldn't they take baby steps into this new in-law relationship they were trying to form?

Could she give him her blessing? In her heart, she still believed that he probably had an affair with someone. She was certain he would cheat on Jen. Maybe not right away, but eventually. Under those circumstances could she give him her blessing? If she wanted to go to the wedding, she'd have to.

"I—" She took another deep breath. "I—" God, she couldn't do it. Something truly horrible was wrong with her.

Mark shook his head. "You can't do it, can you? If you had a way to stop the wedding you still would."

"I'm sorry." She was sorry. After everything, she couldn't say she blessed a union when she believed he'd already cheated on her sister. Jen wanted her at the wedding and given the opportunity to go, she couldn't even say the words. Simple little words. That's all they were.

"Me too." Mark sighed. "Look, I came over here to try to work things out for Jen's sake. You can come to the wedding. Just don't stir up any trouble and ruin this day for Jen, okay?"

Kate nodded. "Of course I wouldn't."

"Right." Mark walked out of the garage and Kate was left feeling as though she'd been given a reprieve.

She'd go to Jen's wedding. She'd plaster a smile on her face. Then she'd get plastered herself at the reception. That should make the whole event easier to bear. And she'd try to remember how lucky she was that they were all alive and not worry about what tomorrow might bring.

Sharing a room with her sister had meant that she'd had to stare at Jen's wedding dress for the last few days. Luckily, it had been encased in a plastic hang bag and she had been able to partially ignore it. Now, the plastic had come off so the dress could be steamed and it mocked her in all its frilly glory.

What had she actually conceded by telling Mark she was sorry? Her sister's future happiness? She groaned. *Stop it, Kate. You have to let it go.* The image of Billy pointing the silver barrel of the revolver at her sister's head clouded her vision. The alternatives were much worse and she needed to keep reminding herself of that fact.

Jen waltzed into the room, her eyes were puffy and red. Had she been crying? She stared at Kate, but didn't say anything.

"Jen, I'm sorry." What else could she say? She was sorry she'd caused her sister any pain. She was even sorrier she'd asked such a stupid question last night. Her emotions weren't exactly in the best shape and she'd just said the first thing that came to mind.

"Did you talk to Mark?" Jen asked. Her voice was hoarse and Kate wondered if it was from a crying jag.

"Yes. He said I could come to the wedding if I behaved." She tried to keep her voice neutral but some of her resentment must have leaked out because Jen frowned.

"Will you behave, Kate? Or are you going to make more accusations?" Jen patted her stomach and it hit Kate that she was going to be an aunt. Did she really want her niece or nephew to grow up without a father? Even if the father was Mark? Or even worse, did she want her niece or nephew to grow up without an aunt?

"I'll behave. I won't say a word."

Jen moved closer until they were toe to toe. "I love you, Kate. And I know just how much you love me after you stepped in between me and that gun, but I won't let you ruin my wedding. I don't want to see a grimace. I don't want to see a frown. I don't want for even a second to think you are plotting anything."

"I won't, Jen. I promise." It wouldn't do any good anyway. Jen was determined to marry Mark despite any evidence or rumors. She'd be best served to keep her sisterly concerns to herself.

"Okay, I'm glad." She hugged Kate and gave a girlish giggle. "I'm so happy you're going to be there. You have to help me get ready."

Kate tried to force a smile but it was difficult. Yes, she'd help Jen get ready and she'd pretend to be happy about it but inside she felt like she was preparing her sister for an execution.

"I'll help you, but first I have to stop by Hancock Memorial and check on Ian. Maybe he'll see me today."

"Meet me at the church at ten?"

"I'll be there with bells on." They would be hell's bells, but she'd be there.

Because she was headed to the church from the hospital, Kate went ahead and dressed in her outfit for the ceremony. The pink dress matched the wedding party colors but was a sleek number with a straight skirt and fitted top with buttons down the center. Silk trim skirted the hem of the outfit and the collar and sleeves.

Her shoes click-clacked on the slick tiles leading to Ian's room. They'd installed him in a regular room. She'd been pleased to discover he was no longer in emergency. She tapped on the door once before entering.

"Ian?"

He sat on the edge of the bed, trying to put on a T-shirt. His face was almost gray from the effort and a thin bead of perspiration sat just above his lips.

Kate rushed to his side. "Let me help."

He didn't protest as she slipped the neck of the shirt over his head and let him ease his arms into the holes.

"Ribs hurt like hell."

"Did they give you anything for the pain?" she asked. At least he was speaking to her. Maybe that was a good sign.

"I hate those pills. They make me groggy." He pulled the shirt down slowly over his bandaged midsection.

"How long until the ribs are better?"

"About a month. I'm being released today though."

"A month! How are you going to work, Ian? You'll need someone to fill in for you." *Please let him suggest me. I could help him to make up for what I did.* She waited but he didn't say a word.

Kate shifted uncomfortably from foot to foot. There had been a time when she'd felt at ease around Ian. But like so many other things in the past week, she'd destroyed that trust.

"Ian—" She stopped. What could she say? She'd already apologized. There weren't words to make up for what she'd done. She bit her lip, unsure of where to go next. How did you tell a man you loved him after what she'd done?

"It's okay, Kate. No hard feelings. I'm flying back to New Orleans. My car is totaled. The towing company described it as a small black metal box with jagged edges."

Kate winced. What if Ian had been killed? She'd never have forgiven herself. Thank God he was okay but he was just as out of her reach as if he'd been dead. She should confess her feelings to him. Let him know how much she really loved him. It had taken almost losing him to an accident for her to realize the depth of her emotions, but she was crazy about him.

Something held her back. She was terrified of being rejected. What if she poured her heart and soul out to him and he rejected her? She shook her head. Unsure of what to do or say, she just stood there.

Ian's smile barely tilted his lips. "Thanks for coming by, Kate. It looks like you have a wedding to attend."

She glanced down at her clothes and then at the clock on the wall. It was already ten o'clock and she'd promised Jen that she would be at the church at ten. She couldn't afford to disappoint her sister. At the same time, she couldn't afford to lose Ian.

"I do have to go," she admitted. "Can I call you when I get home?"

There, she'd put herself out there. She'd taken a risk and suggested she call him.

"Your job is available if you want it. You don't need to phone."

She wasn't talking about the job! She was talking about the relationship. He turned away and stared out the small side window that looked out over a black tar roof. Since it wasn't possible for him to be interested in the view, she assumed it was a way to escape dealing with her.

"I was hoping we could talk about us." Her voice didn't even sound familiar to her, it was so pathetic and whiny. Well, she wasn't a whiner. If he didn't accept this offer, she'd give him more time to cool down and worry about how she was going to win his heart back later.

"There isn't an us," Ian said.

And there it was. Fine. She'd put her heart on the line. Yes, she'd made a mistake but if he couldn't accept her apology and forgive her mistake then there wasn't any hope for them. She jangled her keys in preparation of leaving.

"Take care of yourself, Ian."

She didn't wait for his reply but walked quickly down the hall until she was almost running. She just made it to her car before the tears fell.

Hadn't she heard him? His car was nothing but twisted metal and busted glass. He could easily have been killed and she didn't even respond? The very fact that she didn't say anything spoke loudly about her true feelings. She didn't even care enough about him to be concerned.

"Thanks for coming by, Kate. It looks like you have a wedding to attend."

When she'd walked through the door in that tight pink number, it had been all he could to remember how to swallow. If his ribs didn't hurt so badly, he'd probably yank her down on the bed and kiss her breathless. But what was the point? If she didn't care for him by now, he couldn't make her care for him. He saw her glance at the clock over the doorway. Apparently, she'd already wasted more time here than she really wanted.

"I do have to go," she said. "Can I call you when I get home?"

Her words landed on his heart with swift kicks. It was apparent that she was worried about her job. Otherwise, why would she wait until she got home to call? Well, he would make it very clear to her that their relationship wouldn't affect her job.

"Your job is available if you want it. You don't need to phone."

Ian turned toward the window to hide the emotions trying to escape. The blackness of the ugly tar roof just outside his window matched his mood perfectly. Kate cleared her throat.

"I was hoping we could talk about us," she said.

Her words were soft and her voice sounded unfamiliar. Obviously she was just saying something, anything, to escape the hospital room but not jeopardize her job. He closed his eyes, trying to tamp down the pain. No matter how much he loved her, he wouldn't be played for a fool. After the way that Angela pretended to care, all the while having an affair behind his back with his best friend, he'd sworn he would never again put his heart on the line for someone who didn't love him back. Already, he'd risked more than he should have and Kate hadn't even bothered to meet him halfway. He took a deep breath and decided to let her know that he was well aware that she didn't love him.

"There isn't an us," he said.

The silence stretched into long moments. With each tick of the second hand, his heart closed off a little more. He noticed that she didn't even attempt to deny that their relationship was going nowhere. He heard her keys jangle and realized she was anxious to leave. He felt his lips tilt up but it wasn't a real smile. She couldn't wait to escape him.

"Take care of yourself, Ian."

He turned to watch her leave—she almost ran out of the room and her steps clacked rapidly down the hall. It took everything in him not to run after her, beg her to come back, and give him just one more chance to win her love.

He lifted his hands and covered his face. He'd chased after Angela when she'd left—had followed her car and pulled into the driveway behind her. A split second later, he'd realized that the driveway belonged to his childhood friend Brian. Even in the face of such damning evidence, he'd begged Angela to reconsider. To give their marriage another chance.

"You aren't what I want, Ian," she'd said.

"I can *be* what you want." Even as he'd said the words to Angela, something inside of Ian had cried out. True love shouldn't try to change who you were, should it? It should make you a better version of yourself.

He could hardly accuse Angela of ever making him a better version of himself. With Kate, he'd thought he'd finally found that but her betrayal when she'd tried to test him cut deep enough to reopen the old wounds that Angela inflicted originally.

To be fair, Kate had apologized. She'd also never come out and said she didn't care for him. He stood abruptly, forgetting about his ribs until they screamed a protest. He stopped and tried to catch his breath, holding onto his side. Was he letting his past get in the way of his future? Did Kate actually care more for him than he'd thought? Anyone could make a mistake and he could forgive her for being desperate to save her sister. He glanced at the clock. If he could get the doctor to release him, he could just about make it in time for the ceremony. Forget that, he was going—whether the doctor released him or not.

He'd come to town to romance Kate into choosing him over another man, but winning her heart went deeper than keeping her from falling in love with that goofy cowboy she'd been dating. In fact, he was going to just forget about the cowboy and pretend he didn't even know she'd dated the man. This was about their relationship. Hopefully, once they returned to New Orleans, she'd stop seeing the cowboy and focus on him. At least she hadn't gone to the wedding with anyone else. When a woman showed up at a family event of that magnitude with another man on her arm, it was a sure sign that she was in love. That would have crushed his heart into pieces that couldn't be glued back together.

Her heart pounded with fear for her sister mixed with sadness over Ian. Kate helped Jen pin her veil into place and then stepped back. Blushing bride didn't begin to describe the glow that covered Jennifer's face. Her eyes shone with a strength and maturity Kate couldn't remember ever seeing in her sister's gaze.

"You look beautiful," she told Jen.

Jen's eyes grew moist. Betty rushed to her side.

"Stop that. You'll mess up your makeup. This is no time for tears." Their mother adjusted the billowy white dress and fussed over Jen's veil for another five minutes.

A friend of Jen's poked her head in the doorway. "Ten minutes, ladies."

Kate saw Jen take a long, deep breath. The tension in the room was high and she hoped for a moment that Jen would get scared and back out of the wedding. Instead, she saw her sister take another long look in the mirror while a calmness settled over her face. Her eyes still held fear, however.

"I'd better go find my seat." And give Jen and her mother some alone time before the wedding.

"Wish me luck," Jen said.

"Good luck." Married to Mark, she was going to need it, but somehow after the turmoil of Billy trying to kidnap Jen again, she couldn't bring herself to be as upset as she probably should have been.

Not wanting to sit and think about the pending moment when her sister would say "I do," Kate went ahead and took the long way around the loop that circled the sanctuary and made up the classrooms normally used for Sunday school.

About halfway around, she stopped abruptly. Mark stood just outside a small room, rocking back and forth nervously on his heels.

"Mark." She nodded to him and started to walk past but he reached out and touched her arm.

"Wait. Is Jen okay?" His black tuxedo fit him perfectly and Kate could see why Jen would be physically attracted to the man.

"She's fine."

"Good." His eyes darted nervously down the hallway.

"Is something going on, Mark?" Mark was acting stranger than normal.

He shook his head no, so Kate shrugged and started back down the hallway.

"Wait!" Mark called.

"What is it?" She was trying, so help her, but chit-chatting with Mark wasn't her idea of keeping her cool and not screaming at the top of her lungs when the minister asked if anyone had just cause.

"I never cheated on you, Kate. And I won't cheat on Jen."

"I saw you with Eloise, remember?"

"Two minutes before you arrived she literally threw herself on me and kissed me."

"What about now? She claims that you slept with her last week."

"Are you serious?" he said. God help her but she believed him. "Ask Jerry. He's her brother."

Kate thought she might. Jerry had never lied to her. It was true that he'd gone along with Mark's sabotage, but ultimately he had told her the truth.

"He's here?"

"Saw him come in."

Kate looked him over. "You look nice. Good luck."

What if it had all been a huge mistake? What if Mark was actually a pretty decent guy and she'd just pulled an Uncle Matt and given him a hard way to go? Would he ever be able to forgive her? Would Jen? She sprinted down the hall and into the sanctuary. Her speed drew a few stares, so she slowed down, her eyes searching for Jerry.

He sat near the front of the church, so she made her way toward him and slid into the pew. He'd traded in his typical blue jeans and boots for black denim and boots. She grinned. He looked quite handsome in his thin tie. "Hey, Jerry."

"Kate. Wasn't sure if you'd be attending." He shouldn't have sounded southern, since Indiana was in the Midwest, but his drawl was soft and slow. She supposed it was the cowboy in him.

"I have a quick question for you, Jerry." Possibly one of the most important questions she'd ever asked.

"Shoot."

"You're Eloise's brother. Do you think she and Mark are together?"

"You're kidding, right, Kate? Mark can't stand my sister. Hell, I can't stand her myself half the time. No, he isn't seeing Eloise. Never has and never will."

Kate sat back against the hard wooden pew. Mark hadn't cheated. Wouldn't cheat, at least not with Eloise. Everything she'd thought had just been turned upside down and sideways. She glanced over her shoulder, wishing she had time to let Jen know that she did give her blessing for this wedding.

Instead, she saw Ian walk slowly into the doorway. She met his gaze just as he saw Jerry. His lips tightened and he turned and walked back out the door. *Crap!*

"Excuse me." She slipped out of the pew and rushed back down the aisle, drawing even more stares and not caring. "Ian, wait."

He wasn't in good enough shape to move very fast, so she caught up to him easily. He stopped and turned to her. "I shouldn't have come. It was a mistake."

"No, it wasn't."

"Yes, it was." He took a deep breath. "We'll talk later, Kate. Your sister is almost ready to walk down the aisle. You don't want to miss that."

Kate turned toward the doorway leading to the sanctuary just as the first bridesmaid started down the aisle. The music wafted softly out into the hallway. Her father and Jen stood off the side—Daddy looking nervous and Jen looking scared.

She didn't want to miss the wedding, particularly now that she knew Mark hadn't cheated on Jen, but she didn't want to lose Ian either. Once again, she was being pulled in two directions. Her choice would affect the rest of her life either way.

"Come sit down," she begged.

"No. I should go." He lifted his hand and brushed his fingers across her cheek. "Take care, Kate."

She watched him walk out the door, her heart busting into a million pieces and several skipping behind him. The doors to the sanctuary were closed as Jen and her father moved in front of them, preparing to enter. Kate glanced around in panic. There had to be another way into the sanctuary.

"Jen will never forgive me if I miss this," she muttered. She sprinted past a harassed looking janitor and raced around the circular hallway that surrounded the sanctuary. Mark and his groomsmen had entered through a side door. She just had to find it.

She began opening the doors that weren't locked, searching for the secret opening into the sanctuary. On the third door she broke a nail. Racing to the next door, the heel of her shoe broke. By the time she had completed the circle, she felt winded and ragged and her father and Jen were gone, the final notes of *The Wedding March* straining out of the organ.

Taking a deep breath, she slid in through the now open doors and took a seat in the back of the church to avoid notice. Maybe Jen wouldn't even realize she'd ever left. But her sister was searching the pews and her eyes met Kate's even across the distance of the church. It was a good thing she'd made it. Jen was looking for her.

Twenty

Kate smiled at her sister and gave her a thumbs up. *I wish you only happiness, baby sister.* Jen turned back to Mark and the preacher began with the familiar words that had been uttered throughout the ages.

"Dearly beloved . . ."

Kate watched the joy evident on her sister's face and felt ashamed of her attempts to stop the wedding. She'd told herself she had Jen's best interests at heart but part of her obsession had indeed been because of Mark's betrayal of her. She hadn't believed someone could change, but through it all she herself had changed. She'd just learned a very important lesson in giving people the benefit of the doubt.

When the minister pronounced them man and wife and Mark swept Jen into his arms and kissed her, Kate jumped to her feet and cheered. Even after yesterday, if someone had told her she'd be this happy to see her sister married, she would have thought they'd lost their mind.

Mark set Jen back on her feet. "I present you with Mr. and Mrs. Mark Jackson. The reception will be held at the Country Club. See you all there."

Jen and Mark ran down the aisle, wide smiles on both their faces. Kate followed the rest of the guests out front where they took the bird seed packets her mother had made and wished Mark and Jen on their way. The black limo pulled out

257

with a trail of cars following it—all honking their horns and flashing their lights. She'd have a chance to see the newlyweds at the wedding reception and she intended to try to make amends and make peace with Mark.

Kate arrived at the wedding reception with every intention of speaking to Mark in the receiving line. She stopped outside the front entrance, unsure of which words to use to make things right. Were there any? She practiced what she might say.

"I was wrong. I'm glad you married Jen," she said and then shook her head. No.

"I'm sorry. You're right. You're perfect for each other." No, that wasn't it either.

"I wish you both only the best." Nope.

"Welcome to the family." She snapped her fingers. That was it. Four simple words that said it all. He'd know she was accepting him and that she was sorry.

As she entered the banquet hall, she realized her delay while she'd been planning out her greeting had caused her to miss the receiving line. Jen and Mark were already seated at the long table at the front of the room. She'd have to speak to them both later.

She hesitated for a moment, something telling her that it wasn't good to let a lot of time elapse before she made her statement. She should just walk up to their table, but even as the thought occurred to her, the servers announced that the buffet was ready and the head table should help themselves.

Kate made her way to the table where Sarah and Becca sat, along with a handsome man who stared at Becca as though he were dying of thirst and she was a tall glass of water.

"You must be Jared," she said as she sat down. "I'm Kate."

"It's nice to finally meet you, Kate." Jared stood. "I've heard a lot about you."

She waved him back down. She winked at Becca.

"I thought the wedding was beautiful," Sarah said as they made their way to the buffet.

"Yes, beautiful. I missed wishing them well though." Kate frowned.

"You'll get a chance," Becca said.

"Becca has some news." Sarah's words were sung more than spoken.

"I don't know if I can take the shock of any more of Becca's news." They all laughed.

"We're getting married. Jared still wants to give me a romantic proposal, but I'm happy with this." Becca held out her left hand which sported a pretty little band encrusted with diamonds and a solitaire in the middle. The ring suited Rebecca so well that Kate was at a loss for words.

"Congratulations," she finally said.

Becca's features glowed with happiness. Kate smiled, happy for her friend. Jared hugged Becca and pressed a gentle kiss on top of her head. Often, she got a sixth sense about people and she liked everything about Jared. His personality suited Becca's so well, it was as though they'd been made for one another.

"Oh look. They're cutting the cake." Becca pointed to the front of the room where Jen and Mark stood, ready to slice the cake and feed each other the traditional first bite.

"Maybe I can slip up there and wish them well." Kate stood and made her way toward the front of the room just as Jen crammed a large slice of white icing cake into Mark's face.

He laughed and returned the favor and then they kissed. Before Kate could make it to the cake table, Mark and Jen slipped off to wash one another's faces. One of the brides-maids handed her a slice of cake. She took it and returned to her seat.

"I'm never going to catch up with them," she said. The rich sweetness of the cake melted on her tongue but she couldn't manage more than a bite or two. She really wanted to wish them well so that they could all start off fresh now that Jen and Mark were married.

"You'll find a moment," Sarah said.

After the cake, came the first dance. Jen and Mark made their way onto the dance floor as the disk jockey played a love tune he said was their song. Kate hadn't even realized they had a song. Maybe if she'd taken more time to get to know them as a couple instead of running around like a revolutionary, trying to break them apart, she'd know some of these finer details all Jen's and Mark's friends seemed to know.

Becca and Jared followed onto the dance floor along with most of the other couples in the room. Sarah excused herself to dance with Jerry. Kate sat at the table with the pink candle centerpiece and realized that she felt completely alone.

It seemed as though everyone had a significant other or the promise of one except for her. She'd done this to herself. Her single-minded pursuit without thought for consequences had brought her to this moment.

"May I have this dance?" The husky tones of Ian's voice were like a caress over her nerve endings.

"Ian?" She stood. "What are you doing here?"

"I was invited. Your mother invited me—"

"My mother invited you, didn't she?" they both said at the same time.

Kate didn't quite allow herself to hope that Ian would forgive her just yet but at least he was willing to attend the wedding reception and speak to her. He'd just asked her to dance and she couldn't think of anywhere she'd rather be than in his arms.

"I'd love to dance with you, Ian." She placed her hand in his and they made their way to the dance floor. Tiny butterflies fluttered in her midriff as he pulled her into his arms. She moved closer.

"Ouch." He winced. "Ribs."

"Poor baby." She loosened her grip on him. Her heart was telling her to hold tight and never let him go but his ribs wouldn't allow it.

"My poor car, you mean."

"I'm just glad you're okay." Forget the car, but she didn't say it. Ian loved his car and she knew he was having a hard time over the fact that it was now a heap of rubble in the junkyard.

"I'm glad I'm okay too. So, what do you say we forget about this last crazy two weeks?" he asked.

"That sounds good to me." Relief washed over her in cool waves. "Professionally and personally?"

"Yes. I miss you, Kate. I'm tired of being angry."

"I'm just so sorry I tried to use you to prove a point. I was desperate."

"Jared." He greeted the other man as he and Becca waltzed past and the two men exchanged a knowing grin.

"What was that?"

"We met over cocktails one night and realized we both were dating lipstick diary girls and you both were driving us insane. Now we have a brotherhood. The anti-lipstick diary guys."

She laughed. "You're crazy."

Ian nodded toward where Mark and Jen danced cheek to cheek. "They seem happy."

"Turns out he isn't such a bad guy after all. Isn't that

awful? I spent ten days running around trying to prove he was a louse and all along I was the louse."

Ian chuckled. "I hope you told him that. I almost feel sorry for the guy. When you set your mind to something, there is no stopping you."

"You're lucky you have broken ribs or I'd punch you. Actually, I wanted to wish them well but haven't had the chance."

"You'll find the right time and place. So, when we get back are you going to help me at Ghost Hunters until my ribs heal?"

"Yes, but I have to be honest. I'm only there another six months and then I'm leaving to start my own business."

"What kind of business?" He frowned. "I like seeing you at work every day."

"Then come work with me. I'm starting my own tour company."

"As a partner?" Ian suggested. "If you don't have anyone else in mind."

Kate hadn't really thought that through. She'd never considered a partner, but she wanted Ian in her life. She enjoyed working with him and seeing him often as well and she didn't want to lose that. She noticed that his gaze had settled on the spot where Sarah and Jerry danced. Did he seriously think she'd pick Jerry over him? She placed her fingers on his chin and turned him back to face her.

"I wouldn't dream of collaborating with anyone else." Why not? Ian was savvy at business. He'd make a great partner.

"Personally and professionally?" he added.

"P-personally?" Had she actually just stuttered? "What exactly do you mean?"

"I'm thinking a house in the Garden District, nights in

each other's arms, two or three kids," he paused. "For better or worse; for at least the next sixty years or so."

Kate stopped dancing. "You think you can handle living with me for sixty years?"

"It will be a challenge but I'm up for it." Ian grinned.

"Then the answer is yes."

Ian gave a loud whoop and started to lift her into his arms. He stopped and grabbed his taped ribs. "Just pretend I'm spinning you around."

"How many people are staring at us?" she asked.

"Everyone."

"Good. I love you, Ian."

"We don't have to wait to start the business. I have some money saved."

Had he heard her when she'd confessed her love? "I have money saved as well."

"Perfect. I love you, Kate." He lowered his lips to hers. "Do you want to get married in Greenfield?"

"Yes. My mother will be so thrilled. She'll have another wedding to plan. Oh, maybe we should wait a year. I don't want to kill her. She worked her fingers to the bone—"

"Kate?"

"What?" She came out of her wedding planning daze.

"I think Jen and Mark are leaving." He nodded toward the door.

"Oh, no." She jumped from his arms and dashed for the front door. No way was she going to let Jen leave on her honeymoon without saying something to them both.

She knocked over a chair someone had left pulled out from the table, tripped on the leg, and kept running. She arrived at the front door out of breath.

"Jen, don't go," she gasped.

"Kate?" Jen stopped just as she was getting ready to get

into the limo. "Please tell me you aren't trying to stop us from going on our honeymoon."

"No." Kate laughed and bent over, hands on knees, trying to breathe.

"What's going on, Kate?" Mark put his arm around Jen's waist and stared at Kate.

It was obvious that they both thought she was still trying to stop the wedding. She smiled and straightened. "I never got a chance to wish you well. I missed the receiving line. I didn't get to the front table fast enough when you were cutting the cake and now you're leaving and I almost missed you."

"You want to wish us well?" Mark asked. He looked dumbfounded.

Kate leaned over and hugged him. "Welcome to the family, Mark."

Jen smiled and accepted her hug from Kate.

"Congratulations, sis. I'm so happy for you two and I hope you'll attend my wedding and not be as much of a pain as I was, although I wouldn't blame you."

"Your wedding?" Jen glanced over Kate's shoulder. Ian stood in the doorway watching the scene. He gave a little salute.

"Yes. Ian and I are getting married."

"That's wonderful," Jen squealed and wrapped her arms around Kate's neck.

"Honey, we have to go or we'll miss our flight." Mark waved the tickets under Jen's nose.

"I know. I love you, Katie."

"I love you too." Kate smiled at Mark. "Take good care of her."

"Sure thing, sis. With my life." Their gazes locked and Kate realized that she'd just passed the torch to him. He would protect her sister now.

Had he actually just called her Sis? Maybe he *had* forgiven her. She shut the door behind them and waved as the limo's taillights disappeared around the corner.

Ian came up behind her and put his arms around her shoulders. She leaned back into him.

"This hurts like hell, you know," he said.

Kate laughed and turned to kiss him. "I'll be glad when those ribs heal."

"Me too." He cringed and pulled away.

"So, what do you say we head home tomorrow? We have a lot of planning to do. Are you riding with us?"

"In a car from Indiana to New Orleans with three single women who just witnessed a wedding? Not a chance."

"Hey!" She laughed.

"Seriously, I think a flight will be easier on my ribs."

She nodded. "My parents will drive you to the airport."

"They don't have to do that."

She looped her arm through Ian's as they made their way back into the club house. "Sure they do. You're family."

She'd reluctantly returned home for a wedding she didn't want to happen; learned that appearances could be deceiving; and gained a new brother-in-law and fiancé in the same day. She grinned. She'd have some interesting entries for the diary next Friday. But then, so would Sarah and Becca.

About the Author

Lori Soard has a Ph.D in Journalism and Creative Writing, but she's hardly the stuffy professor type. Her romantic comedy *Housebreaking A Husband* received four stars from *Romantic Times Magazine*.

Thousands of her articles and short stories have been published in magazines such as *Woman's World*. She's served as President of the From the Heart, RWA Chapter; Chairperson and co-founder of World Romance Writers; and has served on the national board for Romance Writers of America. She's currently working as Library Liaison for the Romantic Times Convention.

When she isn't writing, Lori loves to sing and is trying to learn to play the guitar. She often refers to her house as a zoo and, if she isn't caring for her own animals, is taking care of one stray or another and finding it a good home.

The family includes two daughters, three cats, two dogs, and seven hamsters (they kept multiplying). Lori loves to hear from her readers. You can mail her at Lori Soard, PO Box 452, Greenfield, IN 46140; or e-mail her at Lori@LoriSoard.com. Visit her Web site at www.lorisoard.com